Caffeine Nights Publishing

THE AUDACIOUS MENDACITY
OF
LILY GREEN

Shelley Weiner

Fiction aimed at the heart and the head...

Published by Caffeine Nights Publishing 2012

Copyright © Shelley Weiner 2012

Shelley Weiner has asserted her right under the Copyright, Designs and Patents Act 1998 to be identified as the author of this work

CONDITIONS OF SALE

All rights reserved. No part of this publication may be reproduced, stored in a retrieval system, or transmitted in any form or by any means, electronic, mechanical, photocopying, scanning, recording or otherwise, without the prior permission of the publisher

This book has been sold subject to the condition that it shall not, by way of trade or otherwise, be lent, resold, hired out, or otherwise circulated without the publisher's prior consent in any form of binding or cover other than that in which it is published and without a similar condition including this condition being imposed on the subsequent purchaser.

All characters in this publication are fictitious and any resemblance to real persons, living or dead is purely coincidental

Published in Great Britain by Caffeine Nights Publishing

www.caffeine-nights.com

British Library Cataloguing in Publication Data.
A CIP catalogue record for this book is available from the British Library

ISBN: 978-1-907565-20-5

Cover design by

Mark (Wills) Williams

Everything else by
Default, Luck and Accident

O my sister, relate to us a story to beguile the waking hour of our night. Most willingly, answered Scheherazade, if this virtuous King permit me. And the King, hearing these words, and being restless, was pleased with the idea of listening to the story; and thus, on the first night of the thousand and one, Scheherazade commenced her recitations.

> From *Stories from the Thousand and One Nights*
> Translated by Edward William Lane

Other novels by Shelley Weiner:

A Sisters' Tale
The Last Honeymoon
The Joker
Arnost

Part One

1

On her thirty-fourth birthday, Lily told her first lie. Ever.

'Mother,' she announced to the woman who had given her life and shelter but little love, 'I'm engaged to be married.'

Now this, as far as tall stories went, was neither sky-scraping nor hugely creative. From anyone else it would have been questioned, dismantled and laughingly dismissed. But coming from Lily Green, who was virginal in every sense (including, until that moment, the art of deception), it was a whopper.

'You're – *what*?' Eva looked shocked then sceptical, then stretched her thin lips into a semblance of a smile. 'If this is a joke,' she said, 'it is not a very good one.'

She must have known that for plain-talking plain-living Lily a joke was as unlikely as a lie. But then, a secret suitor popping up out of the blue like this was *so* improbable that it might, just might, be verging on the possible. Lily watched her mother's expression reversing from forced amusement, back through doubt and astonishment, and finally settling into the inscrutable mask that Lily had spent the past three decades and more trying and failing to decipher. Her heart sank.

Then she saw that Eva was staring at her intently, something she rarely did. Lily held her gaze as defiantly as she could and for a brief moment the two pairs of dark-brown eyes, identically lit with flecks of green and gold, were locked in the closest thing to mutual empathy they'd ever come to. Lily, dazed, was almost moved to confess.

'On the other hand,' Eva was murmuring, almost to herself, 'you, of all people, wouldn't say such a thing unless —'

'Unless it were *true*,' Lily found herself interrupting, astonished by the confidence and resolve with which she was speaking, the authority she was managing to project. Something was happening. She could make it happen. Excitement rippled through her as the words tumbled out with exhilarating ease. 'It's quite sudden and, for now, has to be kept secret. I'll tell you more about him – us – as soon as I can — '

'Him? Does he have a name?'

'Jeremy,' she said without missing a beat. Where had that sprung from? Which remote crevice in the complex and carefully concealed cave system that was Lily's imagination had harboured an apparition called Jeremy? The utterance of his name had made him happen, fully formed. Tall but not overwhelmingly so, handsome in an approachable way, caring (naturally), intelligent (obviously), with a few endearing imperfections, just enough to make him human. And in case her mother wondered why such a paragon was unattached, she quickly added, 'His *divorce* comes through next week. In fact, we've planned to go away soon after that. As I said, I'll tell you more when I can. Obviously.'

'Obviously.' Eva, nodding slowly, was still studying her with close attention.

Normally Lily would have been daunted by her mother's irony or quailing under her grim scrutiny but now, as the story took hold, she became increasingly convinced of its plausibility. These weren't false words escaping her lips – they were vehicles to another life. She was giddy and a little frightened. A little like she'd felt on the long-before day when she had dared herself to leap from the uppermost diving board into the local swimming pool, the bravest thing she'd ever done. Until now. That time the force of gravity had made an ungainly descent inevitable. Now – goodness! – there were no limits, none at all, *nothing* could stop her. She drew herself to her feet and tightened the belt of her mauve candlewick dressing gown with a resolute tug. She'd have to ditch this gown. Jeremy's fiancée wouldn't be seen dead in it. 'I'd better get back to sorting my stuff,' she announced. Confidently. With quiet purpose. 'There are a million things I have to do.'

'There must be.' Eva's gaze still hadn't faltered. 'I can imagine. I do hope you'll find the time to join me and the girls for tea later on. They're coming specially to wish you happy birthday. Now we'll have something *else* to celebrate —'

'No,' said Lily quickly, desperation rising. Not 'the girls'. Not today. The last thing she needed was the patronising cheer or collective scepticism of her mother's three cronies.

'No? That's mean, Lily. They happen to be my closest friends.'

She recoiled from her mother's sharp, critical tone, then remembered her newfound assurance. '*Your* closest friends, not mine,' she managed, with only the slightest wobble in her voice. 'Anyway, I'm not ready yet for any kind of public announcement. As I said, it's a secret – just between me and you.'

'I understand.' Eva smiled. '*I* won't say anything about – what's-his-name…?'

'Jeremy.'

'Ah – *Jeremy*. You'll be there for the tea party, though? I've ordered a cake, especially. You have to be there.'

There was only the slightest hesitation before she capitulated. 'All right, I'll be there,' she said grudgingly. 'But remember – not a word.'

'Not a word,' her mother promised.

Lily suspected that as soon as she had left the room Eva would be on the phone to Elsie or Matty or Sylvia (probably all three) with the news. Her mother's record in sincerity was not as untarnished as her own.

Until now, she thought with satisfaction, as she swept from the kitchen into her bedroom and firmly shut the door. It was a child's room. A little girl's room, with a single bed, dormer window and a Dolly Varden dressing table all draped in pink chintz. On the bookshelves were illustrated fairy tales interspersed with cuddly toys and small dolls in national costume. On the walls were prints of ballerinas and Lily's single Brownie medal hanging from a nail. It was not, she was aware, a typical bedroom for a woman of thirty-four. On the other hand, she wasn't exactly a typical woman of thirty-four.

She sank on the bed, still aware of the tingling inside her that had started with the utterance of her lie. It was fainter now, more hesitant. The excitement she'd first felt was tempered by the embarrassing probability of her mother and her dreadful friends guessing at the truth. No Jeremy, no engagement – just poor old-maid Lily trudging back and forth from the office, from day to day, meal to meal, every night alone in this fluffy coffin until the day she died. How appalling. How had this happened? Or, more to the point, how had *nothing* happened? How could the years have drifted by with not only nothing happening, but no real belief – on either her part or Eva's – that anything would ever change?

Belief. That was it. Everyone Lily had ever known, even the plainest and most stupid girls in her class at high school, seemed to be convinced they were heading somewhere. A career, marriage, children, happiness, whatever. Lily, it seemed, had been born with a particular form of emotional inertia that seemed to trap her inside a bubble in which 'once upon a time' and 'happy ever after' were conflated into a grey and static present. Not all grey, for there had always been the flights of imagination in her head. And not completely static; she'd once had a gentle father called Max, with an apologetic smile and white powdery flecks on the shoulders of his work suits. Each evening at six he would return from the offices of Eagleton and Nephews, the accountancy practice in which he'd never made it to partner.

'So, Lily Dreamboat,' he would say (no one had ever called her anything so lovely before or since), 'how's tricks?'

Tricks? Lily had never understood what that meant. She'd never tricked anyone; she never knew how. 'Good,' she'd answer dutifully, enjoying his attention nevertheless. And they would sit down for supper, meek Daddy Bear and cross Mummy Bear, and Baby Bear, who ate all her porridge every night, every last drop. Lily had never questioned Max's passivity or her mother's chronic pent-up rage. That was how it was, how it had always been; like the arrangement of the stars in the sky and the Greens' small squat bungalow in a cul-de-sac off the Uxbridge Road and Lily's pink bedroom. Always.

Until the day when she was ten and Max stayed away from work, his first time ever, and she came home from school to find an ambulance, lights flashing, outside their house and the neighbours lurking nosily. 'Poor little girl,' she heard Mrs Fleischmann from next door murmuring to mad Hetty Miller from across the way. And Lily was sure they were talking about someone else, for she'd never considered herself substantial enough to be the subject of their gossip. *Poor little girl.* Who on earth were they talking about?

As she approached her front door, it opened sharply. Her father was being carried out on a stretcher, feet first, still clad in his worn brown brogues. Lily watched dumbly as the stretcher passed her and caught a glimpse of the shiny top of his bald head. That was her last ever sight of him. Eva, meanwhile, stood motionless in the doorway with a strange expression on her face. She seemed oblivious to her daughter, to her poor little girl, and made no move to comfort her.

The end of Max. The end of Lily Dreamboat. Both erased from her life. All that remained of him, his bequest to his daughter, was his tendency towards stoutness and his mathematical mind, both of which played out their relentless destiny – until Lily, frankly plump but with that infallible head for figures, found herself heading for the seat occupied by her poor late dad in Eagleton and Co (the nephews having since retired).

While Lily languished, Eva responded to Max's death with a bewildering metamorphosis. Almost immediately after the funeral, she eliminated all traces of her husband and – overnight, it seemed – acquired a new hairdo, a wardrobe of leisure suits and card table skills. She also joined the charity wing of the local synagogue (Eva? A synagogue? Charity? That made Lily laugh) and acquired the trio of cronies she referred to as 'the girls'.

The same girls who were expected for tea this afternoon and would, after a perfunctory 'happy birthday' to Lily, retire to the sitting room for a few rubbers of bridge and animated chat about their next ocean-going cruise. As far as they were concerned (and she'd overheard the nastiest and most outspoken, Elsie Kramer, more than once articulating the phrase) poor plain Lily had somehow missed the boat.

Maybe she had, maybe she hadn't, she thought, her defiance returning. What did *they* know? And what did Eva know about the daughter she'd managed to ignore for most of her life? All those hours, days, weeks, which Lily had spent ensconced in this very room – as far as Eva knew, she might have been taking drugs or cutting herself or entertaining secret lovers. On the other hand Eva probably had no clue that such racy possibilities would even cross her strait-laced daughter's mind.

But they did. Constantly. Never mind a phantom fiancée, Lily had another dark secret. She bent down and furtively drew from beneath her narrow bed a cardboard box, which she opened to reveal a bulging heap of cuttings culled over the years from almost every glamour magazine in the country. Lily went hot at the thought of her mother getting her hands on this collection, of her derision if she learnt that Lily wasn't just plain because she couldn't be bothered, but that she'd tried and failed to reinvent herself for at least the past fifteen years.

She blamed fairytales, for those had been her first addiction. All the illustrated volumes she'd studied in the children's section of the local library, in which dull oppressed heroines ultimately emerged as gorgeous princesses. With princes at their side, naturally. In real life she'd remained very-ordinary Lily, but in her head, in the lush imagination that took verdant root despite her outer plainness, she was an amalgam of Cinderella, Snow White, Red Rose and every other female who acquired a 'happy ever after' ending on the page.

Then one day, it came upon her that perhaps she ought to do something more than merely wait for recognition by her prince. What, though? Nowhere in her library of fable was there any information about what Cinderella had *done* to expedite her connubial bliss or exactly *how* Snow White had acquired her creamy skin.

Then fate, or possibly destiny, led her one lunchtime to the glamour section of the newsagent's shelves, where a glossy array of beauties grinned as though directly at her. 'Make yourself gorgeous,' enticed *Elle*. 'Bigger and better orgasms,' promised *Cosmopolitan*. 'Catch your man and keep him,' guaranteed *Marie Claire*. Gosh, thought Lily, forcing her attention back to the respectability of the *Daily Mail* and handing over her coins. Then, unable to resist, she quickly grabbed a few of the more alluring editions, emptied her purse and – deeply discomfited, for the cover-girls were so at odds with the dumpiness of her frame – hurried outside.

And so began her systematic study and accumulation of a vast store of advice culled from decades of glamour magazines. Lily believed that here, in the cardboard box she kept hidden under her bed, lay the key to the qualities which would enable her to fulfil her destiny. Beauty, grace, good taste, gourmet cookery skills and the mastery of sexual positions designed to give pleasure to her and, more to the point, her man. Whoever he turned out to be.

What a lot of good that had done her, she thought now, riffling through the contents of the box. Thirty-four years old and, fabricated Jeremy apart, she'd not had a whiff of a fellow to call her own. Why on earth had she preserved that ridiculous *Tatler* piece on preparing and serving pheasant, by Clarabelle Wynne-Stanley? Or 'Two Hundred and Fifty Rules for the Contemporary Coquette'? As for 'The Insider's Guide to Sexual Ps and Qs' and 'Lobster Cookery' and 'A Hundred Ways To Maintain Holiday Hair' – all an utter and complete waste of time. Irritably she pulled out an article from *New Woman* by someone called Carla Devine. Carla had shot up from harlot to heiress in four eventful years and this ascent, she swore, was all due to her extraordinary gift for fabrication.

Fabrication? Confabulation? A genius at the telling of lies? Lily read with closer attention. It seemed that Carla had successfully disseminated anecdotes about her conquest of Everest and neighbouring peaks and how, single-handedly, she had saved whole forests from extinction, small children from abuse and cuddly animals from the clutches of rampant furriers. She also professed to have rescued the endangered fortune of an Indonesian oil tycoon – which she managed to change from fiction to glorious fact. According to the article, she ended up marrying the very tycoon on his deathbed, inheriting his salvaged fortune and surviving to tell the tale.

Like Scheherazade, Lily thought, setting aside the cutting and lying back. Before she had embarked on her magazine dreams, the marathon storyteller of the Thousand and One Nights had been her all-time heroine. With death breathing down her neck, she'd produced tale after tale for close on three years. Lily shivered as she pictured the rapier that threatened to decapitate poor Scheherazade if her narrative flow faltered or failed. Death through beheading. Death through boredom. The living death of an unremitting future in a small pink room in a boxy house in the silent streets of suburban Hatch End. Lily's dream as she dozed was about Carla Devine in Arabian garb giving a masterclass in makeup, in making up, in how invention could elude the scythe-wielding dark-cloaked figure who was lurking in the shadows.

And then she awoke to the clink of teacups and high-pitched peals of laughter. The girls had arrived.

'Lily!' Eva was calling as she tapped ungently on the door. 'We're waiting for you.'

She sat up. Her first impulse was to retreat beneath the bed with the box of cuttings and her fluffy slippers, to lie low and hope that eventually they would go away. She gathered the sheets of paper still scattered on the eiderdown and Carla, atop the pile, seemed to be winking directly at her. Lily found herself winking back, then grinned at the madness of a grown woman in a candlewick dressing gown making faces at a photograph. She felt mad. She was going mad. Carla Devine was off her head, that crazy Scheherazade was almost certainly certifiable, but Lily Green – unless she did something about herself and fast – would be the saddest and maddest of all.

'One minute,' she answered. 'I'll be with you as soon as I can.'

Off came the dressing gown and, from the furthest corner of a drawer she extracted a tightly-bound parcel. It was the result of an impulsive and manic shopping spree on a spring Saturday at least two years before, when Eva had been away on one of her cruises. Lily had spent the day in London's West End and, following the consolidated advice of the country's leading fashion editors, braved the most pricey shops in Bond Street. On the train back to Hatch End, laden with designer carrier bags, she'd kept peeping at the Armani cocktail dress (expensively understated), court shoes by Marc Jacobs (deliciously supple) and the undergarments constructed with the sturdily-built woman in mind. At home she had laid everything out. Carefully, just as the immaculately-coiffed assistant behind the Estée Lauder counter in Selfridges had instructed her, she had painted her face. Then she had dressed and, heart hammering, dared to face her transformation in the mirror.

It had been awful. Unspeakably awful. Instead of dowdy Lily in dowdy clothes (bad enough) she had faced a scarlet-lipped, apple-cheeked woman impossibly squeezed into what was probably the costliest black bin liner in the world. Not only did she look ridiculous, she also faced slipping into overdraft for the first time ever. What an ill-conceived notion this had been. She'd been born to be drab, would live her life out in unremitting drabness and, one dark night when she was as old and drab as a person could become, she would just fade out. Miserably she had compressed her purchases into the smallest bag available and stowed the package away. But now, as though Carla Devine had taken spectral shape and was urging her on, she found herself opening the bag and pulling out item after costly item. 'Go, Lily, go!' she heard Carla whispering. 'Think about Jeremy, your dashing diplomat – ending his ever-so-suitable marriage for you, about to sweep you away with him to far exotic lands. You're an alluring mistress and about-to-be society wife, so dress the part!' But look at me, she wanted to retort. Would a hippo be cast as Madame le Pompadour? Honestly. 'Honesty isn't the way forward, my dear,' Carla rebuked. 'There – give that dress a little shake, get some of those creases out. Not bad at all for having been squashed away so long – good old Armani, you get what you pay for. Now for those foundation garments – heave-ho, cram everything in. There! Dainty you're not, but the overall shape's not bad, in and out in all the right places. Now the dress, stand tall, don't breathe and that zip will close, it will, it will. Excellent.'

'Lily, where *are* you? The tea's getting cold.'

'Coming,' she called. 'I won't be long.'

Hastily, for she suspected her mother's veneer of tolerance and good cheer was wearing thin, she completed her toilette. 'Don't rush so,' Carla was imploring. 'Easy does it. Remember – dignity, decorum, deportment. You're a different person now. Careful with that mascara – oops! No matter. A hint of genteel debauchery is always good. Now for the lips, steady on. And we're done!' Done. As ready as she'd ever be. The newly-glamorous, sultry Lily Green. Automatically, she began opening her cupboard to examine her reflection in the full-length mirror backing the door. 'No!' Carla stopped her. 'Don't look. Just think yourself beautiful, be bold, be brazen – get yourself out there – go, girl, go!'

They had erupted into 'Happy Birthday' at the sound of her emergence from the room. When she appeared at the living room door, they had reached the second 'dear Lily'. Then they saw her. One at a time they stopped singing, until only Eva's reedy voice remained. It would take far more than her daughter's getup to put Eva off her stroke.

And it took almost more than Lily possessed to keep nodding demurely while curving her mouth into what she hoped was a gracious smile. 'Dignity, decorum, deportment,' prompted Carla. 'Run and hide,' begged Old Lily, igniting a blush that would engulf her like the tropical sun. But New Lily ignored her. She kept her gaze fixed firmly on her mother, her stilettos boring deep into the Axminster.

'Thank you, everyone,' she heard herself saying after the final refrain. She sounded remarkably composed. 'Sorry to have kept you waiting. I thought that since you've gone to such trouble to celebrate my birthday, I'd better make an effort.' She indicated her outfit.

There was a long pause.

'You look — very smart indeed,' Elsie Kramer eventually managed. 'Very – different, very – um – *chic*.'

'Indeed,' said Matty Morris, forcing the word out through a succession of tremulous chins.

Sylvia Gold, still in apparent shock, could only widen her eyes, thyroidal at the best of times, until Lily feared they might burst.

There was another lengthy silence before Eva finally spoke. 'So,' she said, surveying Lily from top to toe, and then from toe to top again. 'My daughter in Armani. Well, well.'

'What about it?' Lily couldn't keep the petulance out of her tone. What right had her mother, with her hideous leisure wear and comfort shoes, to be snide about Lily's style? Tears threatened. She blinked hard. Surely a person her age had the right to dress as she chose. 'I *am* thirty-four,' she pointed out with as much conviction as she could manage. Inside she still felt at most fifteen.

'You are indeed,' Eva said firmly. 'We have the candles to prove it. Thirty-four and — go on, Lily, tell the girls! Good news should be shared and celebrated – there's little enough of it around.'

'Mother,' Lily objected. Anger pulsed through her. How dare she betray a daughter's confidence like this? Shared – celebrated – what nonsense. All Eva wanted, all she'd ever wanted, was to humiliate her. 'I told you —'she began, about to deny everything, to back off from this awful, mortifying situation. Then she saw the way her mother was regarding her through narrowed appraising eyes. Was she challenging her? Was she *daring* her to make public her earlier proclamation? *Say* it, Eva seemed to be exhorting. Make it happen. Make it real.

Lily drew herself to her full five-foot-three, sucked in her stomach, smoothed her dress and glanced at each of the girls in turn – at Elsie with her discontented mouth, obese slow-talking Matty, jittery Sylvia. Then she turned to her mother. 'I *particularly* asked you to keep this between us,' she reminded her. How cool she sounded. How controlled. 'But since you've chosen to break your word —' She peered at her disdainfully, then turned to her friends. '— I may as well share this with the three of you as well. I'm trusting you not to tell anyone else.'

Once again, that heady sensation threatened to overcome her as she reiterated and embellished her lie. Jeremy who worked for the Foreign Office, hush-hush of course. Secret assignations. The behind-the-scenes manoeuvrings that had culminated in the (uncontested) divorce, the reasons for the apparent haste with which they were planning to leave the country.

'So tell me,' interrupted Elsie, never one to mince her words, 'is he *Jewish*, this Jeremy? The Foreign Office isn't usually —'

'Yes, he is,' Lily cut in, extemporising fast. He could be Transcendental Mormon as far as she was concerned, but if they wanted Jewish, she'd do Jewish. 'His mother's Jewish, at any rate, which makes him —'

'You're leaving the country?' Matty asked, saving her from further religious clarification, about which she was on weak ground. She'd have to research this.

'We are,' she said quickly, trying not to sound too glad. 'It can't be helped. At this stage I can't be specific about where we'll be settling. Jeremy's talking about eventually trying for transfer back to – um – HQ in London, but we shall have to see. Meanwhile, we're going to have a holiday together as soon as we can. That should be in a couple of weeks.'

'A couple of *weeks*? You mean a *fortnight*?' asked Sylvia, blinking feverishly.

'That's what a couple of weeks usually means,' Eva said dryly.

'But Eva, we're supposed to be flying to *Barbados* in ten days. It's going to be so difficult to find a fourth to replace you at this late stage —'

'You won't have to,' Lily broke in. She'd overheard their excited chatter about a Pan-Caribbean Bridge Cruise. 'There's absolutely no need for mother to miss the cruise. I know how much you've all been looking forward to it.'

There were objections, none too violent, and voices of concern, none too deep. Would Lily manage without maternal support at such a delicate time? Didn't she need help with shopping, with packing, with deciding what to take?

'I'll be fine,' Lily insisted. And with each passing moment she became increasingly convinced this was so. By the time they departed in a flurry of good wishes she was willing them out of the country in hours rather than days. All of them, including her mother, who seemed strangely unmoved by her daughter's imminent betrothal. Was this a natural way to be?

'Well,' said Eva, when at last they were alone. She was squinting closely at Lily. 'You'll have to be a bit more careful with that mascara.'

'Hmm.' She stood up, righteously affronted. Couldn't her mother ever find something positive to say? She'd forgotten momentarily that she was a fraud with a fake fiancé. Then she remembered and, seeing the funny side, smiled, and Eva smiled back without her usual rancour.

'Thank you for the birthday party,' Lily recited dutifully. Like the good girl she was. Or had been. 'I'd better carry on sorting out my stuff.'

In her room she took a deep breath and dared herself to confront her image in the mirror. She shut her eyes, opened the cupboard door – and there she was in her designer finery. Perhaps *finery* was euphemistic, she had to admit as she faced a podgy figure in a tiny black frock that, despite its price tag, bulged and sagged in the least flattering way. That would have to go. So, ideally, should at least twenty pounds and that girlish shoulder-length hair. On the plus side, her breasts were attractive and her brown eyes with their shards of green and gold were – as several people had remarked – striking. Play to your strengths, advocated the experts. Lily fluttered her lashes and flaunted her chest then, feeling like an idiot, slammed the cupboard shut and hurled herself among the magazine cuttings which still littered the bed.

What a mess she'd got herself into with that stupid, stupid lie. What a fool she was making of herself. Even if 'the girls' had swallowed it (and Lily had her doubts), Eva was clearly sceptical. They would go off on their bridge cruise and, two months later, return to find dull old Lily still at home, just a little redder in the face and plumper round the middle. Oh, dear. The prospect was appalling, unbearable.

She wouldn't let that happen, she couldn't. She had willpower, didn't she? Look how single minded she'd once been about teaching herself to stay upright on her roller-skates. Now she would use that tenacity to make her story come true. She had her savings, a marketable head for numbers and, to support her quest for Jeremy or someone similar to fill the slot, a collection of cuttings with all the advice a girl-on-the-prowl might need. She could do it. She *would*. She'd remove herself forever from the stifling confines of home and from the dullness of Hatch End.

Unless something awful happened, Lily resolved to be on the London-bound train within the month.

Immediately – no time to waste – she launched herself on an amalgam of the six most effective Celebrity Diet Plans as listed in *Zest*. Buckets of green tea, lashings of chilli, as many celery sticks as her jaws could tolerate, as much egg white as her stomach could digest and total avoidance of anything containing wheat. By day four, looking haggard, she was furiously applying 'miracle anti-ageing' cream to hide the facial ravages induced by her diet. All in a good cause, she told herself, attending to the emergent spots on her forehead and the new shadows beneath her eyes. On the plus side, she'd never noticed her cheekbones until now.

And on the plus-plus-plus side was her feeling of triumph when she announced to her boss, Ted Eagleton, that she'd be leaving in three weeks to get married. Eagleton looked as astounded as his phlegmatic face allowed.

'You're giving *notice*?' he asked.

''Fraid so.' Lily shrugged and raised her eyebrows. 'We'll be living in London. I can't tell you any more at the moment – it's still a bit of a secret —'

'Of course,' he said immediately. Thank God for English reserve, she thought, relishing his badly-disguised curiosity, his astonishment that plain old Lily might have been harbouring another more glamorous life. 'Of course, Miss Green. Absolutely.'

Discreet Ted hadn't taken over the auditing wing of the family firm for nothing. He would endure torture before telling a soul, that was for sure. Less certain, however (even in her most optimistic mode) was whether, ultimately, there would be anything to tell. At the base of her lie, most fundamental of all, was Jeremy. Nothing would make sense unless she made him exist.

And so, late into each night, as though cramming for her finals, she studied her compendium of cuttings until there was nothing, but *nothing*, she didn't know about how to catch and keep her man. Like a mantra she repeated the guidance of, among others, soap star Gina Woods: 'Be vigilant, keep your quarry constantly in sight. Study his habits, his preferences, his weaknesses.' Thus Gina claimed to have captured a Transylvanian prince, having trailed him for years.

Lily didn't *have* years. Perhaps the advice of that supermodel, Maisie Fitzherbert, would be more immediate?

'Energy is your key to irresistibility. My new Super-Verve Food Supplement is especially designed to boost the bits that make men go wild.'

No, she decided. Jeremy wouldn't be wild, not her Jeremy. The possibility terrified her as much as the prospect of adding a seventh component to her already-nauseating diet. Even more puzzling and alarming were the words of the famous sex therapist, Megan Moffat: 'There is no greater pulling power than positive thinking. Never cloud your vision with doubt. Create a mind-picture of your man in all his burgeoning fullness – and remember: "Out of Figments come the stuff of Fig Leaves". The image made her shudder.

She had almost despaired of finding intelligible guidance when she hit upon the tried-and-tested formula of the millionaire money-broker, Angela Manning: 'Be strong but vulnerable. Beneath that elegant exterior, allow him tantalising glimpses of the little girl within.' That was possible. She could *do* elegant; she could *do* little girl. And – even better – she could couple Angela's dictum with the infallible three-step plan propagated by Jennifer Flower (Flirt of the Year, 1997): One: Make eye contact; Two: Smile; Three: Say something.

Look, smile, say. Elegant but vulnerable. Lily found herself muttering the key words as she worked out her notice and ticked off the days. Impulsively, she experimented on Ted Eagleton (deep eye contact, enigmatic smile, throaty nonsequiter). He stared back mutely and Lily was unsure whether he thought her startlingly sexy or raving mad. There wasn't time to ponder, however. Too much to do, too many glamour items to buy. For the first time in her life, she acquired a credit card, a Premium Platinum, which – to her amazement – was 'awarded' to her with the 'free offer' of five thousand pounds of credit. It arrived in a large metallic envelope which she secreted away. This furtiveness hardly seemed necessary as Eva, deeply absorbed in her pre-cruise preparations, noticed nothing – neither the contents of the mail nor the shopping bags accumulating in Lily's room.

The morning of her mother's departure drew nearer and, when the moment of leave-taking finally arrived, Lily – who had been too preoccupied to think about it – was astounded by the rush of anxiety that swept over her.

'So. How are you going to manage, Lily?' her mother asked at the door. Her taxi was tooting and three sturdy suitcases were piled on the mat.

Lily hesitated. Her mouth was dry. All her lessons in assurance and successful small talk deserted her. She could only manage a nod.

'*I* think you'll be fine.' Eva's expression was resolute. Her garish make-up and baby-blue velour seemed at odds with the astute steadiness of her gaze. Not for the first time, Lily had a sense of her mother in masquerade – a series of costumes in which she'd played suburban wife, then grieving widow, and now crone in glad rags. Were the outfits like onion leaves with nothing inside or, as now seemed fleetingly possible, was there someone *real* beneath the camouflage? Was there an Eva who'd preceded the one who'd settled for domesticity with Max? Lily didn't know. She'd never asked. Her mother, judging by the total absence of anything that hinted at a previous life, had materialised in Hatch End fully formed.

'You do?' Lily asked, sounding and feeling five years old.

In response Eva planted a feathery kiss on one cheek then the other and, in a cloud of Yardley's Lavender, hurried towards the impatiently-revving cab.

Lily's last sight of her was a jaunty, finger-twiddling wave that was disturbingly at odds with her expressionless face.

2

Exactly a fortnight later, it was for Lily that the taxi was tooting and, in conscious parody of her mother, she twiddled her fingers at the now-empty house. Unlike Eva's deadpan expression, though, Lily was smiling. She couldn't help it. That terrible dread had dissipated soon after her mother had gone, but been replaced by a succession of sensations just as extreme. Euphoria, ecstasy, anxiety and hysteria had raced through her in a flurry of hot pursuit. Right until the eve of her departure, she hadn't been certain whether she'd complete all the tasks on her gargantuan lists – and, if she did, whether or not her nerve would fail her at the final moment.

But now that she'd entered the taxi that would deliver her to her destiny, she was serene. Resigned. In a pent-up sort of way, almost happy. There was nothing more she could have done to prepare for this, the biggest test of her life. She was ready. She would crack it. In no time at all she would have her man.

She almost thought she had found him within minutes of boarding the Euston-bound train. Sitting bolt upright and doing a mental check-list ('dignity, decorum, deportment'), she caught sight of her reflection in the window. Not bad at all. That haircut had turned out nicely and the facial exercises had removed any hint of a double chin. She extended her neck and cocked her head and then, with some embarrassment, saw that the man on the seat opposite was glancing in her direction. He returned to his newspaper as soon as was aware he'd been observed, but Lily's attention had been alerted. Surreptitiously she studied him.

Young. Perhaps not *so* young – late thirties, maybe closer to forty. But *nicely* mature, distinguished-looking – and a

Financial Times reader, which augured well economically. Immaculately groomed with (she imagined) good strong teeth. Could this be her Jeremy? So suitable and so soon? Slightly flustered, for she wasn't quite ready but wondered if she'd ever be, she reminded herself of the 'look, smile, say' rule and how it had misfired on Ted Eagleton. This time it would hit the spot.

Silently wishing herself luck, she stared hard at him. He carried on reading. She kept staring. He rubbed his nose. She cleared her throat, continuing to hold him in her unwavering gaze.

He looked back.

Gosh, she thought. It's working.

She smiled. Incredibly, he returned her smile. Now she had to say something, anything. If only that Jennifer Williams had given some suggestions for opening gambits.

But he got in first. 'Pleasant weather,' he remarked.

'*Wonderful* weather,' she answered, with perhaps too much ardour, given the greyness of the day. 'At long last it seems that summer is on its way. Do you know, I read somewhere last week that this has been the coldest spring for eighty-two years. *Eighty-two* years. I can well believe it, though. Those poor little snowdrops haven't stood a chance.' With effort, she forced herself to stop. What had happened to the low, sexy voice she'd spent all those hours cultivating? To meaningful small talk? To the warning she'd been given by at least twenty of her mentors about steering clear of the weather in a pre-erotic exchange? Her man was bored, she could see it. His attention had slipped from her face and back to his newspaper. He was lost. The game was up.

Lily ordered herself not to mind. This was her first proper attempt; she was still at the experimental stage. In all likelihood he was married anyway – and although Jeremy (ostensibly) had been a married man, she had been warned by a multitude of mistresses about how hard it was to unseat a determined extant wife. She put the encounter down to experience and told herself there were many other men, and far better, awaiting her charms. But as the train drew into

Euston, she couldn't ignore the sudden sourness in her throat and the apprehensive knot in her gut.

Then, faced with the logistics of transporting her luggage (two faux-Vuitton suitcases crammed with her clothes, cosmetics, and a thick file containing the cream of her cuttings) across the station concourse and down to the Underground, she forgot her trepidation. Struggling determinedly through the crowd, she regretted her moment of weakness. What kind of intrepid huntress would falter that early? And anyway it would have been far too simple, unsatisfying really, to have captured her prey almost before she had set out. She wanted the thrill of the chase, the pounce, the entrapment, the capitulation. From now on she would operate strictly according to plan. After all the elaborate preparations, she would resist further random sorties or impulsive hits. Wasn't she equipped with the latest and best armoury of expertise that any girl on such a quest could possibly require? Be systematic, she told herself. Sort out a place to stay, then a job. And then, only then, launch the major offensive: the campaign to find him. The man. Jeremy.

Finding accommodation turned out not be as straightforward as Lily had imagined, despite her research. With her small-town fear of the dangers that lurked in big cities (murder, rape, white slavery, larceny and rampant double parking), Lily had noted the names of selected boarding houses that were advertised in *The Lady*. The local librarian had recommended this organ as a reliable source. 'The most *decent* people advertise here,' she'd told Lily with conviction. 'It's where society finds its help.'

That had seemed perfect. So had her first choice, a Mayfair-based 'gentlewoman's establishment' called The Glade, run by Lady Arabella Conilew-Spencer. Three weeks before, Lily had made contact with Lady C-S, who had addressed her as 'Sweetheart' and offered her the last room available with 'all mod cons'. Lily had accepted with alacrity and offered a deposit which had been snootily spurned ('A gentlewoman's *word* is enough for me!').

The location of the said 'establishment', however, turned out to be more Soho than Mayfair and Lady C-S, who came to the door in a purple silk robe, wasn't quite what Lily had pictured as a *lady* Lady. She looked her up and down and said, 'Alas and alack, sweetheart, Cousin Caroline has just landed on me for the Season. Sadly the room has gone.'

'Gone?' Lily had suffered the Tube with her suitcases and then dragged them inelegantly through the teeming streets. This woman (*was* she a woman with that gravelly voice and those beefy hands?) had no right to turn her away. 'You mean —'

'Sorry,' Lady C-S said abruptly. No 'sweetheart' this time. Worse, she was shutting the door in Lily's face. How rude. How hurtful. How deeply *un*gentlewomanly.

Tears began to prickle, but Lily refused to yield to them. She would not be daunted by such a minor setback. The 'establishment' was clearly as wrong for her as she was for it. She congratulated herself on the thoroughness of her preparations, having had the foresight to bring along a back-up list should the promised lodgings fail.

Purposefully, she hailed a black cab. Nothing would persuade her back into the entrails of the Underground. Not with her luggage – not today.

'Where are we off to, miss?' asked the driver.

Miss. That was better. Or was it? Did 'miss' imply freshness and youth or was it an allusion to her blatant spinster state? And where *were* they off to? The meter was ticking. This dithering was costing her a fortune. Hastily she opened her little black book (as advocated by *Tatler*'s Genevieve Olson) and under 'Emergency Accommodation' there was an address in somewhere called Kilburn. 'The Winter Palace Guesthouse, prop. Madame Anastasia Plotnikova. Warm, comfortable, homely food; special rates for single ladies.' That sounded just the thing.

'Kilburn, please,' she said assertively, pleased with the way that came out. Kilburn didn't have the stylish resonance of, say, Mayfair. But for her personal safety as well as a bit of greenery, perhaps it would be best to be away from the centre of town.

Almost an hour and thirty-two pounds later they finally reached their destination, which seemed as grubbily urban as London's hub. There were mucky terraced houses like rows of rotten teeth, with not a tree in sight. The pavements were clustered with disaffected youths and the streets parked up with elderly cars.

'Are we here?' Lily ventured, as the taxi drew to a halt. On the one hand, the idea of being dumped in this derelict neighbourhood terrified her. On the other, the meter now read thirty-three pounds forty, and rising, which meant she was heading for a cash-flow crisis. Not in a million years would her funds stretch to a journey back.

'Yup,' said the driver, switching off his machine and unloading her suitcases. 'There it is, miss – number fifty-eight. Winter Palace Guesthouse.'

'Thank you.' Lily counted out the fare and, before she knew it, she was alone in the alien street, the subject of curious stares. Show no fear, she told herself, as she pulled her luggage along. In 'Sexy-and-Safe in the City' (a free supplement with *Eve*), Marcia Jones had asserted that the scent of panic would attract a rogue to a victim like a blossom to a bee. Or was it a bee to a blossom? Puzzling over the maxim as she strained to seem confident, Lily failed to notice the open door of the unprepossessing Winter Palace and almost stumbled into the arms of an abundantly-endowed woman who stepped back and, in a heavy foreign accent, introduced herself as Madame Plotnikova.

'Pleased to meet you,' said Lily, recovering her composure. 'I'm Lily Green.' She remembered the discount for unattached females and quickly added, '*Miss* Lily Green. Officially speaking, Miss *Lillian* Green.'

'Delighted to meet you, Miss Green. I was seeing that taxi and telling myself that if it is bringing here a lovely lady needing a room then both of us are in luck!'

'We are?' The rapture of this reception was almost as disconcerting as Lady Conilew-Spencer's rebuff.

'No doubt at all' Madame Plotnikova declared. Leaving Lily still hesitating on the doormat, she grabbed the luggage and began mounting the stairs.

'Wait a moment. Excuse me —' Lily hurried after her. 'Madame —'

'Anastasia, please. Or, to make shorter, my guests call me Ana. You can call me that as well.'

'Ana —'

'Yes, my dear?'

'Can we *discuss* this first? You don't know anything about me and, really, I'd like to see the room before I decide. I saw your advert in *The Lady* and —'

'Exactly. All I need to know. A single look at you and I can see a *poifect* lady and a single look at the room and you will see accommodation fit for a queen.'

Gasping, she had reached the top landing and Lily had no option but to follow.

'See? See what I mean?' The landlady swung open the door to reveal a loft bedroom that, while somewhat cramped for the sovereign herself, might have suited a cash-strapped minor royal as a bijoux retreat. Lily had never seen so much gold drapery in such a confined space. It all looked clean, though, and smelled clean. She crossed the carpet to the window and, beyond the crop of TV aerials and satellite dishes that sprouted from the rooftops, saw a patch of grey sky.

'So?' The proprietor was studying her, hands on ample hips. 'Good or not good?'

'Good,' said Lily cautiously. 'But Madame Plot —'

'*Ana*. Please.'

'We haven't talked about the – er – rental or the terms. You haven't even seen my references.'

'All in good time. You like room, I like look of you, now time to talk.'

Reluctantly leaving her luggage in the room (how on earth could she extricate herself from this place, even if she wanted to?) she followed Madame Plotnikova – Ana – back down the stairs. And when they were seated in what she was told was 'the parlour', the landlady became more businesslike as she stated her terms. The weekly rental seemed reasonable and so did the stipulation about paying on time. The only condition that caused Lily disquiet was the strict one, grimly pronounced, about a tenant informing the landlady *immediately* if she changed her single status. In any way. Not that she expected it from Lily, but rules were rules.

'I understand,' Lily said, put out on two counts. About the first, her primary mission to find a mate, she would of course maintain expedient silence. If – no, *when* – it happened, she would decide what to do. What disturbed her more was her new landlady's glib assumption that she was out of the running. Her appearance clearly needed a lot more work.

An hour later, exhaustedly ensconced in the room for which she had paid the deposit and signed a six-month lease, she'd fallen fast asleep with her cuttings around her. Need work, she had been murmuring as she had drifted off, surrounded by the 'before' and 'after' pictures of a miraculously made-over soap star. It wasn't only Lily's allure that was still lacking; more urgent was the attention needed to her fast-dwindling resources. She had to find a job.

The obvious route to a stable income was through the door of the nearest accountancy practice. There was no doubt that her decades of experience combined with the glowing reference from Mr Eagleton would find her a spot behind a desk somewhere. But when Madame Plotnikova had asked her how she was to support herself in London, Lily had found herself saying with perfect aplomb, 'I'm taking up quite a senior position in a magazine publishing company – I was head-hunted, in a way.'

'*Head*-hunted? Like in jungle?'

Lily had hesitated for but a split second. What was she getting into now? What kind of compulsive liar had she become? It was scary. Mind-boggling. In fact, rather thrilling. 'I was approached, discreetly of course, with the offer of, well, an excellent packet of benefits. I think it's my *creative* ability that they're after – writing, editing, commissioning articles. I'll tell you more about it when I begin.'

The next morning she was still fired with excitement about the new career she'd invented for herself. Media Executive. Impressive. She hurried out to buy *The Times* and braved the shiny-suited sales staff in the Carphone Warehouse to equip herself with a modestly-priced contract-free mobile phone. In a coffee shop she bought a latte, feeling ultra-sophisticated, and settled down to ring executive recruitment agencies that specialised in the media.

'Where did you say you had worked, Miss —'
'Green. Lily Green.'
This was the tenth call she had made and, according to a message on her mobile, her remaining balance was eighty-seven pence. Her confidence, too, had diminished.
'My *actual* experience,' she said, trying to sound poised, 'is in finance. But I do have extensive knowledge about media matters. Particularly the whole field of women's magazines.'
'I see. But what exactly have you *done* in this field?'
'Oh, I *can* do anything. I would, truly I would. Isn't there a place somewhere for a person who has a sort of *overview* of what's in and what's out – someone who really *understands* what a woman wants to read?'
'Perhaps. I'm not sure. I'll have to come back to you on that.'

She didn't. No one did. After three futile days Lily looked in desperation for direction from Martha Smithson (author of 'Top Jobs for Dummettes'), who wrote: 'Flatter your potential employer, embellish what you've done and concoct what you haven't done; if black sludge can be sold as Marmite, you can sell yourself.'
'I've been told,' Lily began cautiously to the first firm she called on day four, 'that you're the UK's leading media

employment consultancy. Let me introduce myself: I'm Lily Green – *the* Lily Green – I imagine you've heard of me?'

'I'm not sure. Not offhand. But then —'

'This call is in strictest confidence,' Lily went on, getting into her stride. She was doing well. 'At this stage I don't want it made public that I'm thinking of making a move. You know how gossip spreads in our little world? Shall we do lunch? Somewhere discreet, where we can run through my ideas?'

'Sounds good. But listen, Ms – er – Green, perhaps I'm not the person you should be speaking to. I'm the cleaner, actually – shouldn't even be answering the phone. But they all get in so late and I can't stand to hear it ringing.'

'Oh,' said Lily.

'I'll leave Mrs Harroway a message, though. She's always game for a lunch. What was it again? Lily Green?'

'With an e at the end,' put in Lily with a charge of inspiration. That was it. A subtle but powerful touch. A single vowel that would enhance her name with irresistible distinction.

But after another three silent days it was clear that, Green or Greene, Mrs Harroway wasn't biting. Nor were the twenty-or-so other potential employers she called, who seemed impervious to Martha Smithson's 'Flatter-Embellish-Concoct' formula. Lily's cuttings yielded no further guidance on the matter, beyond the insistence that she should keep pampering herself in the face of disappointment. But how many face packs and long soothing bath-soaks could an unwaged person afford? By the end of the week her spirits had plummeted, and her assets had sunk to an all-time low. She was almost ready to consider crawling back to the Hatch End half-life she'd so defiantly ditched

But a core of resilience stopped her. Lily was stubborn. Out of her passive daydreams and the dreary sameness of her previous existence she had managed to weave the possibility of some sort of future and she was damned if she'd concede defeat. Not yet. She would hold onto her principal goal –

finding Jeremy – and downsize her vocational ambitions. After all, with her newfound talent for mendacity, she could always exaggerate the status of her job for anyone who asked about it. So far it seemed that her only potential audience was Madame Plotnikova whom, until now, she had mostly managed to avoid.

Resolutely she turned from 'Creative and Media Opportunities' to the less enticing 'Jobs for Secretaries and PAs' and called the first temping agency that caught her eye.

'A qualified book-keeper with a sixteen-year employment history in *one* job!'

'Yes,' said Lily cautiously. She'd been put straight through to the boss without any need to flatter or concoct. Could this woman be mocking her?

Apparently not. 'There's a *huge* demand for mature women with a solid track record and computer skills,' she was saying. 'Come in immediately and we'll fix you up.'

This was more like it. Lily was relieved but, at the same time, a little deflated by the image. Mature. Solid. What a compromise after all her grand plans. A means to an end, she reminded herself, as she carefully followed Smithson's step-by-step instructions on 'dressing for that vital interview' and, with her certificates, the reference from Mr Eagleton, her make-up purse and mobile phone (now completely out of cash), she set off for the office near Holborn Station. She was wearing her most uplifting bra and her complexion was aglow with instant highlighter. She'd show that woman, *mature*.

Triumphantly, she did.

'Gosh,' said the manager, who couldn't have been more than twenty-one and said her name was Emma. 'Lily – can I call you that? – you don't look *anything* like I expected you to! Great suit you're wearing. I like those shoes as well and the way you've done your hair. It's a pity *more* women your age don't make the most of themselves.'

'Well,' Lily demurred, unsure how to respond to the compliment, if indeed it *was* a compliment.

But Emma wasn't waiting for a response. While Lily was assimilating her remarks, she was babbling on about a job that had, that very morning, come into the office, the most exciting vacancy she'd handled for years. 'When I spoke to you on the phone earlier on,' she said, 'I didn't want to say anything because we were particularly asked to supply someone *presentable*. But now that I've seen you —' Beaming, she held out a sheet of paper.

'You mean, I've got it?'

'Not yet. But you will. I'm sure they'll take you on. Here, take this with you and ask for Mr Paterson. The firm's called Global Perspectives. It's a literary bureau and features agency in Panton Street – not far from here. What do you think about that?'

Lily was afraid to think in case this potential workplace (which sounded like it had sprung straight from the chapter on 'Ultimate Super-Jobs' in Martha Smithson's manual) proved as illusionary as fiancé Jeremy. Was she hallucinating? Had she made it up? 'It's small-ish,' Emma had said. 'Small-ish and new-ish, but definitely on the way up.'

Like me, she thought – then reminded herself that, despite her weight loss and efforts at rejuvenation, she wasn't small, nor would she be new again. But she was 'on the way up', that was for sure. As she followed Emma's directions to Panton Street, she imagined how she would impress her potential boss with tales of her aristocratic background and the family's temporary fall into hard times. She would demonstrate the breadth and depth of her insights into what the glamorous woman wanted to read. She'd be *devastating*.

So engrossed was she in this reverie that she almost walked past the door bearing a tiny and tarnished brass plate on which GLOBAL PERSPECTIVES was engraved. She pressed a buzzer and a gruff voice instructed to take the lift to the seventeenth floor.

'Small-*ish*' turned out to be an understatement. The international headquarters of Global Perspectives PLC (its reception area, surely?) was barely able to contain a filing cabinet and two battered desks. One, unattended, had a keyboard and screen and behind the other was a lanky and unkemptly-bearded middle-aged man. He was bashing away on an old-fashioned typewriter and paying absolutely no heed to Lily, who was hovering at the door. Was he a writer? A journalist? She couldn't help being slightly disappointed by the shabbiness of the office, its diminutive scale and the scruffiness of its sole occupant who, even from the distance of the doorway, reeked of smoke and beer.

And continued to ignore her.

She coughed discreetly.

'Eddie,' he called through the side of his mouth, neither looking up nor interrupting the staccato foxtrot of his two-finger-tapping. 'She's here.'

There was a firmly-shut door at the far end of the room. From behind it Lily heard voices, followed by peels of laughter. Then it opened abruptly and a younger plumper man with slicked-back hair appeared, adjusting his jacket and straightening his tie. 'Hiya,' he said, extending a hand to Lily.

'Hi,' she answered, trying to match his brisk informality. His hand was damp. As unobtrusively as she could, she wiped hers onto her Chanel-inspired skirt and hoped it wouldn't stain. 'I'm Lily Green.'

'Oh yeah – sent by Emma, right? I'm Ed – Ed Paterson. Emma says you can do the business, so let's get on with it. Charge a bloody fortune, these agencies – hope you're worth it.'

Lily, flustered, found herself being directed to the empty desk with its dated PC. Not a single word of her meticulously-rehearsed speech. Not a question or appraisal. But it seemed she had the job. 'Mr Paterson,' she tried, wanting him to perceive her as more interesting than a mere run-of-the-mill clerical employee, someone with creative edge. 'Mr Paterson, I just want to say —'

'Tell it to Gordon,' he interrupted, and disappeared back through the door from whence he had come.

Lily, was left sitting there, mouth open, while the man she gathered was Gordon kept tapping away. A moment later she heard laughter resuming from behind the door, louder and more piercing than before. And at least three long minutes later, Gordon finally ceased typing and, with a flourish, added a final sheet to the pile on his desk. 'Right,' he said, straightening the pile and pushing it in Lily's direction. 'All yours, babes.'

'Mine?'

He exhaled and looked at her properly for the first time. 'Sorry. You must think we're barmy round here. We are, a bit.' He grinned wryly and Lily saw that despite his dissolute appearance and dental discoloration there was something engaging about his smile. 'I'm Gordon, as you've probably gathered. Gordon McCloud. And you're the latest Miss – er – Green.'

'The latest?'

'Perhaps not the latest Miss *Green*, as such. Certainly the latest in a long line despatched here by your very agency and occupying that very seat. But not for long.'

'Oh?' Lily was finding it hard to summon repartee. She kept telling herself that this was the most fascinating place she'd ever been in, that life was happening to her at last. Truly, though, she felt out of her depth. Being honest, she was drowning. 'I do usually stick at things, you know.'

'I'm sure you do, Miss Lily Green. A word of advice if you want this one to last for more than five minutes, though: don't take too much notice of our Ed, and give him as wide a berth as you can.'

'Our Ed? You mean Mr *Paterson*?'

'The very one. He's been through more secretaries than I've had whisky sours. So, as I said —'

'*Avoid* him? But isn't he the boss?'

'Mind you,' he went on, looking at her properly for the first time. 'Unlike most of the others, you're not exactly fifteen. So you should be ok.'

Lily bristled. No, she *wasn't* fifteen or even thirty, but was this wreck of a human being implying she was beyond charm? 'I'll be all right,' she said defiantly. 'And I'd be better still if you could explain what my job is and what you'd like me to do with this pile of papers you're thrusting my way.'

'Touché,' he said holding up his hands. 'I'm sorry.' He got to his feet, groaning, and patted the pockets of his tweed jacket. 'Bugger, I need a smoke.' Despondently, he sat down again. 'Given up. Again. Liver's gone, mind's going, why the hell I'm suddenly bothering with the lungs, God only knows.'

'The job?' Lily prompted.

'Ah, the job.' He inhaled and spluttered into a chesty cough. 'Where shall we start?'

'How about right here?'

'I was only thinking aloud. But – yes. Here's as good a place as any. Take a look around you, Lily. What do you see? This may appear to you a small and humble office. In fact, it's the nerve centre of a vast organisation supplying newspaper features to publications all round the world.'

'Really?' said Lily, not sure whether to be sceptical or impressed. There was a note of permanent mockery in Gordon's voice and she couldn't decide if he was teasing her or it was just his unfamiliar Scottish accent. Or both. Scots in Hatch End were few and far between.

He nodded. 'And here,' he continued, pointing a nicotine-stained index finger at himself, 'is the hub of the operation. The manufacturing plant. Your one-man production team. You, dear girl, are looking at Madame Katinka, who sees the future in the stars, and Marge Scott the famous agony aunt. Not to mention Marge's sidekick Pete Preston, who deals in troubles afflicting the male psyche (and his thingummy of course), plus about a dozen or so other persona filling thousands of column-inches each week —'

'Hold on!' Lily was bewildered. '*You* are Madame Katinka?'

'Pleased to meet you.'

'But I *read* Madame Katinka. I *believe* in Madame Katinka. I've been following her for years. And all the while —'

'Whoa – keep your trousers on, Miss Green. Let me take a good look at you. Gemini. I'm right, am I not?'

Lily nodded her head, dumbstruck. How had he guessed? 'So,' she challenged, 'what's in store for me, then?'

'One sec.' He pulled out a sheet from the typewritten pile he'd just assembled. 'Here we are: "Gemini – Now that you're on track career-wise, it is time to attend to romance. Your perfect partner will reveal himself during this sensual and liberated period. Make use of your considerable charisma to ensure you don't miss your big chance." What do you think of that?'

There was silence while Lily struggled to hide the mix of emotions that were threatening to overflow into inappropriate tears. Embarrassment mainly, plus exhaustion, confusion and disillusionment. 'Very good,' she said eventually, hoping she'd hit an appropriately sardonic note.

'See?' He'd cheered up considerably and was now preening himself like a conceited six-year-old. 'How plausible is that! An old hack like me can make up anything. You should read some of the agony columns I've invented – problems that would have made the toes of my detested late mother curl. Oh, the deviants I have created and consoled.'

Lily couldn't listen any more. She covered her face with her hands. Never would she admit to this seedy imposter that once, in a fit of misery, she had sent off a letter to Marge Scott imploring her for a way out of her lonely grey life. Week after week she'd awaited a reply, which had never come. Now she knew why. It was clearly far too dull a predicament for the likes of this Gordon McCloud, who was eyeing her quizzically as he awaited her response.

She sat up as tall as she could. If it killed her, she wouldn't let him see she was in any way disturbed. 'So what's *my* part in all this?' she asked. 'What does the dolly bird do?'

'The dolly bird,' he answered, acknowledging her irony with a wink, 'punches all my immortal prose into the bowels of that computer. I've never got the hang of it and, frankly, am too far gone to learn. That's her main duty. In addition, she does bits and bobs for Uncle Ed.'

'And what does – um – Uncle Ed do?'

'Ah well now, that's a puzzle. It's not for the likes of us to question too closely what goes on in there.' He tilted his head in the direction of the door, through which guffaws of laughter (sometimes loud, sometimes muted) had been sporadically emanating all the time Lily had been there. 'All I can say is that it sounds like their job is a whole lot more enjoyable than mine.'

As he spoke, the door burst open and a deeply tanned woman slid out. She wore black leggings, a scanty orange top and gold jewellery either draped or pierced almost everywhere else. On her arm Lily noticed an intricately-wrought snake tattoo that seemed to disappear inside her top. She wondered where it ended and what it signified.

'Bernadette,' Gordon was saying. 'We were just talking about you.'

'Cool. Oi, Vince,' she called over her shoulder. 'Get a move-on.'

A male version of Bernadette – similar tan, tight black jeans, orange vest, gold trimmings and matching tattoo – emerged from the doorway. Lily had never seen such a pair outside a circus tent and, since an outing to Zippos had been a one-off treat with her poor late father thirty years before, her memory of its artistes was hazy.

'About bloody time,' said Bernadette, grabbing hold of Vince's left bicep. The tattooed one. 'We're late.'

'Okayee,' he said in a stupefied drawl. He seemed dazed, maybe exhausted by whatever had been going on in that room. 'Give me a fucking chance, will you?'

'Language, Vince, language,' said Gordon. 'We have a lady in the room. Meet Lily, you two. She's our new PA.'

Lily knew that PA stood for Personal Assistant but somehow Gordon made it sound rude. 'Hello,' she said shyly.

'Hi,' mumbled Vince.

Bernadette didn't say anything at all. She threw a quick up-and-down glance in Lily's direction, nodded cursorily and, with Vince's muscle still in a pincer hold, hustled him out of the door.

'So there you have it,' said Gordon when they had gone. 'Global Perspectives and its merry workers – a pimp, two porn stars and a drunken old queer.'

'A *what*?' asked Lily, not sure she'd heard the last correctly.

'Do you think I'd be sitting here writing this shite if I hadn't been kicked off every paper in town? Which reminds me – time for a quick one. You'd better stick round here, pussycat, and get cracking with that stuff I gave you.'

'Will do,' said Lily, sounding as bewildered as she felt.

Gordon, almost at the door, wheeled round to face her. He approached her and bent so close to her face that she had to hold her breath. 'What's with *you*, babes?' he wanted to know.

'Me?' What did he mean by that? What was she meant to say?

'You look concussed. Even Vince has more spark, and that's saying something. But you have stunning eyes, Miss Lily Green. Has anyone told you that before?'

She managed to shake her head.

'Don't *worry*.' He patted her shoulder. 'What's your story then? How did you land up here?'

She was on the brink of answering him truthfully. He had so unbalanced her with his admiration of her eyes that she was about to tell him about her big lie and leaving Hatch End on this lunatic quest, the lot. Then she caught herself. 'I'm a bit strapped for cash at the moment,' she improvised smoothly. How on earth was she achieving this self-confident voice? 'Nothing serious. Just a temporary blip. Tax and stuff on the family property, a real nuisance, but what can one do? I don't normally take on this kind of work.'

'Ah,' he said enigmatically, and *again* she didn't know whether he was teasing or not. He raised both eyebrows in playful farewell and withdrew.

Lily worried for hours that night about whether Gordon had believed her and if he had meant 'homosexual' when he'd described himself as 'queer', and whether Ed, Vince and Bernadette were somehow breaking the law and, if so, whether Lily could be implicated. And if Gordon was a fake astrologer, how could he have known her star sign? And if he *was* gay, could he still be attracted to her, given that he'd so adored her eyes? So many of her magazine mentors had placed The Office high in their lists of male entrapment grounds but Global Perspectives seemed, at best, barren and, at worst, downright dangerous. It would be much more sensible to go along with the opposing school of thought, the one that urged caution about romance in the workplace. *New Woman*, for instance, was insistent that work and sex were like water and oil, never the twain to mix.

By the time Lily eventually drifted off, she had decided that her job, such as it was and as long as it lasted, would be strictly aimed at paying her rent and other sundry expenses. There were plenty other hunting grounds. The experts, after all, were in total agreement that vibrant London was *teeming* with ripe and gullible men. If so, there was no doubt that out of this multitude Lily would somehow nab her quarry.

3

In her little black book, on the page calligraphically headed *Operation Find Jeremy*, she made a list of recommended tactics. She would approach this as a military campaign. Stage One: ambush the local laundrette. That was easy. Armed with a pile of her least spinsterish undies (the new Agent Provocateur knickers she'd bought with that special man in mind were, sadly, 'hand wash only'), she'd reconnoitre the field. If that proved fallow, she would move directly on to Stage Two: lurk irresistibly in the exotic fruit section of a posh supermarket. Several authorities, Jennifer Flowers among them, had suggested that prolonged but artful lingering near the melon varieties, in particular, would yield positive results for the buxom and the brave.

She was certainly brave and in her Janet Reger DD-cup bra she looked gratifyingly uplifted. So if he popped up between the papayas and the mangoes, she'd snap him up, no question.

If not, there was Stage Three: the cinema. Lily hoped against hope that she wouldn't have to resort to this. A lone woman venturing out to see a movie? That sort of thing wasn't done by nice girls in Hatch End. As it happened, Lily wasn't nice – she was a raving liar. Plus, she was no longer a girl, sadly not; she was a woman, a woman on a particular quest. Which was *exactly* why she'd left Hatch End and come to London: she was brave, well-endowed and anonymous. She would go to the cinema, if that's what it took.

She would also, if necessary, hang out in the 'car maintenance section' of the local library (Stage Four) and join a gym (Stage Five) and – at a push – advertise her romantic requirements in *Time Out*. The last made her as nervous as the possibility of Speed Dating – a matchmaking method that she'd read about but had never, even remotely, considered trying for herself.

She wouldn't need to, though. Without a doubt in this testosterone-laden metropolis she'd find her Jeremy within Stages One to Three. She'd plan her outfits, diet like mad, and launch her first incursion the next weekend. She was sure that Madame Plotnikova would be more than happy to oblige with the necessary local information.

The following Saturday afternoon, Lily seated herself demurely on a wooden bench opposite a row of washing machines and leafed through a frayed two-year-old copy of *Country Life* while she waited. It had taken all her determination to resist the laundrette proprietor's urging that she leave her washing to be 'serviced' for an extremely modest fee. 'No – thank you anyway,' she'd asserted. 'I'd rather see to it myself.'

'I know what you mean,' the proprietor had said, leaving Lily to wonder *what* she knew. Was it that the service she provided was unreliable? Or that Lily's laundry was of such exceptional refinement that it demanded her personal care? Or that she had guessed the mission was more about entrapment than ablution. If the last, was Lily following a path that had brought success to others who'd sought and conquered before the Final Spin? Each time the door opened she looked up hopefully – to be greeted by yet another gust of cold air and a load of washing hastily deposited for 'service'.

By the end of the cycle (and Lily had selected the longest one possible, given the synthetic nature of the fabrics she'd selected for the purpose of this exercise), the only possible candidate had been a dark-haired Adonis, slightly too young but extraordinarily handsome, who had flirted and bantered with the proprietor and even directed a smile at Lily. But close on his heels had come an equally good-looking fellow, who'd popped his head in and called, 'Get a move on, Milton!' in a way that prohibited any further speculation. Two hours later, Lily conceded defeat. Not only did she emerge into the Finchley Road without having made a single promising encounter, she'd also managed to ruin all her whites by allowing a non-colourfast pink T-shirt to slip into her load.

But she wasn't daunted. Not even slightly. Chin in the air, she returned to her lodging and extracted what she could from the damages of the fray. A few items of underwear were light casualties in such a vital war. Which would now, she avowed, be extended to several more fronts – laundrettes, supermarkets and libraries, simultaneously occupied in a kind of pincer campaign. Perhaps not *simultaneously*, since her army was limited to one, but closely following one after the other until not a single stone remained unturned. Or whatever. It might be hard on her wardrobe and a little tight on her pocket (the salary at Global Perspectives barely tipped the National Minimum), but she had to keep her objective in mind at all times, in the face of minor defeats, and despite heavy costs.

After such a rousing rally to arms, Lily went to bed exhausted. Her last waking thoughts were about where, in particular, she should position herself when Waitrose Finchley Road – enthusiastically lauded by Madame Plotnikova as *the* purveyor of tropical fruit – opened for business the following day. Should she be standing, deep in thought, above the passion fruit (a bit obvious), or perhaps contemplating the pineapples or musing over the nectarines?

But her supermarket foray, alas, proved as futile as the laundrette strategy. Fired up, she'd made an early start – forgetting that retail outlets of a certain size only opened for trade at midday on Sundays. Which had meant loitering on the pavement for almost an hour. She had also failed to take into account the demographic of the area and, when the supermarket finally opened, found herself adrift in a tide of Madame Plotnikova-clones, shrieking at one another in foreign voices and cluttering the aisles. The exotic fruit counters proved lacklustre; not even Lily's fanciful imagination could enhance the guavas and mangoes with sex appeal. She tried to appear as seductive as she could for as long as she could – but after forty-five minutes that seemed like a lifetime, she felt herself under the suspicious scrutiny of a security guard. And hastily, empty-handedly, scurried away.

The line of attack that led to Kilburn Library proved equally unproductive. Lily realised as soon as she entered the main entrance that her image of a sanctuary for intelligent and cultured Jeremy-types was wildly out of touch. Instead of finding herself among contemplative intellectuals, she was almost knocked off her feet by young lads on skateboards noisily competing for computer terminals. And instead of emerging with her prize, or even the promise of her prize, Lily came out an hour later with a borrower's card and a copy of *Anna Karenina*, which she'd finally got round to starting while passing the time. Dejectedly she headed for the underground station. Perhaps a trip to Oxford Street and a couple of purchases would cheer her up. At least she had a job. At least ...

Small comfort. She stood on the crowded platform, jostled and elbowed by strangers. Would anyone care if, like Anna K, she decided to throw herself in the path of an oncoming train? Not a chance. Anna's tragedy had been immortalised in the profoundest book in Kilburn Library. The suicide of Lily Green, however, would be a mere 'incident'. She could almost hear the words crackling over the loudspeaker:

'London Underground apologises for the temporary delay in services due to a passenger incident in West Hampstead Station.'

They'd write that down in their daily report and people might murmur for a day or two about an unexceptional thirty-something woman who had done herself in. What story would that be? Even in its unexpurgated version, it would hardly be the stuff of great literature: woman tells a lie and doesn't have the gumption to see it through, to transform fantasy into the food of fiction. At least Anna K had given Tolstoy some meaty material; even a master chronicler like him would have struggled with Lily's abortive attempts at finding a match.

Thus far, she reminded herself, gazing down at the track and spotting a rat scurrying along. Was it frightened? Or curious? Watching the creature, it came to Lily that she was both frightened and curious – still. Frightened by the likelihood of oblivion, for she'd never been convinced by a Higher Being or the possibility of an afterlife, and – despite her gloom and persistent failures – interested still in what might happen to her next.

Which meant – no, she wouldn't end it here or now. She would brave the cinema and sign up for Soul Mates and Love Matches and any other scheme, online or otherwise, that might artificially transform her from singleton to someone's Special Other. She might, God help her, even tip a tentative toe into the terrifying world of Speed Dating, if it came to that. Or, if all else failed, she'd narrow her campaign to the ethnic roots she vaguely acknowledged and try (God help her) *Jewish* Speed Dating. As a final, desperate last resort she could drain her reserves (and her Amex card) and cough up for the services of a marriage broker.

Meanwhile, she would pass her days at Global Perspectives and, while the work she did was hardly riveting, at least it was more interesting than the number-crunching at Eagleton and Co. Only a single consonant distinguished her old boss, Ted, from the current one, Ed, but in that letter was a whole new world. Not that Lily felt part of any world; not yet, perhaps not ever. A floater – that's how she thought of herself. One of life's floaters. In Hatch End she'd drifted almost mindlessly between her small pink bedroom and the office. Now, despite her dreams, in spite of the life change precipitated by her enormous lie, she found herself wafting between another small bedroom, this time in the Winter Palace Guesthouse, and another dreary desk. As far as engagement with the outside world was concerned, she had merely exchanged her daily chit-chat with the Hatch End postman for equally meaningless (yet unaccountably pleasant) conversations with that dark-haired and blue-eyed good-looker in the ticket booth at West Hampstead Station.

The fellow in the ticket booth.

Lily found herself smiling at the thought of him, then felt foolish. Wasn't it enough that she'd been hovering at the platform edge, almost about to cause an incident? Now here she was, grinning to herself like a demented bag-lady. He was pleasant, she thought, perhaps slightly more than pleasant. Maybe *pleasant* wasn't quite the word to capture the small tingle at the base of her spine when he shook his head in mock reproof as she approached his booth. 'Look who's here again,' he'd say. 'Return to Holborn?'

She'd nod, ridiculously glad that he'd remembered her. How lonely she must be for this to be so significant.

'If you don't mind my saying so, madam,' he'd remarked more than once, 'you're wasting your money buying these tickets every day. You'd be much better off with an Oyster Card.'

'Thank you,' she'd said haughtily, but not too haughtily to put him off. 'I prefer it this way. Saving money isn't a priority for me.'

'Well, lucky for some.' His sarcasm had been softened by a mischievous grin. 'Have a good journey, then.'

'Thank you,' she had repeated, conscious of how stupid she seemed, aware that he was looking at the person behind her and waiting for her to move on. But she couldn't. She was stuck. If a pane of glass hadn't separated them she'd have reached out and stroked his cheek. Such a beautifully sculpted cheek, textured with faint stubble, firm yet strong. She had wanted to trace her finger down it, and along his jaw line, and over his finely-shaped, sensitive lips.

'Anything more I can do for you, madam?' he was asking, more than a touch of impatience in his voice.

'I'm so sorry,' she'd said, embarrassed. 'I was dreaming. Silly me.'

And now even thinking about it, him, was silly beyond words. She was behaving like a schoolgirl, fantasising about someone who was unsuitable in every possible way. The trouble was, she'd never been *that* sort of schoolgirl and wasn't sure what *those* sort of fantasies were, not beyond the graphic descriptions of her magazine mentors. She had tried, how hard she'd tried, to follow *Cosmopolitan*'s step-by-step instructions to get 'in the mood'. Was being 'in the mood' what she felt about this stranger? If so, it frightened her. She would put a stop to it now. She would resist Mr Wrong and redouble her efforts to find Mr Right. She would succumb to an Oyster Card, use another station, walk if need be.

In the week that followed she resolved each morning to sort out her card, but was drawn irresistibly to the ticket booth. The week after, she avoided West Hampstead altogether and grimly marched to Finchley Road. She took herself to a movie, wept over *Brief Encounter*, and left the cinema in the same unaccompanied state with which she'd arrived. Directed by an advert in the *Jewish Chronicle*, she reached the main door of a Soho venue for a riotous night of 'Jewish Over Thirties' speed dating – but at the last minute her courage (and energy) failed her. She couldn't do it. And nor could she stop herself from thinking about Underground Man; her body kept sending signals that she was unable to ignore.

What could she do? Write to an agony aunt to say she'd been beset by an uncontrollable desire to see, to touch, to be touched by, a strange male person? And have her plight land up on the desk of someone like Gordon McCloud, who'd *laugh* at her?

It wasn't long before Gordon noticed her state of distraction. 'What's up with you, babes?' he asked when, for the third day running, she arrived late. 'Has our Lily fallen in love?'

She pulled herself up sharply and managed to assume the nonchalant air which, until Underground Man, she'd been wearing so effectively for work. 'You must be joking, Gordon. *Love*? After what *I've* been through, it's the last thing on my mind. I'm done with men, that's all I can say. Done with them all.'

'Oh?'

His raised eyebrows signalled his interest in hearing more, but Lily wouldn't oblige. Normally – or what had *become* normal since she'd broken the lying barrier – she'd have easily come up with a torrid account of love and betrayal. Now even that minor confabulation had exhausted her creative powers. All she wanted was for the day to pass so that she could get to bed – to dream.

This meant evading the human stumbling block imposed, almost on a daily basis, by Madame Plotnikova, who would clearly die of some nosiness-induced disorder if Lily didn't feed her with juicy anecdotal scraps. So promptly did she appear to greet her tenant that Lily suspected she spent the better part of each evening lying in wait.

'Velcome home, my dear,' she'd say, popping into Lily's path on the landing, the stairway and sometimes barring the door to her room. 'And so? How is our busy-busy lady?'

Until the incursion into her consciousness of Underground Man, she had found it easy – amusing, even – to elaborate on the part she'd created for herself of high-powered career woman. She had elevated her workplace into an international media hub and her role within it to Executive Chief – for what did Madame Plotnikova know about chiefs and hubs? Even less than Lily did, for she would gulp it all down eagerly and beg for more. This evening, having materialised from her Private Sitting Room, she was studying Lily intently and shaking her head.

'You looking terrible tired,' she remarked.

Lily couldn't help wondering whether this state of fatigue was exhibited by puffy pouches beneath her eyes or, worse, a stale odour? Was she pale and interestingly wan or just old and knackered. 'I'm exhausted,' she agreed. 'There's been a lot of pressure at work.' It was the best she could come up with.

'Is that so?' Firmly planted in Lily's path, Madame Plotnikova awaited elaboration.

'I'm sorry. I'm dead beat. Please excuse me, I need to go to bed. Tomorrow's going to be another long day – wall-to-wall with meetings —'

'Meetings, meetings.' Madame Plotnikova sighed heavily. 'Too hard you are working. Like my late husband, Igor, and look at him now. I am saying to Mrs Rosen only this morning that I worry about you, you will wear yourself out.'

Mrs Rosen, another resident at the Palace, was a septuagarian widow who sported two walking sticks and an unlikely blonde bouffant. Lily had met her twice. She had managed to avoid socialising at the guesthouse and, thankfully, not yet encountered Mavis Fishburn or Elizabeth Harris, two other occupants frequently referred to by the landlady. Everyone, it seemed, knew everything there was to know (and how little it really was) about Lily.

'I'll be fine,' she said, with what she hoped was the measure of grit and optimism required of the determined high-flyer.

'I hope so.' Madame Plotnikova looked doubtful. 'I really do.'

Rallying all her limited resources, Lily edged past her and emitted a decisive 'Good night' as she ascended the stairs. Alone in her room, though, she broke into a convulsive fit of sobbing that was as far removed as it was possible to be from the sardonic personality she affected for Giles and the career-woman sophistication she feigned for her landlady. She held her pillow over her face to muffle the gasping noises she couldn't repress and, when she had finally cried herself out, diagnosed her malaise as a potentially lethal mix of loneliness and – a condition she'd read about in a thousand advice columns but thought would never apply to her – *sexual frustration*.

The only remedy, as far as she could determine, would be to lift her self-imposed ban on West Hampstead tube station. Just to see her Underground Man would alleviate the pain.

The next morning she took her place, third in line, in front of the ticket office. By the time it was her turn, her heart was thumping and she was afraid she'd lose her voice. 'Hello, there,' she managed, determined that he would look at her. With the two customers preceding her, he had conducted transactions while chatting to a friend on the phone.

'Cheers, mate,' he said – not to her, to his mobile. He smiled, not at her but at his own musing. Damn. Then his gaze rested on Lily – on her – yes, definitely on her. 'Oh, hi.' This time his smile was addressed to *her*, without a doubt. 'Been away then?'

He'd noticed. He'd been aware of her absence. That must mean something, surely? 'Well, yes – I travel for work,' she said, which sounded plain boring. She had to hold his attention, somehow. She had to sustain the focus of those keen blue eyes. 'I was wondering —' she began.

'What were you wondering?'

She could sense the queue growing restive behind her. In a few seconds he'd lose his patience too. 'Remember you – er – mentioned that maybe I'd be better off with an Oyster Card?'

He nodded. His phone started to ring.

Quick, she thought. 'Is there any chance that you could help me? I'm not very —'

'Yup,' he was saying. Into his phone again, that bloody phone. 'Not *now*, mate.' Then to her – *to her*. 'Sorry?'

'Oh, that's ok. Maybe I should come back later, when you're not so busy?'

'Sure. Sure thing.'

'After work, maybe – at, say, six-ish? Will you still be here?'

He leaned forward and propped up his chin with his hand, staring at her intently. 'You bet,' he said. 'I'll be here.' And smiled.

She couldn't answer, for her mouth had dried. All she could manage was a cursory nod as she tried to decipher his gaze and his smile. Was it condescending? Conspiratorial? Invitational? Sympathetic? She'd find out when she returned there at six. But meanwhile how on God's earth would she get through the day?

With excruciating difficulty. In her head ran a constant compulsive refrain about the idiocy of what she was getting herself into, countered by her commonsense reminding her that she was merely seeking appropriate advice for her travel arrangements.

'What?' asked Gordon.

'Huh?'

'You're muttering to yourself. That way madness lies, lovely Lily.'

'Oh. Sorry. I was trying to work something out.' She stared at her computer screen, hoping she'd seem too engrossed in her work for interrogation.

But Gordon, she knew, wouldn't leave it at that. As he often remarked, he hadn't become a newshound, even a failed one, for nothing. 'Well,' he said, 'if at any stage you wanted any help with your calculations —'

'No,' she said quickly, adding 'thank you', so as not to sound churlish. 'By the way, I must leave at five-thirty sharp today. I have a very important appointment after work.'

'You do?' He sounded sceptical.

'Yes, I do.' She pursed her lips, resenting the doubt he seemed to be casting on her story – it wasn't even a story, a mere statement. He had no idea of the true nature of her liaison, which of course it wasn't. At all. After all, she could be meeting a client or a financial advisor or … 'It's with an estate agent,' she heard herself explaining. Gosh, that came out smoothly. This lying business was getting easier every day. 'An adorable little flat in Chelsea has come up for sale and I've managed to get some funds released from the family trust. It all has to be done very quickly in case the owner changes his mind.'

'I see,' he said, still in that irritatingly cynical way. 'That's a quick turnaround, if you don't mind my saying so. Didn't you tell me only a few weeks ago that you'd taken this job because you were strapped for cash?'

She glowered at him. 'I said *cash*, didn't I? The *real* money's all impossibly tied up – or it has been until now. So that is why —'

'Whatever.' He was rummaging through the papers on his desk. 'Before you rush off, though, will you please make sure to get this piece out to the *Bangkok Echo* pronto – Ed's been making noises about the deal being off if it's not there by today. Bloody deals. I think he's going too far. One of these days it will all come crashing down on him, the whole bang shoot.'

Normally, she'd have been offended by his peremptory tone and curious about Ed's deal, and why there'd be crashing, and what Gordon meant by 'the whole bang shoot'. The intricacies of Global Perspectives were still as mysterious to her as the origins of the universe and the workings of the World Wide Web. Today, though, the only thing that occupied her mind was the impending appointment. What would he say? What would happen? Her fingers danced across the keyboard, transmitting to the popular press of Thailand some lurid insights into the sexual proclivities of select soccer stars, but her thoughts were on him, on *him*. His face. His chiselled cheeks, so manfully defined by that hint of stubble. His intensely blue eyes.

Goodness or badness or madness or whatever it was – she, Lily Green, was obsessed.

At five twenty-nine she shut down her computer and a minute later, calling out a hasty farewell, she was out of the door. She joined the tide of homebound commuters surging into Holborn Station and, for the first time, felt there was a purpose to her journey. This evening she wasn't merely returning to her sad little room in the Winter Palace. Even the lithe blonde in the travel poster and the miraculously youthful model touting anti-wrinkle cream didn't faze her. Look at them, plastered onto the tunnel wall, while Lily had somewhere to go, someone to meet. *She* had an assignation.

But when she emerged through the barriers and into the ticket hall at West Hampstead Station she became apprehensive. Uncertain. People pushed past her, leaving, returning; this was a transition point, not a destination. How could she have inflated a random encounter into the stuff of romance? And

Shelley Weiner

look – the ticket booth was empty. A few dislocated souls hovered in front of it, but the window that usually framed his dark hair and his smile revealed nothing but a blank wall. Ah, well. She should have expected nothing else. He'd no doubt forgotten all about her, had never given her a thought, and was out on the town with his gorgeous young girlfriend, the two of them giggling hysterically at his mimicry of the flaky female who'd needed help with her Oyster Card.

But, wait. He was there. He'd appeared. He had taken his place in his booth and was squinting out into the concourse. To the right, to the left, and then he saw her. 'Hi,' he said.

'Oh, hi.' She tried to sound offhand but was sure that, even at this distance, he could hear her hammering heart.

'It's you. You turned up. I was wondering if you would.'

He had remembered. More than that, he'd been wondering. Wondering about *her*? All she could manage was, 'Yes.'

He, meanwhile, had turned away and begun talking to someone at the inner entrance to the booth. 'Bloody hell,' he was saying. 'Can't a person even go and take a leak? It's like working for the Gestapo.' Then, facing the window again, he remembered her. 'Sorry about that,' he said, with a smile that made her weak. 'I wasn't meant to have left my post till Joe came to relieve me. Anyway —'

'The Oyster Card?' she reminded him. This had, after all, been a professional appointment. Such private matters as his bladder control, his choice of vocabulary and the logistics of his job were not, strictly speaking, on the agenda. She wanted him to respect her, not to jump to conclusions.

'Of course. You wanted some extra information. Hang on a sec – let me pop out of my cage and take you through it.'

She held her breath for what seemed like an unendurable gap between his disappearance and manifestation at her side, then released it when she saw that his bottom half was as good, if not better, than his head and his shoulders. He was solid, chunky in his jeans, a fine figure of a man.

'Here we go,' he was saying as he held out a leaflet. She accepted it. His hand brushed hers and she shivered at his touch. 'Have a read. I'd say that Pay As You Go would be the best way to get you started – it's easiest for someone like you.'

'Ok,' she said, obligingly. 'If that's what you think.'

Someone like you. Had he considered what she might be like, then?

'Anyway, I'll leave this with you,' he was saying, 'and if there's anything —'

'No, wait!' It came out before she could stop herself. He was ending this. The meeting was over. She'd been utterly mistaken; he hadn't thought about her, didn't see her as a woman at all. 'Don't go. Please —'

'What's up?' He looked baffled. 'You don't have to feel pressured in any way, you know, miss —'

'Lily,' she said, so hastily that she almost tripped over her name. 'Lily Green. And you're —?'

'Me?' He smiled, as though amused by the rarity of a transport attendant being asked his name. 'Oh – I'm Thomas Kennedy. Tom to my friends.'

'Tom,' she said, savouring the compact virility of it. 'I like that.'

'Cheers – be my guest.' He raised his hand, clearly about to offer it to her, when a face appeared in his ticket booth. 'Joe!' he said. 'At fucking last, mate!' He headed for the booth, calling over his shoulder to Lily something about being glad to have met her and she should take a good look at the leaflet, no obligation of course…

This time she was too distraught to protest. She watched dumbly as he retreated and thought how she had blown it, the only encounter she'd ever cared about, the only fellow she'd ever care for. Everything else, all her reading, all her hanging about in public places, her meticulous grooming, her reckless lying – it had all seemed to be in preparation for this. For him. For *Tom*. She stood there, unable to move, and was hardly aware that she had started to cry.

'Hey.' She felt a sudden pressure on her arm. 'What's up, then? Is discussing an Oyster as upsetting as all that?'

'Sorry,' she said, mortified by her heaving shoulders and running nose. How deeply unglamorous. As if that mattered now. 'It's not the card – honestly. It's – nothing. I'm fine, I'll be fine, I didn't mean this to happen.'

'Course you didn't. Blubbing in a public place isn't something one usually plans on. As it happens, though, I have just the thing for you – I wasn't a Boy Scout for nothing.'

Through her tears she saw that he was pulling something out of his trouser pocket.

'Here,' he said. 'Get a load of this – a genuine linen handkerchief, white as driven snow. You don't see many of these about – an extinct species, as a mate of mine once told me. Go on, then – er – Lily?'

She nodded. 'Lily,' she affirmed nasally.

'Have a good blow and wipe off those tears. I was hoping this would come in handy one day.'

What was happening? From the bowels of the underworld she had unaccountably floated to heaven. Soft clean cloth was being dabbed on her eyes and a velvety voice was caressing her. 'Thank you,' she managed.

'My pleasure.' He was studying her, and there was something different about his scrutiny. Something, Lily sensed, had changed.

'I'll wash this and let you have it back tomorrow,' she offered.

'Nah, keep it,' he said expansively. 'One never knows when these kind of emergencies will strike again. You're ok now, aren't you?'

She nodded but was unable to staunch another torrent of tears. The embarrassment. What an emotional wreck he must think her to be. None of her mentors, not a single one, had advocated weeping as a come-on. 'Cry in company,' Carla Devine had once written (misquoting someone else), 'and next time you'll be crying alone.'

'I'm f-fine,' she stammered.

'You don't seem that fine,' he said, looking closely at her and proving Carla Devine wrong, *utterly* wrong. Never would Lily trust her advice again. 'I'd say you could do with a very stiff drink. Can I be the bloke who buys it for you?'

What a question. She tried to suppress the hysterical joy that bubbled up and threatened to transform her unattractive sobs to even less alluring snorts of laughter. She couldn't trust herself to answer lest she sounded too keen or, conversely, not keen enough. Instead she merely shrugged her acceptance, waited till he was free to leave, and mutely stepped beside him along West End Lane and into a pub called Ye Old Black Lion. Was this real? Was this truly happening to her, Lily Green?

'So,' he said, when he had ushered her into a seat, 'what can I get you?'

'A Scotch,' she said boldly, not knowing where this came from but thinking how cool it sounded, how in-the-movies cool. 'Actually,' she added, 'could you make that a double?'

'Sure thing,' he said, looking impressed. Or taken aback?

'Medicinal, you understand,' she felt obliged to add in case he was thinking she was not just a plain snivelling mess but an alcoholic snivelling mess. Which wouldn't enhance her attractiveness at all.

But when he brought the drinks and slid in beside her, she felt his sapphire-eyed gaze resting on her face and took a throat-scorching sip of her whisky and felt like the most beautiful, sophisticated woman in the world.

'Is that better?' he was asking.

'Yes, much,' she answered, trying not to cough. And thinking of the multitude of articles she had read about The Art of Seductive Small Talk and What the Stylish Woman Should Drink and Say. And of the advice of Jennifer Flowers, who had sworn that vodka was the aperitif of choice for the visible enhancement of sex appeal. Instead, here was Lily, monosyllabically swallowing a two-tot serving of single malt while this beautiful man was studying her with blatant fascination.

'So,' he said. 'What were those tears about? Or don't you like to say?'

He had moved a little closer to her and his distracting proximity impeded any recollection about her ever having been in tears or why. She sighed theatrically. 'It's a long story,' she hedged.

And somehow the pronouncement of the word 'story' cleared her head. A tale. A fairytale that ended with the two of them here, now, on the brink of endless rapture. Surely a consummate liar like Lily, someone who'd invented her fiancé and career and aristocratic family, someone who had successfully deceived her own mother, would be undaunted by the concoction of a poignant sob story?

'Tell me about it,' he said, as though he cared; as though he – like her – found stories irresistible. What a perfect match they were.

'In a minute,' she said. 'Let me collect my – er – thoughts.'

She told him she had lost a lover in a plane crash. She'd been much younger, twenty-three to be exact, and she and Josh had been desperately in love, with everything before them. So many plans. He'd been an architect and she – she had only lived for him, would have done anything to help him fulfil his dreams. Such ambitious dreams. He might have changed the skyline of the great capitals of the world, if he'd lived. Why, of all people, had Joshua gone and died so young?

'How?' Tom ventured. 'How did it happen?'

'The plane – an executive jet owned by a client – was bringing him back from Paris where he'd been working on a design for a new art gallery. Something happened – they never quite – it's so hard to talk about, even now —'

'Don't.' He reached for her hand and squeezed it gently. 'Not if it upsets you.'

'I want to,' she said stoically. 'I want you to know.'

For years after Josh's death – she went on – she had been inconsolable. Luckily she'd had good friends who had taken care of her and made her see that she *had* to carry on. When she'd been strong enough to do anything at all, she had immersed herself in work – her own career in the magazine world as well as voluntary work that filled all her free time so she wouldn't have space to grieve. She had tried to put Josh behind her, had various boyfriends, even found herself engaged to one. But no man had moved her since Josh. It was as though her heart, her whole being, had turned to stone.

'Until today,' she said softly.

'Today?' He had ceased drinking and was listening avidly.

'Probably before then. It was when I first saw *you*.'

'Me?' He seemed genuinely surprised. 'Why me?'

'There's something about you, something that reminded me of Josh. It struck me immediately.'

'I look like him? Poor bugger.'

'He was very handsome.' She dared to raise his hand, still enveloping hers, towards her cheek. 'It's been – it has been a long time since I've felt – like this. That's why I started to cry.'

There was silence. He seemed moved by the story. She herself was almost stirred to a resumption of her tears.

Meanwhile there was a part of her – the same part that had triumphantly witnessed the success of her other lies – that was agog with admiration at the plausibility and conviction with which she fibbed. What a talent she'd unearthed in herself. Who would have guessed that beneath the bland façade presented to the world by plain Lily Green lay this conniving creature who, even now, had duped a young man into rapt adoring empathy? 'D'you know something, Lily,' he was saying, 'you have the most amazing eyes.'

'So I've been told,' she managed serenely, hiding the thrill that pulsated through her and trying to ignore her fear of perhaps having reached the portal of a great unknown.

'So,' he said, having drained the last of his pint, 'I'd say some food would come in handy. Hungry?'

She considered. There was a hollow somewhere, but the idea of filling it with food made her nauseous. On the other hand, the possibility of ending the evening now was unthinkable. 'I might be,' she said cautiously.

'Good.' He stood up and indicated that she should do the same. 'There are some places round here we could try —'

'No.' Something within her had forced out the word. 'Let's stay here a bit longer, Tom – another drink would be good.'

Another drink! Was she crazy? As though her head wasn't swimming already. 'And then, maybe —'

'Maybe what?'

'Well, perhaps...' She couldn't believe she was about to say this but couldn't, wouldn't, stop herself; it was her chance, she had to grab it, her only chance. And the whisky had made her bold; more would make her bolder still. Or sick – no, she wouldn't be sick. 'Perhaps we could go back to —' She was about to say *my place*, but the prospect of smuggling him upstairs past prying Madame Plotnikova was too horrible to contemplate. '— to *your* place and have something to – um – eat there?'

'My place? It's in Shepherd's Bush.'

'That's perfect.' How romantic, she thought. How rustic. 'We can get a cab there. I'm happy to pay.'

The combination of alcohol and apprehension made the journey seem shorter and the fare less exorbitant, but there was no denying that their destination was hardly the pastoral idyll Lily had imagined. She stepped into a grimy street copiously littered with fast food containers, indolent youths and the indigent old. 'It's very lively,' she said politely.

'Isn't it great!' he enthused. 'I love it round here.' He steered her through a blistering brown door set between an off-license and a camping shop, and they picked their way through a narrow hallway and into a tiny lift that creaked up to the fourth floor. Halfway along a corridor lined with stained mattresses and cast-off chairs, he stopped and produced a key. 'Home sweet home,' he proclaimed, ushering her into Flat 435. 'Well?'

'It's a nice size,' was the best she could say.

'Isn't it?' He seemed unaware of her uncertainty. Striding ahead, he opened the curtains to reveal a sitting room that contained a sofa, a small table and a giant flat-screen television set balanced on a cardboard box. 'Two bedrooms as well. Thing is, I used to share it with a friend – someone my dad once knew. It was his flat.' He paused.

'And?' Lily asked, struggling against a strange floating sensation. Had she really come all the way to this squalid, alien place? It wasn't happening. It couldn't be happening. Here she was, a vulnerable woman with a stranger about whom she knew nothing and who might, at any moment, drug, rape or strangle her, and she had brought it all on herself.

'He – er – snuffed it.'

'Who – your friend?'

He nodded and for a moment looked young and forlorn, and her apprehension dissipated. Then he seemed to catch himself. 'Anyway, anyway,' he said cheerily. 'The good thing was that he left this flat to me.'

'That *was* good,' she said doubtfully.

'And even better,' he went on, 'he introduced me to this!' He reached up to a shelf for a squat brown bottle, which he dusted off and placed on the table. 'Tia Maria. Nectar of the gods. Want some?'

Without waiting for an answer, he ducked into an adjoining room which she took to be the kitchen. Deep breaths, Lily, she told herself. In, out, in, out. There was nothing unusual about her situation, nothing at all. She was on a date, having a sociable evening with a lively and attractive man. Intelligent, too. There were several books on his shelf. She couldn't make out the titles and didn't want to be caught snooping but there, unmistakably, was the Shorter Oxford English Dictionary. Now that *alone* said something about him; it had to.

'Here we are.' He'd reappeared bearing two surprisingly elegant cut-glass goblets. 'Tell me these aren't classy? Jimmy left these to me as well.'

'Jimmy,' she repeated as she accepted a brimming glass.

'My friend.'

'I gathered that. He had good taste.' She sipped her drink. 'And *this* tastes excellent.'

'Cheers.' He leaned over and brushed her forehead with a kiss.

'Oh,' she said. And next thing they were kissing, properly kissing, and his hand was caressing her, and hers was —
'Tom.' She pulled away. 'I need to tell you that I haven't – I'm not —'

'What? Oh, don't worry, I'll use something.'

He didn't understand. 'I've never done this,' she confessed, fearful and close to tears again.

'Never?' He frowned. 'You mean you're a —'

'No,' she said quickly, remembering her story. 'It's not that. It's since – Josh. It's been a long time.'

'And you're sure that now —'

'Yes,' she broke in. 'I do. I want to. You won't – hurt me – will you?'

'Lily,' he said, unbuttoning her blouse and tenderly stroking her breasts, 'I'll be gentle, truly. I'll awaken every part of you. I'll be your prince and you can be my sleeping princess.'

Forty minutes later Lily's timidity had gone the way of her virginity and she was applying playful pressure to Tom's earlobe. The path of her awakening could be traced by the items of clothing randomly strewn between the sitting room and his bedroom, which boasted an extremely large and very bouncy bed. Now he was snoring deeply and she, wanting his attention, tweaked his ear again.

'Ouch!' he said.

'Wake up.' She applied light kisses to his eyelids. 'Let's talk.'

'Talk?' He reached out and pulled her towards him and was about to start the awakening process again.

But she restrained him. She wouldn't have minded another session, but a chorus comprising Clarabelle Wynne-Stanley, Carla Devine, Maisie Fitzherbert, Megan Moffat, Angela Manning, Jennifer Flower, Genevieve Olson, Marcia Jones, Martha Smithson and a few random others were beaming forth their warning that now, when she had him, was the time to hold back. Strategy was all. 'Yes, talk,' she declared. 'I want to know everything.'

'Me too,' he said sleepily.

'But you already know about *me*. Maybe not everything, but the important things.' As she spoke, she managed to forget entirely that she had invented them all. 'I've told you about Josh. And then there's my job, which I'm sure I've mentioned. At the moment I work for an international media agency based near Holborn. I live, temporarily, in a small private hotel in – well, quite near West Hampstead Station, as it happens. One of the better streets. But as I said, it's not forever. There's the possibility of a flat coming up for sale in Chelsea quite soon.'

'Chelsea,' he repeated, studying her with interest. 'A *Chelsea* girl.'

'Not yet,' she said hastily. She must be careful not to get out of her depth. 'You know what it's like with buying property – it goes on and on and on. Very boring.'

'Not to me. I wouldn't be averse to having myself a small pad in that part of town.'

'So where do *you* come from, Tom?' she asked, quickly changing the subject. 'Where did you go to school? How did you end up working for the Underground? Tell me all!'

'Now *that's* boring.' Again he pulled her towards him and this time she didn't resist. He gazed into her face. 'There's one thing I *will* tell you, though – even at the risk of repeating myself. Lily Green, you have the most extraordinary eyes.'

Part Two

4

She certainly did have great eyes. They were amazing. Tom meant the compliment in all sincerity. But the reason his heart was pumping like a steam engine, the *real* reason, was neither those eyes nor her not-bad boobs nor even the passable sex, but the fact that he'd made it.

At last.

The woman was loaded.

Every clue confirmed it, they all added up. Number one: the way she dressed, expensive stuff, understated. Number two: the way she threw her cash about, a full price Tube ticket every day, that taxi fare without blinking. Number three, the clincher: her place in Chelsea, well not *yet* her place, but the way she spoke made it just about a done thing.

And, bingo, to cap it all – she fancied him. Mightily. All that crap about Josh for fuck's sake. He didn't believe it for a moment, it stood out a mile that she was making it up. Did she think he was some kind of sucker? Likelihood was that she needed to justify her attraction to Tom (fair enough) and the blatant fact that she'd never done it before. Basically, all she'd wanted was a good shag and fortunately for her she'd come knocking on super-stud Tom's front door. Lucky Lily. More to the point, lucky him.

'I'd better get back,' she was saying, sitting up bare-chested and then, suddenly self-conscious, crossing her arms to cover herself.

'Don't do that,' he said. 'You're spoiling my view.'

She frowned at him suspiciously.

'What?' He pulled her towards him, gently; one had to be gentle with a dame like this. 'I'm not being funny. I mean it. I like looking at you. You're beautiful.' A bit of strategic exaggeration always went down well, but the last might have been too much.

It was.

'I'm not,' she said. 'You know I'm not.'

'Maybe not *classically* beautiful,' he moderated, then saw her face falling. Christ. He was mucking it up. Next thing she'd start blubbing again. Tentatively he stroked her cheek. 'You're just very, very attractive. And I meant what I said about your eyes – truly.'

She gave a sceptical half-laugh, but he held her gaze intently. And when she repeated the crap about having to 'get back' (Where to? Where was she running?), he wrapped his arms round her and could almost hear the cheers of his mates as he felt her dissolving into his embrace. Wey-hey! He was melting her again, masterfully melting her. And now she was writhing against him, her excitement knowing no bounds. What a player he was and what a quick learner she was turning out to be. Physical compatibility, that's what they had. Despite the age gap, which was big but not what you'd call a chasm. He was twenty-four and she was – say, mid-thirties? It wasn't a *great* age; it wasn't as though she was old enough to be his mother.

His mother. Beatrice. Tom didn't like thinking about her, it was easier not to. Even now, when he came upon a particular smell or gesture or tone of voice, a muddle of feelings shot through him. There were sweet memories of her holding him close, trying her best to keep him safe, but these were quickly overtaken by the shivers he got recalling his father's sneering voice. 'Three daughters and then you,' his dad would say, looking disparagingly at his only son. '*This* is what I waited for? This pathetic sissy – my son and heir?'

He would prod Tom's bony shoulder, but Beatrice would protect him from anything worse. 'Give him a chance, Hector,' she would plead. 'He's little. He'll grow. You'll be proud of him one day, just wait and see.'

She would urge him to eat. 'Finish your food, Tommy. It will make you big and strong for your daddy.' But no matter how much he ate or how hard he pushed and pulled on the Multi-Function Chest Expander he was given for his seventh birthday, he remained tiny. Far too small and weak and scared to go to the rescue when he heard the thumping of his father's fists and his mother's cries in the night.

'It's not like that, Hector,' she would sob. 'I promise, I *swear*, it's not like that at all.'

Then the girls, his big sisters, would chime in: 'Leave her, daddy. Please. *Please*.'

And finally there'd be silence and Tom would lie there, not knowing if his mother was dead or asleep or had run away. Each morning he would almost faint with relief when he saw her, but then at night the scuffles and shouts and thumps would begin again. Terrified, he'd try not to think about her fate, her ultimate fate – and his own too if his oldest sister Eugenia was telling the truth. 'We're *all* going to turn into skeletons in the end, arsehole,' she taunted. 'All of us. Every single one. Think about that!'

'No, no, please no – I don't want to,' he protested, fighting against tears.

'Cry-baby, cry-baby,' she jeered, summoning Florence and Midge to join in the teasing. They loved teasing Tom. It was the only thing they totally agreed upon – the subjugation and humiliation of their puny brother.

'I'm not crying,' he insisted, knowing they couldn't *wait* to regale their father with this further evidence of his weakness and flinching in dread of the beating that would come his way.

But this time Hector didn't hit him. Nor did he join in with his daughters' mocking laughter. His face was grim. 'Your mother's sick,' he announced.

The four of them looked at him silently. Tom didn't dare ask the questions he wanted to – had *Hector* made her sick, and would she die? And if so…?

'What's wrong with her?' Eugenia asked.

'Brain tumour.' Hector's voice was flat. 'Inoperable. Not much to be done.'

They went to visit her in the hospital – Hector, Eugenia, Florence, Midge and Tom all arranged round a big white bed with Beatrice upon it, as shrunken and still as —

'A skeleton,' Tom screamed, unable to contain his horror. 'She's turning into a skeleton.'

Eugenia dragged him outside and slapped him. 'Wait till daddy gets hold of you,' she warned. 'Arsehole. Cry-baby.'

He braced himself for Hector's retribution but Beatrice's death, quicker than anyone had predicted, intervened to save him. Even then.

She wasn't there, though, to save Tom from being packed off to boarding school which, his sisters told him gleefully, was his father's firm intention now that Beatrice was gone.

'What does it mean, going to boarding school?' he wanted to know. At eight, he had no concept of the fate that was being handed to him.

'What does it *mean*?' Eugenia repeated scornfully. 'You tell him, Midge.'

Midge, the youngest, had always been Hector's favourite and had now become his Right Hand Girl. 'Whatever it means,' she said in a superior way, 'Daddy says, that if it doesn't turn you into a poofter it will make you a man.'

'Oh.' He didn't dare risk further ridicule by asking more. Maybe boarding school was like the chocolate factory he'd once been taken to, but instead of making Mars Bars and Smarties it turned out poofters, whatever they were, and men? He could imagine it, all those moving belts and the sorting and the trucks waiting to carry them away...

'Stop dreaming, arsehole,' Midge was saying as she poked his arm. 'Daddy wants to see you in his study now.'

'*Now*?' Tom's stomach contracted.

'Get a move on. You know he gets twitchy if he's kept waiting.'

Nervously Tom tapped on the heavy door of his father's study. He could hear Hector's voice on the telephone, then a barked, 'Come in!'

Tom slid inside. 'An agreement's a fucking agreement, Geoffrey,' Hector was saying. 'And you can tell your hedge fund man that if he doesn't come up with the goods pronto, there's going to be trouble. Yeah. Right. Cheers.'

He frowned, muttering expletives, and Tom surreptitiously scoured the dark-oak-and-leather-dominated room for any clue to the tone of this interview. His father's huge desk was littered with papers and empty glasses and a granite ashtray brimming with cigar butts. The air was heavy with the smell of drink and tobacco and sweat. Tom coughed.

'Be with you in a sec, Thomas,' his father said, dialling a number distractedly. 'Fucking morons.' He shook his head and gave Tom a wry man-to-man look.

A *man-to-man* look. And he'd called him *Thomas*. And he wasn't sending him away while he finished his business talk. No – he'd got someone called Arthur on the line now and was *giving* it to him, effing and blinding and meanwhile glancing at Tom and rolling his eyes. *Including* him. Tom inhaled the acrid air which, with each breath, made him manlier and manlier until, by the time his father terminated his conversation with a flourish of blasphemy, he felt six foot tall.

'Nicely handled, sir,' he said to Hector out of the side of his mouth. It sounded good. Mean and menacing, like a tough guy's sidekick in a movie.

'Don't *sir* me, you little runt.' His father was squinting at him with the old contempt. 'How old are you anyway?'

'Nearly nine,' answered Tom. It was like he'd been pricked and deflated and was small and motherless and weak again.

'Nearly nine,' Hector mimicked. 'And look at you! That boarding school will have its work cut out, that's for sure.'

'Where is it?' ventured Tom.

'Somewhere up north, who knows? Your mother's poncy brother Edwin went there, so I could pull some strings. Better be good is all I can say – costs a fucking arm and leg. You're a bloody privileged little fucker getting this opportunity, which is more than I had I can tell you. I learnt the hard way, and we're not talking book-learning here. We're talking survival. Beating the system. Do you know what I was, lad?'

'I'm not sure.'

'A nothing. A nobody. And what am I now?'

Tom didn't want to get this wrong. He could feel the impending thrashing. 'Rich?' he tried in a small voice.

'Stinking rich. And fucking powerful. They call me The Hedge, did you know that? *The Hedge*. I had this mate once, a bloke called Jimmy Henderson – tried to convince me that with my abilities I should maybe go legit, start a proper business, pay my taxes. We even fell out over it. He came to London before I did and who-the-fuck knows where he is now. Last thing I heard he was earning peanuts on the railways or something.' Hector seemed to have softened during the course of his musing. Tom almost starting relaxing again. But then his father drew breath and turned on him, bellowing: 'The point of this story is that there are life's travellers and life's stickers-in-the-mud and *The Hedge* always knew he was one of the slickest movers around. *Always*. I have gone *places*, lad – unlike that fuckwit Henderson. And if *you* want to go places too, you'd better start looking sharp.'

There was a long pause. Tom wasn't sure whether or not the interview was over, but thought it prudent to wait till he was properly dismissed.

His father, meanwhile, was studying him. 'I want to show you something, Thomas,' he said at last.

'What?' Tom no longer trusted the conspiratorial voice.

'Something.' Hector smiled. 'Something secret.'

Tom stared back, not daring to speak. Had his first instinct been right, then? Was he now man enough to be taken into his father's confidence? He returned the smile, trying not to reveal too much delight.

'This school I'm sending you to,' Hector went on conversationally. 'It's meant to be an excellent place, guaranteed to turn you into the kind of gent your mother's family'd been proud of. The thing that worries me, though…' His voice trailed off.

'What?' Tom prompted, eager to allay his father's concern.

'I'm afraid that with all your learning and posh new connections, you'll get soft —'

'No,' he interrupted fiercely. 'Never!'

'You'll start thinking that your old dad's an ignorant fart.'

'Not *ever*,' said Tom emphatically. But he was getting panicky again for Hector's tone had sharpened.

'Just in case you did, though, I thought there was a little spelling game we could play. Me and you. Don't worry – it's an easy one. Are you good at spelling?'

Tom nodded warily.

'Here goes then: OMNIPOTENT. Try that.'

'O,' Tom began. 'M.' He faltered. Such an easy word. He knew it. But his mind had frozen.

'Go on, clever-clogs,' his father urged.

But Tom couldn't.

'Come to think of it.' Hector stood up, stretched languidly, and began to examine the shelves above his desk, which were stacked mostly with black-bound files. From the highest he pulled down a hefty volume which he placed on Tom's lap. 'Seems daft to have a spelling quiz when there's this fine reference book in the house. Feel the weight of it.'

Tom could. It was pinning him down. 'The Shorter Oxford English Dictionary,' he read aloud.

'Surprised? Shocked that someone like your old man would own such a fine – er – tome?'

'No. Not really.'

'Go on, then – open it and look up the word. We know it begins with O, then M —'

Tom slowly opened the book and stared, at first uncomprehendingly, at what he saw. Into each page had been carved the silhouette of a gun – slide, frame and handle – which turned the volume into a nest. And snugly encased in this nest was a black metal pistol. Deadly. Menacing. He shivered.

Hector started laughing. He carried on for a minute or so, then stopped short. 'Omnipotent,' he said. 'O – M – N – I – P – O – T – E – N – T. Having infinite power.' He leaned down, so close that Tom could feel his breath on his cheek and smell its sour tobacco odour. Then he reached into the book and stroked the weapon. Tenderly. 'Omnipotent,' he said again. 'This is our secret, son. *Our* secret.'

Even now Tom could summon the fear and excitement of the moment Hector had revealed the black Luger P08, their secret; the rare gentleness with which he had taken Tom's hand and placed it on the cold metal, then sharply pulled it away. He shuddered. Fifteen years ago, and it could have been yesterday.

'What's up?' Her voice, concerned, jolted him to the present. She was frowning, her astonishing eyed fixed on his face, a tentative finger on his cheek.

'Nothing's up,' he said quickly and resumed the melting process. 'Why,' he asked, nuzzling the back of her neck, 'should anything be up?'

'You went all quiet.'

'That's contentment,' he murmured.

'And you shivered?'

He removed his nose from her neck, his hand from her left breast and her finger from his cheek. Sighing deeply, he drew himself up to a seated position alongside her. 'Lovely Lily,' he said, 'this luxury flat of mine has one fatal flaw – it's fucking cold.'

She yanked at his arm with surprising strength. 'Come back here – I'll keep you warm,' she whispered. 'Let's snuggle up and tell each other stories —'

'Stories? How about that – I *love* stories. I'm a complete story freak.

'— Stories and secrets.'

Secrets he wasn't so sure about, he hardly knew the dame. 'Nah, not secrets,' he said, restoring his lips to the back of her neck. 'Stories are for telling but secrets – they're for keeping.'

He'd certainly hung on to his, like a Rottweiler with lockjaw. 'Our little secret.' Tom had buried the words deep into his head and the malevolent image into his mind, taking them out now and again for private scrutiny, but never telling. Never *ever*. Hector's revelation had changed Tom's perception of himself from puny mummy's boy to mean Son of the Underworld.

He waited for the old man to take it one step further – to show him 'the secret' again and maybe brief him about his future role in his empire; to tell him exactly how he'd made it to the status of The Hedge; to regale him with stories of skulduggery and vice. Tom practised whistling through his teeth and persuaded Midge to take him to see *The Godfather* and *Scarface* and *The Long Good Friday*, and didn't know what the fuck they were about but tried to ape the heroes. He started using fuck a lot. And whistling under his breath. He carried on waiting for Hector to summon him back. But in vain. Weeks passed. Hector went away 'on business' and would – according to Midge – be gone for some time. By now Tom had been expensively equipped and packed into a northbound train that would carry him to boarding school.

'Good riddance,' sang Eugenia and Florence and Midge as they waved him away.

'Bitches,' he muttered. But without conviction. London flashed past, then the alien countryside, and it seemed to Tom that he was being hurled into oblivion. He shut his eyes and tried to picture himself with the father who had shared with him his most dangerous, vital, intimate secret. They would return, The Hedge from his travels and Tom from school, and pick up where they'd left off.

But it never happened. The term passed, then another and another and Tom, enduring cold showers and tepid dinners and unrelentingly cruel banter, kept hoping to no avail for another audience with his father. Hector was 'away'; Hector was 'unwell'; Hector was 'otherwise engaged'. The only sign that Tom received of the conversation with Hector ever having happened was an unsigned postcard delivered to the school and bearing a single word: OMNIPOTENT.

And this was only a few months ahead of the next auspicious word that came to the school – of his father's sudden death.

'*How?*' he asked, when he'd found his voice. As a sixteen-year-old late starter, it had only just broken. 'How did he die?'

'In mysterious circumstances,' answered his House Master with enigmatic emphasis.

'Oh.'

'Bad luck, Kennedy.'

Tom nodded. 'Can't be helped,' he said, trying for matching nonchalance but unable to prevent the catch in his throat that somehow spoilt the effect. Bugger. Next thing he'd start bawling. 'Better get back to London, then. They'll need me.'

This wasn't true; the last thing his sisters would want or need (even in a crisis, especially in a crisis) would be arsehole Tom. But it sounded important and gave him a reason to leave the dreaded school in dark-suited dignity, at least that. In London he was told that Hector had been in an accident – or what they'd assumed had been an accident for want of any other explanation. His Merc, apparently, had been involved in an unaccountable collision with a tree in a dark Essex lane. The car had sustained only minor damage but The Hedge had been instantly killed.

And by the time Tom arrived he'd been buried as well.

'Couldn't you have waited?' he asked Eugenia. 'I'm his son – his son and heir.'

'Heir nothing, snotface,' his sister retorted, with a galling lack of respect given that he was now man of the house.

'What do you mean?'

'I mean that Daddy's so-called accident happened to coincide with a period of – how shall I put it? – financial slump. There was some kind of link, they're saying, between the crash and his debts and a couple of unexplained tyre-marks on the road.'

'I don't understand.'

'Nothing much to understand, moron. The car's been impounded and the house repossessed. We're broke. Totally and utterly skint .'

'I see. You mean we have nothing.'

'You got it, dumbo. Nothing. Not a single bloody thing.'

There *was* something left, though, after the bailiffs had cleared the house in Mill Hill and taken Hector's fake Chippendale chairs and his batch-bought paintings and his rugs and his 1975 Vintage Port and almost everything else. What was left, in lonely splendour on the shelf above the space that until now was his desk, was his copy of the Shorter Oxford English Dictionary.

'Didn't they want that?' Tom asked his sisters, pretending he didn't give a damn.

'Does it look like it?' Eugenia retorted. The loss of their legacy hadn't improved her temper.

'Do *you* want it?' He put the question very carefully for fear of making it seem in any way desirable.

'Do I *look* like I'd want a bleeding dictionary?'

'Do you think that – uh – *I* might hang on to it, as a kind of memento?' he suggested.

'Suit yourself,' she said with a shrug.

Yes, he thought. Yes, *yes*. Casually he retrieved the book from the shelf and bore it away. 'Omnipotent,' he mouthed to himself as, in seclusion, he opened it and looked inside. And the Luger was there, hard and black and deadly. *His* now, all his. Tom would restore (never mind restore – *exceed*) Hector's fortune. The underworld would tremble in his wake. The Hedge's reputation for unscrupulous, merciless double-dealing would be like that of a kid's for nicking sweeties compared with the infamy of his son.

What a moment that was, he thought. What a glorious fucking moment. Everything before him, struggles and humiliations in the past. Like now, with his conquest, his rich Lily Green.

'Tom,' she was saying, 'I'm suddenly starving.'

'You are?' He lunged playfully towards her, but this time she held him at bay.

'I mean it.' She rose unsteadily to her feet. 'I need food.'

She was gathering her undergarments. The woman meant business. He'd have to forage in the kitchen and see what he could find, which wasn't likely to be much. On the other hand, there was always the Balti Tandoori downstairs. 'Fancy a curry?' he asked.

'A curry?' She hesitated briefly, and he thought he'd blown it; he might have guessed she'd be too cultured for curry. Then she smiled and he relaxed. 'I'd love a curry,' she said.

Which solved the catering problem but not the subsidy issue, for Tom had long exceeded his credit limit with the Balti and was now, as usual, out of cash. He pulled on his clothes and began to rummage ostentatiously in various pockets.

'Need money?' she asked.

Dead right he did. 'If you could just – er – advance me a tenner or so, that would be great. I'll get some cash in the morning.'

'Don't worry about it.'

Worry about it? He forced himself to look uncertain when she handed him a twenty instead of a ten then, clutching the note to his chest, joyfully trotted down the stairs.

5

After they had swallowed their Lamb Rogan Gosh and Special Pilau Rice, Tom started thinking, what next? He had the woman and she had the wherewithal, but how the hell was he going to put them together on a basis that would result in long-term profit for him and not too much collateral damage to her? His brain hurt.

It was like the dip that had followed his euphoria when he'd taken possession of the deadly weapon that was going to launch his career in crime. Having decided that this was his destiny and true vocation, the big question was where and how to make a start. And, in the meantime, how to keep himself alive until the job began to pay. He'd scoured the Situations Vacant pages of the local papers for something that would keep him temporarily in pocket – a position that would use the articulacy of an expensive (if incomplete) public schooling and prepare him for a life of successful felony. Something in finances, maybe, or in the leisure industries? A night club bouncer, or a trainee hit person? Maybe a flexible cop?

Nothing doing. Not a single thing. He was reduced to pedalling a frigging bicycle (not even a moped!) round West London at a menial rate for a Mafia front called Pizza Pleeze. Gasping from the traffic fumes and recoiling from the abuse of customers whose order was late or cold or both, Tom consoled himself that at least his thighs were hardening and he was earning enough, just, to afford a bedsit in Acton.

When Pizza Pleeze folded, his fast food distribution skills quickly found him a new position with Doorstep Tandoori, then Kebab on the Hoof. Months passed, a year, and Tom's delivery technique became as impressive as his rock-like quads – but his criminal record remained crystal clean. Not that he didn't have the chance for a spot of larceny – there were takings to be pinched and customers to be mugged. But Tom couldn't bring himself to do it. Each morning he would put his hand on the Shorter Oxford English Dictionary which he kept at his bedside, and resolve that *this* would be his day, his criminal deflowering. And each evening he'd come home with his innocence intact.

It got to the point when he couldn't face looking at the dictionary. Instead of inspiring him it reminded him of his father's contempt. 'Didn't I always say you were a useless little runt!'

Tom hid the book in a cupboard, but Hector's mockery haunted him night and day.

The only place he could silence it was in the local Crown & Anchor, with a few pints of bitter in his belly and a receptive audience at hand. Then his bravado knew no bounds. Drunkenly he would expand on his violent but lucrative exploits, his dastardly associates and the trail of splattered organs in his wake.

'It's all a matter of having the right connections and the right mind-set,' he would explain, trying not to slur his words. 'And then of course there's the genetic link. It's no accident that I'm in this field. You might say it's in my blood.'

He would pause dramatically, then announce himself as no other than the son of a notorious gangster, one of the most infamous crooks in underworld history.

'A legendary *late* crook,' he'd add with sombre deliberation. 'Died a few years back, did my old man – it's a high-risk, big-reward occupation. But even now people shudder when I mention his – er – professional name. Bet you've heard of him – go on, have a guess.'

There would be wild conjecture, punctuated by the clues offered by Tom. 'Think privet,' he'd suggest. 'Bush? Shrub? *Topiary*? No? Give up?'

They'd grow silent while he made his revelation. They liked him or maybe liked the rounds he sponsored when they pleased him, but what-the-hell difference did that make in the end? 'My dad,' he'd declare, 'was no other than Hector The Hedge.'

The revelation would be met with gasps and applause. There'd be questions met with expansive tales which Tom vaguely recalled having related before, but his listeners didn't seem to mind as long as the alcohol flowed with his progressively incoherent diction. Until at last he'd dry up, broke and drunk and spent, and stagger off in the direction of home.

Which was a hit-or-miss endeavour. On a good night he would make it into bed. On an average night he'd reach the bedsit and find himself the next morning on the not-too-clean bathroom floor or maybe just inside the doorway. Increasingly, though, the pavement would rise up to greet him long before he'd made it home and there he would lie until the kick of a cop, or worse, returned him to consciousness.

On one particular Friday evening, when his intake and output were especially high, he only managed to stagger a few feet from the doorway of the Crown and Anchor before succumbing to gravity. Hours later, there he was, still lying on the dark deserted kerb, soddenly asleep. In an inebriated dream his father was punishing him for his cowardly fibs. Pinching him. Sneering at him.

'No,' he groaned. 'Leave me alone, sir – please – please. I'll do better next time, I promise…'

But his entreaties were ignored. Gradually he perceived that someone had crouched down beside him and now, instead of squeezing his arm, was shaking it violently.

'Fuck off,' Tom managed, now half-awake. No way was this his father; it was some ancient perv. 'Get off me,' he slurred. But the bugger ignored him. Tom tried to wriggle free but couldn't make the connection between his brain and his limbs. 'Leave me alone,' he moaned.

To no avail. With dogged persistence (surely he wasn't such a catch?) his assailant dragged him to a seated position and then, gasping asthmatically, stared him in the face.

'Hector's son,' he said, shaking his head. 'Who'd have believed it.'

'Who the fuck —' Tom began.

'Oi. Watch the language. Meant to be a gent, you were – cost him a fortune. Get up off the street – here, I'll give you a hand. There you go…'

Weakly he complied, finding himself supported – bloody humiliating – by this interfering geriatric. Who was he? He seemed to know Hector. He even knew that Tom had been sent to a private school.

'I heard you talking that crap in the pub, couldn't help meself,' the old guy was saying. 'First I thought you were just another bullshitter and I was right, of course, but when you said The Hedge I realised —'

'You knew him?'

He didn't answer. Breathing heavily, he guided Tom forward step by stumbling step. 'Where to?' he wheezed at last.

'What's it your business?' Tom tried to sound aggressive and to free himself with dignity, but his voice came out all whiny and he almost fell to the ground again. 'Past that traffic light and second to the left,' he mumbled and then, after they'd made some slow progress, asked again, 'My old man. The Hedge. You knew him?'

'I did. I certainly did. Name Jimmy Henderson mean anything to you?'

'Jimmy — no, I don't think so.' Tom paused to ponder and the name trickled through his befuddled mind until it struck something. An image. His father's study, as it had been in his heyday; Hector on the brink of sharing his secret, his voice dangerously mellow, talking scornfully about a friend called Jimmy Henderson who'd tried to convince him to go legit. A *fuckwit*, although Tom didn't want to say as much to this elderly Samaritan. 'Actually, I think it might just ring a bell.'

'Thought so.' He sounded pleased. 'He probably told you I was a bit of a fuckwit for going straight —'

'No, not at all.'

'— and he might have been right. But who's laughing now, eh? Which of us is six feet under?'

Gloating bastard. Tom pushed him away and was now angry enough to remain on his feet. 'Get off. Loser.' He turned and, with difficulty, headed off.

'Wait,' Jimmy called. 'Hold it there, lad. It's *you* who's the loser, not to mention a complete bullshitter – one minute listening to you in the Crown & Anchor told me that. Even so, you're the son of one of my oldest friends, which counts for something. Here. Take this. Get in touch if you feel like it – I may have an interesting proposition for you, something that'll turn things around.'

The next morning Tom awoke with a hangover and an ornate business card clutched in his hand. *James Henderson – Mercenary Consultant* was written in an elaborate cursive font. Who was James Henderson and what on God's earth was a 'mercenary consultant'? Through a befuddled haze he recalled his late-night encounter, but there wasn't time to ponder. He was running late. With a pounding head he put the card aside and set off for Kebab on the Hoof.

But the day was a disaster. He lost his way four times, fell off his bicycle twice and misdelivered three orders. When he finally stumbled in to collect his pay, he was told by the Operations Manager that he wouldn't be needed again.

'Do you think I give a shit?' Tom asked belligerently. The booze lingering in his bloodstream and relief at the prospect of sleeping it off lent him a laddish braggadocio that was rather thrilling.

But a week later his elation had vanished. He had tried every local home delivery outlet he could think of but, as the man in the Jobcentre put it, his track record was 'erratic'. On the dole he could barely pay the rent, never mind treat himself to a pint or so at the Crown. He'd reached rock bottom. What would Hector say if he saw his son now?

Thinking of Hector reminded Tom of his meeting with decrepit Jimmy Henderson. An 'interesting proposition', he'd said. Whatever that meant. On the other hand, any proposition at all was better than Tom's current state of despair. Where was that card he had been given? Having randomly stowed it away, he almost tore his bedsit apart trying to find it and then, when it came to light, hesitated before dialling the number. Could he face Jimmy's derision over the fact that The Hedge's son and heir was crawling to him for help?

Yes he could. He had to. There seemed no other way.

'I was hoping you'd call,' Jimmy said. 'I had a feeling you would.'

'Really?' Tom asked cautiously, on the lookout for sarcasm.

'God's my witness.'

'Oh.' Such a high-level alibi had to mean either sincerity or that the old boy had got religion, or both. Could Jimmy's mercenary consultancy have something to do with being a Soldier of Faith? Well, Tom would try anything once. 'I'm a Believer too,' he tried, with as much conviction as he could manage.

'Yeah?'

Now there *was* mockery in Jimmy's voice. Unmistakably.

'In an expedient kind of way,' Tom amended, trying to moderate his ardour.

'And how expedient,' Jimmy wanted to know, 'is your devotion to a nicely-seared rump steak washed down with a few well-chosen pints?'

Was this another catch? Tom paused to think – and to swallow back a surge of saliva – before he answered. 'Steak and ale,' he said at last, 'is beyond religion. It's fucking paradise.'

'Good lad.' Jimmy laughed, properly laughed, which was a relief. 'And how about I treat you to paradise tomorrow night? There's a nice steakhouse a few doors down the street from the Crown – see you there at eight?'

He hesitated. What was the bugger after? Why was he so keen? The meal was tempting, though, and the old boy was probably just lonely and sentimental; if he tried anything on with Tom there was no doubt who'd land up on the floor. 'Tomorrow at eight,' he prevaricated. 'Hmm. Not quite sure.'

'You're wondering what's in this for me?' Jimmy asked, picking up on his disquiet.

'No – well, yes.'

'Meet me at the Crown at seven and I'll explain. No obligations and no commitments, right?'

What the hell. Nothing ventured, et cetera. 'Right,' he agreed.

The steak proved heavenly indeed and the brown ale pure nectar. Tom savoured each mouthful and when his plate and third pint glass had been thoroughly emptied he sat back and sighed. 'Beats kebab,' he said, patting his belly.

He glanced at Jimmy who, he noticed, had eaten little and was studying him intently.

'And so?' Tom suddenly felt vulnerable. And angry with the old fart for witnessing his greed and gratification. 'What's the deal, fuckwit?'

'The deal?' Jimmy sat back, nodding sagely, unfazed by Tom's crudity. 'For a start, lad, I think we'd better decontaminate the language. Ladies like a bit of slap and tickle, but you go too far.'

'Ladies?' He'd got him wrong then. Maybe he wasn't a poofter after all. But a *ladies'* man? Some kind of gigolo? Was he joking?

Jimmy smiled at his puzzlement. 'As you might have noted on my business card, sonny, I practise as a Mercenary Consultant,' he explained. 'As such, my particular area of expertise is with the female sex. Putting it plainly, women fancy me. They find me irresistible. Always have.'

'Really?' Tom couldn't hide his scepticism. He was trying his best not to insult his host, whose generosity had been impeccable. But honestly. Look at him. On the edge of decomposition. Maybe, he thought, glancing surreptitiously downward, the bugger was exceptionally well endowed? 'But what's that to do with —?'

Shelley Weiner

It was a long, long story, an interminable story, which Jimmy – having extracted a substantial cigar from his jacket pocket, ostentatiously examined the wrapper, and ignited with painstaking care – settled back to narrate. It all began, he said, with Hector The Hedge.

'My dad,' prompted Tom, wishing he'd get a move on.

'The very same. The Mister Big who had the nerve to laugh his pants off when I told him that he could transgress and violate as much as he liked, but Jimmy Henderson was going straight.' He drew deeply on his Cuban and almost failed to suppress a cough. 'Funny, that. With all Hector's bragging and his wife's upper-class family, landowners the lot, he's the one feeding the worms, his family destitute, while Jimmy Henderson sits on a tidy little fortune. Comparatively speaking. Huh!'

Tom's palms itched. If the bill had been paid and if he hadn't been desperate, he'd have rammed that cigar down Jimmy's throat. 'And so?' He tried to look menacing. 'Get on with it.'

'Patience, lad. You have nowhere to run, I can vouch for that. So. Here I came to London town, as broke and miserable as can be, thinking Hector was right and what a fool I'd been. I can tell you something, if he'd as much as crooked his little finger at me in those early months, I'd have gone hot-footing it back to his side. Crappy little jobs here and there, hardly enough to keep me in trousers. Finally, something a wee bit steadier – with London Transport as it happened – but it wasn't till the penny dropped that the real money started the flow.' He re-ignited the cigar, watching for a response.

'The real money?' Tom echoed obligingly.

'Moolah. Dough. Cash. Loot. Get it?'

He nodded. 'So how did that happen?'

'I had an epiphany. You're familiar with the term? An awakening, so to speak. It came upon me one day as I was dealing with Joe Public – or let's say *Josephine* – that I had this way. With women. I decided to milk it for all it was worth.'

'*All* women? Across the board?' Tom couldn't help but be impressed.

'Possibly. Probably. But in this age of specialisation, I thought I'd concentrate on the rich and the ripe. And what I discovered was that, properly handled, the London Underground system could deliver more gold than the whole bloody Klondike.' He paused to give this announcement dramatic effect.

Tom widened his eyes obligingly.

'I can prove it to you,' Jimmy went on. 'Think about females such as Lady Catherine de Montfort. The Honourable Amanda Jenkins. Baroness Bartlett. Jemina Pudlock-Irving.'

'I'm thinking.' Tom hadn't heard of any of them but had to admit they sounded well off.

'Two things in common, all of them. Number one, they found themselves at the window of my ticket office. And I can see you wondering what the hell a rich dame would be doing on the Tube when there's a perfectly respectable cab service available? Think rain, my boy. Think no taxis for miles around and a handy, warm station beckoning, with the most efficient transport system in the world. Anyway, that was number one.'

'And number two?' Tom asked.

'I had them all. Them and their money.'

'You mean they gave you money, like that?'

'I *earned* it, lad. On my life, I haven't laid my lily-white hands on a single dishonest penny since the day I went straight. It's been quid pro quo all the way. I've given them pleasure and they've given me cash.'

'Even – uh – now?' Tom enquired, trying for tact. Wasn't there an upper age limit for all this?

'Well,' Jimmy answered, exhaling a perfect smoke ring and sitting back expansively. 'I must confess I'm slowing up a bit these days. Also, there aren't that many older women left – not from my perspective at any rate. In fact, I happened to be thinking just the other day what a pity it would be for me not to pass on some of my business experience to a promising neophyte. A kind of partner-protégé. Someone like you, as a matter of fact.'

'Why *me*?'

'You're young, in good health I presume, nicely spoken thanks to that schooling of yours. I have a feeling about you. I can usually sense when a lad has the gift.'

'Really?' Tom was suddenly suffused with fondness for the old fellow. A gift? It was the first time in his life that he'd been attributed with any special aptitude. 'You think I may be *talented*?'

'Possibly, possibly not,' Jim answered.

Bloody hell.

'And another thing,' he continued, brushing away Tom's stillborn protest. 'We were close, me and Hector, even though things soured in the end. I never had kids. So it seems fitting that I pass my legacy down to my old mate's only son.'

'I see.' He tried to sound cold and mean. He felt cold and mean. Who'd given this antiquated goat the right to condescend to him with his idiotic legacy? As though Tom didn't have one of his own from the heart of The Hedge's inner sanctum. His father had shared with him his most precious secret and one day, any day now, Tom would be strong enough and bad enough to use it. One day.

Then into his mind came an image of the dictionary which had been taunting him so relentlessly that he'd had to hide it away. And here, right in front of him, was Jimmy Henderson who claimed to have spotted his potential and was offering him tuition, a roof over his head, and the assurance of untold wealth.

There seemed no choice in the matter at all.

A week later Tom had moved into Jimmy's flat in Shepherd's Bush.

'It's much – er – larger than I imagined,' he said, to cover his disappointment that it wasn't nearly as smart.

'A handy size,' Jimmy agreed. 'Two bedrooms and all mod cons, for under two hundred grand. Tell you, lad, I'm blessed with a nose for property that's as finely honed as my ability to sniff out a rich lady.' He scratched the said olfactory organ meaningfully as he set off to show Tom around, stopping now and again to embellish on a particular feature. The telly, the German dishwasher, four lava lamps, forty-seven (at last count) erotic DVDs. 'And now,' he said, leading Tom into the main bedroom. 'Feast your eyes or whatever on *this*.' He flung himself rather awkwardly onto the vast king-size bed and patted the space alongside him.

'Hang on a sec.' For a sick-making moment, Tom thought he'd made a huge mistake. 'What do you think I —'

'Come off it,' Jimmy said dismissively. 'We're talking *ladies* here – a veritable honey pot.' He bounced up and down with voluptuous appreciation. 'This here is the ultimate in orthopaedic luxury.'

'Orthopaedic? Doesn't that sounds a bit geriatr —'

'We're talking comfort layers, here,' he went on breathlessly, ignoring the intervention. 'Heavy-gauge spring units. The firmest and most supportive orgasm generator in the world, for male and female alike. I've been in the bed business. I know.'

Tom, silenced, watched him subside in exhaustion. 'In our profession,' Jimmy said, when he'd caught his breath, 'one can't cut corners with the mattress. It's our number one accessory.'

Our profession. Despite himself, Tom liked the sound of that. He'd been chosen and was being initiated by his master. All of a sudden he was rearing to go. 'So when can we start?'

'That's better. A bit of enthusiasm at last.' Jimmy drew himself to his feet. 'This evening. After dinner. I was thinking I'd begin by taking you through the basic principles.'

'Sounds good. And when do I – we – start practicing?'

'Whoa! Hold your horses. As you'll learn, composure is essential in the trade. Meanwhile, though.' He beckoned Tom closer and whispered confidentially. 'I've put in a word with my old colleagues on your behalf and they're trying to sort out a position.'

'A position?' Tom stepped back. His mind leapt to the illustrations in the battered copy of the Karma Sutra which had been secretly passed round at school.

'On the Jubilee Line,' Jimmy was saying.

That sounded wild. Tom raised his eyebrows.

'A *job*, lad. *My* old job. In the ticket office at West Hampstead tube station. It's where I got my first big break – and look at me now.'

Tom looked a little doubtfully. He saw a fairly dapper but unmistakeably lonely post-mature man. 'So why,' he ventured, 'didn't you end up with one of your – er – conquests? You know, marry her or something?'

'Marry?' said Jimmy scornfully. 'Would you honestly see marriage as a sound growth proposition for a Mercenary Consultant?'

No, course not. Silly question. Tom decided to stop quizzing him, to do his best to suspend his disbelief. He was getting his bed and board, after all. And a job, apparently. His best course was to shut up and listen.

Shutting up didn't prove too hard as the evening progressed, for the codger didn't give him a chance to get a word in. Listening was harder. Several times Tom found himself nodding off and being prodded fiercely.

'Oi!' Jimmy's breath, not the sweetest, gusted into his face. 'Concentrate, boy! What was the last thing I said?'

'Something about – the older woman and the – er – lovable rascal?'

'Correct. That's the spirit. Mature women adore a rogue. Nothing mean, though, mind – that scares the shit out of them. Now see if you can answer this. Who foots the bills?'

'She does,' he answered wearily. 'You know I haven't got a bean.'

'I have. We're partners, remember? The rule here is that you pick up the small tabs and the big ones will take care of themselves. It's always a good investment to pay for round one – after that, it is champers all the way home. Talking of pricey booze —' Jimmy drew himself to his feet. 'How about a drop of top-class after-dinner liqueur? This is another of my secret weapons. Infallible. Has them panting for it.'

He disappeared into the kitchen and returned with a dusty bottle. 'Tia Maria,' he announced. 'Only a mouthful, mind.' Carefully he filled two miniscule goblets. 'Costs an arm and a leg and we don't want you panting for *me*.' His chuckle quickly turned into a spluttering cough.

'No fucking chance.'

'And no *effing* chance that anyone at all will be panting for *you* unless you tidy up that language,' Jimmy drained his goblet. 'Culture, lad. They like evidence of culture. For instance —' From beneath the sofa he produced a cardboard box and extracted from it two compact discs, *Mozart's Top Tunes* and *Madame Butterfly*, a small glossy volume entitled *Art for Dummies*, the 1996 edition of *Burke's Peerage*, a condensed version of Sir Richard Burton's *Arabian Nights* and *The Complete Works of Oscar Wilde*. Ceremoniously he placed them on a shelf.

'By the end of the week,' he said, 'we'll have you whistling eight bars of the Clarinet Concerto and half an aria by Puccini. You'll be spouting the names of six Post-impressionist painters and three quotes by Wilde. How about that?'

'How about it?' Tom's head was buzzing. He yawned extravagantly. 'Bedtime?'

But Jimmy was relentless. His verbal flow seemed as inexhaustible as his store of advice. 'Take it from me,' he kept repeating with such veteran authority that Tom forgot his scepticism and started believing the bugger had really put in the work. By midnight he was cross-eyed enough to believe anything. 'Take it from me, she'll be all over you if you bamboozle her with exotic potions. Siberian ginseng mixed with royal jelly, for instance – the Imperial Courtesans of the Forbidden City couldn't get enough of the stuff.'

'I'll certainly —'

'— And another thing – instead of coffee, offer her Catuaba bark infusion. Got that? Cat-oo-ah-ba. Never mind

Spanish Fly, this is the best aphrodisiac in the world. I can get hold of it for you.'

'Thanks, mate. Now I really must —'

'You'll have go into training. Look at me and look at you. To be honest, you've got the staying power of a paraplegic limpet.'

'Bloody hell,' Tom objected. 'It's late. I'm fu – *rociously* exhausted.'

Jimmy glared at him. He cleared his throat. 'And now,' he said, sententiously. 'One last thing before we turn in. I want you to pay attention now – it's important.'

Tom tried to look animated. He was almost on the floor with fatigue and boredom, but there was something comforting about the drone of Jimmy's voice. When last had he been given such undivided attention?

Jimmy, meanwhile, had taken out yet another prop from his box of tricks. It was a square of white fabric which, like an old-time conjurer, he was waving aloft. 'Here we are,' he said, presenting it to Tom. 'A pristine linen handkerchief to keep folded in your jacket pocket for an emergency. Never fails. Generations of women have fallen flat on their backs for the Classic Hankie Ploy.'

Tom fell on *his* back, fully clothed, when he finally reached his bedroom which was substantially smaller than Jimmy's and with a single and markedly non-orthopaedic bed. Surely, he thought as he sank into sleep, his head swirling with unsought and unseemly images, Jimmy had said everything there was so say on the subject and more?

Not a hope in hell. The first evening was only an introduction. Tom's apprenticeship had several weeks to run. Every night he wondered what on earth he was doing with this sad superannuated Casanova, and every morning he resolved to leave. Where to, though? Another dead-end job, another grim rented room? Apathy triumphed, abetted by that glorious thirty-two inch telly with its soporific emission of daytime shows.

Until at last, one evening, Jimmy produced the Tia Maria for the second time since the lessons began. 'Chin chin,' he said, raising his glass.

'Cheers,' Tom answered hopefully, wondering what was up.

'Good news, lad. You're on.'

'On?' Tom's throat constricted. It was what he'd been waiting for, but he now quailed at the challenge imposed by the word. It reminded him of when he'd been summoned from the reserve bench of the under-fourteen cricket team and missed every ball. He didn't think he wanted to be *on*.

'Your position's come through. This is your big opportunity. Report to the manager's office at West Hampstead Station tomorrow morning at seven.'

Bloody sparrow's fart, thought Tom, but forced himself to smile. 'Great,' he said, faking relish. 'G-r-r-eat!'

It wasn't great, though. It turned out to be far from great. Up Tom crawled long before dawn and got himself dressed while the old boy – who never seemed to sleep – kibitzed non-stop about what he should or shouldn't wear. Wear for what, for fuck's sake? For snoozing on the first tube with a bunch of labourers and then a day trapped in a kennel that made the working life of your average pizza biker seem exhilarating. As for the women – *what* women?

'Patience,' Jimmy would urge when Tom dragged himself home with nothing to show for his efforts but a stinking headache. Wasn't there a point when a person graduated? Did a bloke really have to know how to dismantle an artichoke or repeat ten French ballet terms in order to land a dilapidated bird?

Then, one night, it happened. Not the conquest, far from it. Tom's tolerance reached breaking point and snapped.

It had been an exceptionally frustrating day. His journey to work had been delayed by signalling problems and staff shortages and, when he finally got there, they had the nerve to issue him with an official warning for poor timekeeping.

Shelley Weiner

He had the beginnings of a cold and a minger of a headache and all he wanted, when he finally got back to Shepherd's Bush, was a pint and a bath and a bit of peace and quiet.

Instead of which there was Jimmy waiting for him with a Beef Bourguignon. He swallowed it with good grace and forced down a glass of pukey Merlot, making himself listen to Jimmy's commentary. He even managed to invent a lacklustre tale of romantic mishap – a mark of extreme goodwill, given how grotty he felt. But when it came to enduring yet another rendition of the Second Act of Madame fucking Butterfly —

'No!' Tom blocked his ears. He couldn't bear it. Truly he couldn't.

'Lad, you'll thank me for this one day. This is what gives a chap cultural – er – *gravitas*. If only I'd been able to hum it in *my* heyday —'

'Jimmy, please, I really need to get to bed.'

'Ten more minutes, that's all. I specially chose it for you.'

'No. I said NO!'

'*Five* minutes then —?'

Something exploded in his head. He went crazy, started ranting like a psycho, yelling the most awful hurtful things – to this poor harmless bugger who couldn't *help* being a pain in the arse, had meant well for Tom, only wanted to be kind. 'I don't believe you,' Tom shouted. 'Nothing about you, nothing. You're a randy old goat. I don't believe you had any of those women, it's all in your head. A *fraud*, that's what you are. A fake and a fraud. You've never had it in your life. I bet you can't even get it up.'

There was a terrible silence. My God, thought Tom. Fuck. What had he said?

Jimmy sat there quietly. Then he got up.

'I'm going out,' he said. 'Don't wait up for me. I may be some time.'

Of course Tom waited. He went to his room and sat on his bed, fully clothed, dreading the worst. A policeman. They were sorry —

No, Jimmy wouldn't top himself, not him. He wasn't like that. Or was he? No, never. He'd come home eventually and Tom would apologise, meaning it from the bottom of his heart. It was a joke, he'd say. He hadn't meant for it to come out so nasty. He'd had a miserable day, a headache. He wasn't himself.

Hours passed. Finally he heard the key turning. Jimmy was turning it. He was alive, he'd come home! Tom was about to call out his name. He opened his mouth.

Then he heard a high-pitched giggle.

'You naughty thing! Ouch! Do it again – I like it!'

A woman, Tom thought. He's gone and found someone to prove I was wrong. That's the spirit. He lay back, exhausted and relieved; laughter welled up in him he was so relieved. They'd piss themselves about it tomorrow, he and Jimmy. His taunts were already in the past tense. Harmless. Nothing to get fussed about. He'd probably done him a favour by challenging him.

Listen to them go, he thought. Not bad for a bloke close to seventy. That mattress was getting a good work-out and the woman was yelping and moaning like a cat on heat. Where had he found her? Listen to her, shouting and yelling. Yelling? *Shrieking*!

Tom went cold.

She screamed again.

He couldn't move. What he was hearing wasn't passion. It was terror. Something was wrong, very wrong. Her shrill voice pierced through the bedroom wall.

'He's dead,' she was crying. 'Help! Someone help me – I think the old man's dead!'

6

Nonsense, he thought. Jimmy wasn't dead, couldn't be. The woman was hysterical. People didn't die like that. He was faking it, having her on. Maybe he'd fainted or, more likely, he was trying to frighten Tom as a way of getting back at him.

'Someone please *help*,' she yelled again.

Unable to ignore her any longer, he emerged from his room and opened the door to Jimmy's. 'What?' he asked crossly, hovering on the threshold. 'What's going on?'

The words dried up as they left his mouth. There lay Jimmy, a shrunken form on the king-sized bed, as still as stone and as naked as the day he'd been born. And the woman, a stranger with tangerine hair awry, was whimpering as she squeezed herself into a purple shift, her face a patchwork of mascara and rouge.

Tom backed off. This had nothing to do with him, nothing at all.

'Don't leave me!' Zipper still undone, she rushed up to him and was clawing at his t-shirt. 'Look – look – at what's happened. We need an ambulance, call 999, call someone quick —'

In a daze he walked towards the motionless figure. 'Jimmy – wake up. It's ok, mate – I didn't mean it – please wake up?'

'999,' she kept repeating like a maniac. 'Call 999. Call 999.'

The paramedic shook his head and said he was sorry. Too late. A classic case of – uh – misadventure. Probably instantaneous. 'I'd say he croaked as he peaked as he croaked, sort of thing,' he said, with supreme indelicacy. 'I couldn't think of a better way for a fellow to go.'

Easy for you, thought Tom, who knew the truth. His mentor, his friend, had died of humiliation. The only person who had ever cared about him, and Tom had mortified him into his grave.

'Such a lovely man,' the tangerine-head was saying. Her hysteria had subsided to a trickle of tears. 'A fine man. A gentle man. A witty man.'

All those things were true. Yet Tom had wronged him. He had doubted and baited him. He felt as though he'd killed him as surely as if he had removed his weapon from the OED and shot him at point-blank range.

'Who's the next of kin?' asked the paramedic.

'Not me, dear.' With a flourish, the woman blew her nose. 'No sirree. Maybe it's the young man over there?'

They turned to Tom with what might have been sympathy but he saw as accusation. They would judge him, sentence him; he deserved to be hanged. Arms outstretched in a gesture of supplication, he felt tears spilling down his cheeks.

'Are you —?' the paramedic began in a gentle voice.

'I was his best mate, his pupil. Almost his son.' Tom was crying properly now. It seemed he would never stop, that the regret would never stop, that he too would die, not of heart failure but of interminable, incurable remorse.

It turned out that Jimmy had left him everything. His last will and testament, signed only weeks before his death, named Thomas Henry Kennedy as his sole beneficiary.

'Did he have a *sense* that this might happen?' Tom asked Jimmy's old London Transport colleague, Dave, who'd come back to the flat after the funeral. 'It's almost like he had some kind of premonition.'

'Could be.' Dave was sombre. 'On the other hand, his ticker was dodgy – landed him in hospital quite a few times. Two heart attacks, as I remember – one major, one minor.'

'Funny.'

'Funny?' He gave Tom a sharp look.

'Well, not funny, but you know what I mean. The old boy was the gabbiest bugger I ever met – didn't shut his mouth for a second. It's strange that he never mentioned his heart.'

Dave shrugged, muttering something about 'Nowt so queer ...', as he examined Jimmy's bookshelf. 'Interesting stuff here,' he said. 'Never knew my old mate was the literary type.'

Tom handed him *Burke's Peerage*. 'Here you go. Look at this for a laugh. You can take it as a souvenir.'

When Dave had left with his bequest, Tom looked around the flat and tried to convince himself that this was now his. All his? He ventured into the main bedroom and dared himself to approach the bed on which his friend had expired. Someone had stripped it. The orthopaedic mattress looked vulnerable and virginally clean.

The dressing table, too, had been denuded of any evidence of Jimmy's life or death. His blood pressure pills, his Brylcreem and his dentures were gone. He'd gone, Tom thought. Well and truly gone. Leaving hardly a penny in his bank account, despite all his grandiose swanking. All that remained was this shabby flat, a few bleeding books and some music by dead people.

He eyed Jimmy's collection, Oscar Wilde and the like, and wanted to clear that out too, but didn't have the heart. Instead, perhaps he should add to it – make it more his own. After all, this was Tom's cultural heritage now. For the first time since he'd moved into the flat, and he'd been there almost six months, Tom drew out his suitcase from beneath his bed, opened it, and lifted out an oblong object wrapped in an old T-shirt which he'd safely secreted from Jimmy's prying gaze. Slowly, cautiously, he removed the rubber bands securing the Shorter Oxford English Dictionary. Holding it gingerly and making sure he didn't open it, he carried it to the sitting room and placed it on the shelf.

There. That looked good. Tom smiled for the first time in a week.

Which was when he started to recover. The next morning, with a flourish, he shook out the white linen handkerchief and carefully folded it into his jacket pocket. On the way home from work he stopped off to buy two matching sets of linen for the king-sized bed and a fresh bottle of liqueur. That evening he moved his possessions across to Jimmy's room, where he endured a sleepless night. It's what his mate would have wanted, he kept telling himself. He had to overcome his aversion. He would fail on the most elementary variations if he was too squeamish to get it up. He couldn't falter. He had to make sure he succeeded beyond Jimmy's wildest confabulations. He'd draw them in like iron filings to a magnet, like kittens to a fish stew, like bees to a honey pot...

Tom was so intent on imagining how it might be if the right woman, suitably bankrolled, fell for his undeniable charms, that when Lily Green chanced along he almost missed her. There she'd come, a prime candidate, wanting to know about Oyster Cards; and Tom, sitting there and counting out his change and the hours till the pubs opened, failed to notice. Not once, not twice, but morning after stinking morning.

'Look who's here again,' he said, without properly looking. He liked her name, though. It was certainly prettier than she was, the way she ogled him with those strange eyes. Bonkers. A flaky female like her needed to be saved from herself. She wanted Oyster Card advice? He gave it to her, no holds barred. A hanky for her tears? Bingo. Bona fide on both counts. No ulterior motives which, coming from someone whose entire persona was ulterior, was a bit rich. Or, as Jimmy would have seen it, piss poor. Tom simply felt sorry for her, standing there and blubbing, looking so hopeless.

So when did hear the ker-ching? Maybe not until they were seated in the pub and, cool as a Cornetto, she ordered a Scotch. Never mind a Scotch – a *double*. Now that was a famous first. He'd expected her to ask for a light cider, maybe a shandy, at worst a glass of wine. But a double

Scotch? Did the woman have a drinking problem or had she no idea what whisky cost?

It didn't take him long to put two and two together. Her face, when she took her first sip, told him straight away that this wasn't habitual. Nor was it, as she claimed 'medicinal', did she think he was dumb? Which meant, by a process of elimination, that to her money was no object. And *this* probably meant —

Even so, he probably wouldn't have proposed what came afterwards if she hadn't mentioned it first. Among other things. Bloody hell, she could talk! All that stuff about the lover Josh, as though he cared, as though he believed her for one second. A good story, though, and he'd always been a sucker for stories. And at a certain point her eyes didn't seem so much strange as hypnotic. And when she suddenly ran her finger along his jawbone and down the collar of his shirt she didn't turn out to be as awkward as she seemed, not at all; he rather fancied it, he fancied her. Especially when, without blinking, she offered to pay for the taxi that would take them back to his lair.

Blimey.

Talk about your Thunderball, EuroMillions, Dream Number and Lotto HotPicks all coming up simultaneously. Mind-blowing. And Jimmy would have been so proud and impressed with his performance, his response to this jackpot bonanza. Without thinking about it, Tom followed all his golden rules – from picking up the first tab in the pub (and not wincing too obviously when it was whisky) to remembering each of her erogenous zones. And to think that – far from pulling either a dragon who happened to have money or maybe a pretty tart without a bean – he'd landed this trophy, a paragon of creditworthiness and sensuality.

'Lily,' he mused, practising her name.

'What?' she said contentedly, getting to work again on his earlobe. It wasn't his prime spot, but she seemed to like it and he couldn't afford to be over-picky. He couldn't afford much. She didn't seem to mind that, though. On the contrary, she was lapping him up.

'How about staying the night?' he suggested.

'Shall I?' she asked, sounding coy and a little scared.

'Go on. Be a devil.'

She giggled. 'What about work? How will I get to work?'

'Shepherd's Bush,' he said loftily, 'is renowned for its proximity to a wide range of public transport services. All covered by your trusty Oyster Card —'

'But I don't —'

'— which I'll personally sort out for you.'

'Gosh, thank you —'

'But not tomorrow. Tomorrow,' he went on boldly, 'I think you should bunk off work. *Both* of us should. We can bunk off together – call in sick.'

'I couldn't!' She sounded appalled. 'I can't *lie* like that!'

What an innocent, he thought, feeling a rush of tenderness for her. Such a sweet blameless creature. 'Oh yes, you can, Lily Green,' he said. 'Isn't it shocking to suddenly discover all the things you can do?' He winked suggestively and made a lunge for her which she didn't resist. She was falling for him. She'd fallen.

But then, sudden reversal. She pushed him away. 'Wait,' she was saying.

'Wait? I don't think I can —'

'One minute.' She hopped off the bed and disappeared into the sitting room where, hours before, she had lodged her large and expensive-looking leather handbag. Moments later she was back, clad in nothing but a bright red gauzy, lacy, vest-thingummy that barely skimmed her thighs. 'My baby doll,' she announced, indicating her apparel. 'That's what it's called.'

'Very – uh —' He was gobsmacked. Maybe she wasn't such a sweet blameless creature? 'You came *prepared*?'

She shrugged and looked embarrassed, then held out a floral zip-up pouch. 'If I'm staying the night,' she said, like a well-trained toddler at a sleepover, 'I'd better go and do my teeth.'

Lost for words, he padded after her to the bathroom. Her teeth? How many ravishing sex kittens bothered with that level of dental hygiene? 'Oi – Lily,' he pleaded through the firmly-bolted door. 'Let me in!'

'Hang on,' she called through a mouthful of toothpaste.

He heard splashing, gargling, scrubbing noises that went on and on and on. 'Lily,' he called again. Personal cleanliness was one thing, but this was verging on the obsessive compulsive, and anyway he needed to pee.

At last she emerged. 'I thought the bathroom was meant to be private,' she said sniffily.

'And *I* thought that after all the things we've got up to, the concept of privacy disappeared.'

She considered for a moment and he watched her indignation turning to perplexity. 'Is that so?' she asked. 'Maybe you're right.'

When he had hastily concluded his own far less rigorous ablutions, he hurried back to bed. But already she was asleep, the picture of purity, curled on her side and demurely covered by her bedclothes. Tom studied her, intrigued. What kind of hybrid had he reeled in – a well-heeled child-vamp with early middle-age spread? He bent down to examine her closer, and found himself pressing his face to her hair. Soft tendrils tickled his nose and he inhaled a scent that reminded him of a sweet grassy meadow. It was soothing. Pleasant.

Careful not to disturb her, he crept into bed and almost immediately he fell fast asleep and began to dream.

But despite the peaceful chastity that reigned in Jimmy's orthopaedic wonderland, his dreams turned out to be lavishly obscene. He was engaged in wild and abandoned copulation – but not with Lily. His partner was someone else, someone he began to recognise as *that woman*, the hooker who'd been in this very bed with his late mate. But then, all at once, it wasn't Tom in the bed – it was Tom as voyeur and Jimmy in the bed.

'Go for it, Jimmy,' he was calling, like an Arsenal fan cheering on a free kicker. 'You can do it! I know you can do it!'

'I'm getting there, lad.' Panting, straining. 'I'm getting there.'

But where was the hooker? She'd gone, disintegrated in an orgasmic blast. Now it was Jimmy on his own – triumphant, happy Jimmy. 'See, lad?' He was beaming.

'I saw. You were great.'

'And how about you, Hector? What do *you* have to say about it, old dead lag you?'

Tom swung round, for Jimmy seemed to be addressing someone behind him. *Hector?* What was he doing here, smiling maliciously, knowingly – and holding a gun, a grey-black Luger with its mean barrel trained on Tom's thumping heart.

'Stop!' Tom cried aloud. 'Don't shoot – please don't. *Please?*'

Part Three

7

His restlessness disturbed her, all that thrashing and moaning and shouting, 'Stop!' Stop *what*? She couldn't quite make it out. Was it *normal* for men to act like this? Could it be what, post-coitally, they usually did in bed? This being a totally new situation for her, she didn't know.

But, gosh, how rapidly she was learning! 'Hush, Tom,' she whispered, touching his shoulder to calm him and then shivering luxuriantly as, in his sleep, he grabbed her hand and pressed it to his mouth. 'Tom,' she murmured softly, then, practising it: 'Thomas.' *Thomas*. Yes, that sounded better. More substantial. More like *Jeremy*, in a way. He'd be Thomas for the world and Tom – lovely, loveable, sexy Tom – in bed.

Was Lily really *in bed*?

She smiled to herself at the feat she'd accomplished. That Big Night Kit had proved its worth. Maybe she'd write a letter of appreciation to *Cosmopolitan*. 'Everything a Girl might need when Sudden Passion sweeps her off the floor,' the ad had boasted. In Lily's opinion, £49.99 had been a bit steep for a fire-resistant baby doll, a pair of lacy knickers, a six-pack of condoms, three feathers and a jar of Pure Venezuelan Chocolate Spread. On the other hand, the zippered pouch in which everything was packed would always be useful. Being practical and hygienic, she had discarded the feathers and the chocolate spread, replacing them with a small tube of Colgate, a toothbrush and some travel floss. Then, almost forgotten, the kit had languished in her handbag, just in case.

And – how about that! Sudden Passion had arrived and swept her straight off the floor and onto this incredibly bouncy bed. She wriggled in sensuous ecstasy and he groaned a little louder.

'Don't – *shoot!*'

Was *that* what he was saying? Could he be having some kind of macho weapon dream? She'd read an article on male fantasies that focused on phallic warheads and wondered if he needed reassurance in that area. Steeling herself, she reached under the bedclothes.

He sat up with a start. 'Who —?'

'Oh, dear – I didn't mean to frighten you.' Hastily she relocated her hand and lightly traced a small archipelago of freckles on his left bicep.

His expression softened. 'Lily,' he said. And he lay back and sighed into sleep.

She watched him, thinking again how unfamiliar she was with male behaviour, with the whole sexual thing. Despite all her reading. No one had warned her, for instance, about how messy it was. Who needed massage oils or whipped cream or even Venezuelan Chocolate Spread when there was such a superfluity of natural stuff? And the surprising thing was that Lily – normally an extremely finicky type – hadn't minded in the least. On the contrary. To think that she had once scored ninety ('Get hold of a sex therapist!') on an 'Are You Frigid?' quiz and a dire twelve percent ('Steal, beg or borrow some Viagra!') on a New Woman Libido Rating. What did these people really know? Probably as little as Gordon, with his hollow opinionising for the gullible readers of the *Kuala Lumpur Morning Post*.

Gordon. What would he think if he discovered how sedate Miss Green had passed the night? Would he be shocked or impressed? His propensity for insinuation would certainly be stirred. 'I think, dear Lily,' he'd say, with a smirk, 'that you're wasted as a mere PA. I'll recommend to Eddie that you hook up with Bernadette and Vince instead.' No. She wouldn't have it. She would never let him know how readily she'd jumped into bed. She might hint, of course, that there was a 'new man' in her life. 'He's called Thomas,' she would say, fluttering her eyelashes demurely. 'An up-and-coming flautist with the Royal Philharmonic. Not much money in that, as we know, but such a genius —'

'Wassatime?' Tom had sat up and was looking confused again.

He seemed nervy. One would think that *he* was the stranger in the bed.

'The time,' he managed, more distinctly. 'Please?'

'That's better,' she said primly.

'What?'

'Saying *please*. I've been taught that *good manners* is a prime virtue in the boudoir.'

He grunted. 'And so —?'

She glanced at her watch. 'It's two in the morning,' she said. 'If you really want to know.'

'Ta.' He lay back and, clutching an excessive share of the duvet, returned to a more restful repose.

And Lily, settling beside him, wondered why he'd been so intent on wanting to know the time. What difference would it have made if she had said, say, three? Two a.m., three – both nothing-hours, empty numbers floating in a void between one day and the next. Except that now, for the first time ever, it seemed to her no longer a void. Within it, gloriously suspended above Shepherd's Bush Green, was a miraculous turreted palace in which the handsome prince and the princess he'd awoken were lying side by side. Her Underground Man, now Prince Thomas of Shepherd's Bush, with his true love Princess Lily, late of Hatch End. His breathing had now become slow and even, and she began to time her inhalations with his. In, out, in, out. Sedated by the rhythm and her magical vision, she drifted off to sleep.

Almost immediately, it seemed, to be shocked awake by the screech of an alarm clock.

'Oops!' her prince was saying. 'I forgot to turn the fucking thing off.'

'S'okay,' she said sleepily, thinking that although his voice seemed cultured enough, his highness's language tended to be somewhat rough. She'd have to talk to him about it, subtly, if she wanted to present him to polite society.

'Try and get back to sleep.' With hands much gentler than his idiom, a *million* times gentler, he soothed her cheek.

But she was awake now, good and solid. 'Tom,' she said, taking hold of the back of his neck and gazing into the intense blueness of his eyes.

'Yeah?'

'You are real, aren't you? You exist?'

He laughed. 'Pinch me.'

'Pinch *me*,' she said playfully.

But he didn't. He patted her perfunctorily and slid out of bed.

'Don't go,' she said, alarmed. Was he leaving her, already? Could this be the end of her fairytale dream? She tried to stem her rising panic, reminding herself of Angela Manning's counsel about repellent neediness. The strangulatory properties of the clinging vine. She'd let him go graciously and, with a little luck, he'd return of his own accord.

He did.

'Now *that* was an Amazonian piss,' he declared.

'Glad to hear it,' she said with heavy irony that he didn't seem to notice. Was it sensitivity he lacked? He certainly seemed devoid of a work ethic. Which was *good*. Lily certainly needed a lighter approach to life. But then again, she couldn't afford to lose her job, whatever she'd led Tom to believe about her unlimited wealth. 'Tom, I have to get to the office,' she said. 'I'll need to leave quite soon – I knew I shouldn't have stayed —'

'It's *five-fifteen*, Lily.' He sounded irritated, then seemed to catch himself and smiled at her indulgently. 'Much too early to worry about work. Later we'll concoct some sort of story.'

A story. She returned his smile, conscientiousness dissipating at the prospect of a partner in deceit. He had no idea of the depths to which she'd already sunk. 'Let's concoct the story now!'

Fondly – he was definitely fond of her, she could see it – he planted a kiss on her forehead. 'You're funny,' he said.

'Funny?' This wasn't what she'd studied half her life for, not in the least.

'Funny – sweet,' he amended.

'Ah. That's all right then. So what shall we —?'

'Your story. Ours – *I* need one too. How about some bullshit excuse about rotten prawns or a twenty-four-hour virus? The usual kind of thing.'

'They wouldn't believe *that*,' she said, disappointed. Perhaps she'd overestimated his imaginative capacity. A simple young man like that, he'd probably never told a decent lie.

'Of course not. Nobody *believes* stuff like that. Nothing much they can do about it, though. Can't even demand a medical certificate, not for a single day.'

Her capitulation was almost instantaneous. A single day, he'd said. An incredible single day. 'What shall we do?' she asked, sounding even to herself like a wondrous, mischievous child.

He didn't answer immediately. Instead, he kissed her again, this time on the eyelids. How did he guess what response that would trigger? However could he have known? 'We'll find ways to amuse ourselves,' he said, drawing breath. 'You can leave the agenda to me.'

By four that afternoon, Lily was wondering whether she had now fully compensated for thirty-four years of corporal abstinence. Part of her hoped she had, for now. Her wish for a hot bath had become desperation; she longed for fresh underwear and the laundered smell of Madame Plotnikova's sheets. She also needed space to consider this *thing* that had happened to her, to grasp its significance and relive each astounding moment.

'I'm so hungry I could eat a dead skunk,' he suddenly announced. 'What do you say to a bite somewhere?'

'Where?' she asked cautiously. Something alarmed her about the prospect of emerging into the street in broad daylight with such a ravenous carnivore.

'Oh, I don't know. For a classy lady like you, I'd recommend something in the Holland Park vicinity. Nice little bistros round there – much smarter than our local cafes.'

Shelley Weiner

She hesitated. Holland Park sounded a respectable hunting ground, if expensive. She didn't want to rush this, though – her first public appearance with him. Thomas. Her man. She wanted to anticipate it and dress for it, to consult her sources for all the right moves. 'I have – um – some urgent paperwork I need to catch up on.'

'Go on, Lily,' he urged. 'Forget the paperwork. Be spontaneous.'

Again she hesitated. 'Be spontaneous,' was the motto of so many experts that she'd opened a file dedicated to 'The Gentle Art of Spontaneity'. And now Tom was quoting the same adage. It must be a sign, confirmation that all her legwork had not been in vain. 'You're on,' she said decisively. 'Give me five minutes to freshen up and we'll go.'

Wandering into the sitting room to gather items of apparel cast off with such abandon the night before, Lily's attention strayed again to the presence of the Shorter Oxford English Dictionary on the shelf. 'Tom,' she called. 'Do you have a fondness for crossword puzzles, by any chance?'

'What's that?' He was in the bathroom, shaving.

'This dictionary here. It's exactly the same one as my father used. It was a hobby of his, crossword puzzles. He'd sit down with me and try and teach me – but I was only ten when he died and have never been a great speller —'

All at once he appeared, breathless, shaving cream dripping into his collar. Lily reached for the dictionary but found her way barred.

'Crossword puzzles?' he said with unexpected vehemence. 'Even the *idea* of them bores me.'

'No need to get uptight about it,' she said as she retreated beneath the sofa to find a stray shoe. Gosh, his moods were unpredictable. She hoped he wasn't bipolar or even *tri*polar; she'd been warned against such men. 'In fact,' she added brightly, waving aloft a stiletto she'd retrieved, 'crosswords aren't particularly *my* idea of fun either. You probably know by now how *I* like to enjoy myself.'

The Audacious Mendacity of Lily Green

'How?' he asked, still standing and scowling between her and the bookshelf.

'My goodness, Tom – what's got into you? I'm teasing. I think you should add a few joke books to that sombre collection on your shelf.'

He had the grace to smile, but she could tell he was forcing it. 'Come,' he said, and his tone had softened. The resolute way in which he guided her out of the room, however, made her uneasy.

Not for long, though. She'd forgotten her disquiet by the time they'd settled into their upholstered banquette in a French-Oriental fusion place off Holland Park recommended by the cab driver Tom had ebulliently hailed on Shepherd's Bush Green. The journey to Chez Wong had taken forty minutes and the balance of Lily's emergency stash. Now, studying the menu, she worried about who would foot the bill. Traditionally, of course, paying was the male prerogative; but as a modern liberated woman, should she offer to go half? Then again, as the ostensibly wealthier and blatantly older consort, perhaps *she* ought subtly to pick up the tab? Or would that undermine him? ... oh, God.

'So,' he was saying. 'Isn't this nice?'

His face came into focus, that beautiful sculpted face. 'It's lovely, Tom,' she answered, meaning it, her anxiety immediately dispelled. Gosh. This was her day, *their* day – how could she desecrate it by thinking about such a mundane matter as cash? 'This is a *wonderful* occasion. In fact,' she added, a rush of blood carrying extravagant spontaneity through every vessel in her body, 'I think it's fully deserving of a bottle of champagne.'

In an hour and ten minutes they drained sixty-two pounds worth of Bollinger NV and did their utmost with the forty-pounds-a-head 'lunchtime special'. Lily, remembering all the rules governing refined dining in the face of repulsive food, managed better than Tom, who massacred his Dim Sum Escargot and only managed to swallow his Pâté de Won Ton

109

with the aid of a hefty Coke. Which swelled the final total to a stomach-knotting £210.

Tom whistled loudly when he'd checked the addition. 'A complete swizz,' he said, 'but all seems correct.'

He passed the slip to her and she, having regaled him throughout the meal with accounts of her high-flown career and the Chelsea apartment, could do nothing but accept it. Obviously. Had that really been in question? Ignoring her panic (never had she spent so much on a meal, never, ever, *ever*), she gritted her teeth and opened her purse to produce her pristine Premium Platinum Card. Mr Wong, the dapper proprietor, who, until now had treated them with unmitigated contempt, examined it and bowed obsequiously.

'*Merci*, Madame,' he said. 'I 'ope you 'ave enjoyed our repast.'

'We certainly 'ave,' answered Tom, mimicking him with drunken fervour. Hastily Lily gathered their belongings and ushered him through the door where, hardly waiting for it to shut, he hugged her fiercely and planted a series of huge damp Coke-and-prawn-scented kisses on her face and neck.

'Don't!' She was embarrassed, disapproving, dizzy, more tinglingly happy than she could recall ever being. If only they could remain like this forever, her joy frozen by life's camera into a heart-throbbing fade-out finale.

But no. 'Where to next?' he was saying. 'Shall we head for your place now?'

'We can't,' she said more sharply than she'd intended, breaking free. 'I mean,' she went on, moderating her tone, 'I really, *really* need to get some work done – catch up with stuff. Have a bath, catch up with a bit of paperwork —'

'Fine,' he said. 'Cool.' His accession was immediate and disconcerting. 'See you anon, Lil. Take care.'

For ages that night, as she fidgeted in her single bed, she analysed their final exchange. Had she erred irrevocably by so abruptly calling it a day? Was that *it* then? Ah, well. So be it. Lily was hardly what Carla Devine termed an 'Urban Slag' and there was no way she could have smuggled him past

Madame Plotnikova. He liked her, though – surely he'd see her again? Why couldn't she relax and enjoy the memory of their night and day together – the fluency of her responses to his caresses and his persistent questions? He had certainly shown interest in her.

'Tell me again,' he'd said, draining the last of the champagne. 'Let me get that right. Your family —'

'There aren't many of us left, now.' She had affected an air of wistful melancholy. 'Basically, it's just me and my mum, the old dowager. She's always kept a tight hold on the various trust funds. Only now has she finally agreed to release money for the flat.'

The old dowager. Where had she dreamed *that* from? She smiled to herself, thinking of Eva in her baby-blue velour, cerise lipstick gleaming as she pouted across the bridge table at Matty Morris's bad call; Eva giggling, that high-pitched shriek of hers, sharing a joke with her pals at someone's expense – often Lily's; Eva gazing at her intently with those dark-brown, green-and-gold-flecked eyes that identically mirrored her daughter's. 'I think you'll be fine,' she had said when she'd left for her cruise. 'Perfectly fine.'

And I am, Lily thought defiantly. She was. She had felt like a woman of the world, sitting in that pricey restaurant and holding forth to her rapt young paramour. What a pity that no one had been there to witness her triumph. Anyone. Someone. *Eva*. Would she have been impressed? Would she have cared?

A small tear trickled through Lily's tightly-shut eyelids, which she knew was inappropriate after such a remarkable day. She was emotionally labile. Megan Moffat had written at length on Cunnilingus and the Sensitive Mind. *Was* Lily sensitive? She supposed so, in a contained way. Surely her mother might have understood that her bland imperturbability was merely a front? Surely, at the very least, she might have responded to the card that Lily had sent, giving the address of the Winter Palace and an emergency contact number? There might have been *some* word from her after so many weeks at sea.

Resolutely Lily sat up. She would *not* torture herself with negative thoughts, not tonight. Look at how well she'd done, how self-assuredly she'd behaved, and how readily, deferentially even, that waiter had accepted her credit card. She had *five thousand pounds* to spend, which – even if she subtracted £210 for that dreadful meal – meant a fair amount of squandering ahead. Her bookkeeper's head told her that there was sufficient credit for 77.258 further bottles of Bollinger (at the current rate), which made her lover's heart beat wildly. She lay back and calmed herself with erotic imaginings until, shattered, she finally fell asleep.

The next morning she attended to her toilette even more carefully than usual. Well-heeled yet hot-blooded, prim yet passionate. Pearls and a hint of cleavage, she decided. A dusty-grey twin-set and tightish pencil skirt hovering discreetly over her knees. Emitting a sophisticated suggestion of Chanel No 5, she made her way to the tube station and joined the ticket-office queue.

He was there.

Looking a little worn, a young man like that. Pale and unshaven, which made him look paler still. 'Just piss off now,' he was muttering to someone behind him. 'I told you I was sick, didn't I? Fuck it, Joe, if you don't —'

Then he saw Lily. His face immediately brightened. 'Hello,' he said with a smile that weakened her legs. 'Same as usual?' He winked.

The wink, she thought, was gratuitous. But, not wanting to be a spoilsport, she smiled. 'Same as usual,' she confirmed. Then, daringly, she leaned forward and whispered, 'See you tonight?'

His affirmation was unmistakeably eager. He nodded vigorously and she was gratified to see colour rising in his cheeks. 'Seven, in the pub?'

She dipped her chin in agreement, taking her ticket and change, murmuring, 'We must do that Oyster Card sometime.'

'We must.' His hand brushed against hers and lingered a little longer than necessary.

At Global Perspectives, it didn't take long before Gordon noticed her state of distraction. 'Anyone home, Lily?' he asked.

'Home?' She frowned. 'Well, if you must know —'

'For goodness sake, girl — it's a manner of speech. What I'm trying to say is that you're away with the fairies today. Is something the matter?'

'Well,' she said indignantly, 'I *was* ill yesterday, as I told you on the phone. These things take time.'

'They certainly do.' He'd resumed filling the weekly horoscope order. 'Hmm,' he said to himself. 'Something benign for the Bangladeshi Scorpions — they need cheering up.' He glanced up at Lily. 'Any ideas?'

'How would I know?' Sighing, she gathered the pile of papers on her desk and settled to work.

'How would I know?' he echoed mockingly. 'All *I* know, Lily dear, is that I barely managed to convince Eddie to keep you on. Luckily for you he has bigger problems right now. And, if you don't mind my saying so, you don't *look* very sick.'

Assailed by the barrage of threat and contempt and — was she imagining it? — underlying concern, Lily sank her head in her hands. It was noble of him to have saved her job but mortifying that he should feel sorry for her. Sorry? She didn't need *anyone's* pity. She looked up at him defiantly. 'Gordon, I think I'm in love,' she said.

'Ah.' He gave her a crooked smile, adding amusement to the already-infuriating mix of sympathy and derision. 'Well.'

'Well, nothing,' she said crossly, to hide her embarrassment.

'I thought you told me you were done with men. Isn't that what you said to me?'

'It was. I was. But then I met Thomas and — um. I *was* sick yesterday,' she pointed out, trying to retain at least part of her pretext. 'I'd never have stayed off work otherwise. He just happened to pop by and took care of me – that's the sort of person he is.'

'I see.' Gordon's smile broadened. 'And, this Thomas person, does he by any chance happen to be an estate agent?'

'An estate agent?' She puzzled for a moment, then remembered about her supposed viewing appointment in Chelsea two nights before. 'Oh, that – no, of course not. Thomas is a musician. He's senior flautist with the Royal Philharmonic and known to be incredibly talented.'

'I see. And you, of course, will give him all the help and support you can.'

She didn't like his tone. 'Naturally,' she said.

'Well, ducky,' he said, after a brief pause. 'What a surprise this is, coming from you. And here I was, thinking that *I* was the one who fell for artistic young men. Shows you how wrong a person can be.'

'Shows you.' She tried to match his nonchalance, hoping to hide her discomfiture by total immersion in the pile of transcripts awaiting her. 'Oh, well,' she said wearily. 'I'd better get on with it.'

'So you had.' Gordon was on his feet, jacket in hand. 'I'm off now for a while – nicotine siren calls. See you later, lover.'

Lover, she thought. Lover. On a cloud, despite the tedium of deciphering at least a year's worth of haphazardly-typed horoscopes and twenty agony aunt columns, she decided to pop home after work and freshen up before her seven o'clock rendezvous with Tom. Madame Plotnikova, as ever, was poised on the landing.

'Hellooo,' she called out. 'And how is Miss Green today?'

'Very well,' she answered. 'And how is Madame?'

'I can *see* you are very well,' she said, ignoring the question. 'A little more tired, maybe, than usual? But be what will be. Nice outfit you have on today, I must say. So.'

'So?' Lily tried to edge past towards her room.

'So I am chatting with some of my other ladies this morning – Jocelyn, in particular. That Miss Green, I says to her, is perfect tenant. Quiet, decent, pays on time, career-girl as well.'

'Thank you.' There was more. Lily waited for it.

'Anyway, all four of us were agreeing how nice you can look when you dress yourself up – and when you didn't come home last night Mavis was suggesting maybe – you know the sort of mind she has —'

'What?' Lily asked indignantly. 'How rude!'

'I agree.' Madame Plotnikova's chins trembled with the vigour of her assent.

'Actually,' Lily went on, her anger fired more by the qualified compliment than the insinuation. 'As it happens, I'm currently working on an extremely high-level and complicated media contract that involves a fair amount of overnight travel.'

'Of course. Exactly. That's what I imagined. That's what I said.' Her tiny black eyes became even smaller and blacker as she studied Lily closely. 'But you must *not* overdo things, Miss Green – I speak from experience. Mine late husband Igor learnt bitter lesson from overdoing things – may his soul rot in hell. A gentleman in Minsk, a bastard (forgive language) in London. But that's another story – one day I will tell you all.'

Lily nodded in a way she hoped showed interest, compliance and contrition, and made a determined lunge past. 'One day soon,' she called over her shoulder, finally making the escape to her room where, behind a firmly-bolted door, she prepared for the evening ahead.

'You're here,' he said when she arrived at the pub.

In accordance with the Second Law of Dating Dynamics she had arrived twelve-and-a-half minutes late. But there he was, waiting for her – at the same table, on the same chair. *Their* table. *His* chair. Their first little ritual, already! 'Did you think I wouldn't be?' she teased.

'I certainly *hoped* you would.'

'That's nice to know!' Boldly she leaned forward and kissed him. He raised his lips to hers and the ecstasy made her almost pass out. With difficulty she remembered the Fourth Law, which urged the Enlightened Datress to show an independent spirit by braving the bar. 'Tom – um – shall I? What are you drinking?'

'I'll get them.' He sprang to his feet.

She sank back, relieved, for the Laws didn't elaborate on ordering techniques. And did she really care about female self-sufficiency in the face of his endearing male gallantry? 'A glass of sauvignon blanc for me, please,' she said, having done some hasty research. 'Chilean, if possible.'

As a token of her independence, she reached out and pressed a twenty-pound note into his hand; after the briefest hesitation, he took it and applied to it a jaunty kiss as he headed for the bar.

8

Thus began a season of bliss – forty days and forty nights of it. There were minor dips in Lily's elation, but these only served to emphasise the state of giddy happiness into which she'd arrived. Was it really her, cavorting in these extraordinary positions on his bed, on the floor and even – not too comfortably – on his Ikea kitchen table? Could it be dull Lily Green taking the initiative as they conjugated upside down and inside out and (a couple of times, although neither much liked it) backside front? It was as though she were headlining in a spot-lit arena, with Clarabelle Wynne-Stanley, Maisie Fitzherbert, Carla Devine, Megan Moffat, Angela Manning, Jennifer Flower, Genevieve Olson, Marcia Jones and Martha Smithson all signalling their approval from the grandstand, each one of them agog with wonder and admiration.

'Go for it girl,' they were shouting – all apart from Wynne-Stanley, who didn't do shouting. The author of *New Manners for Old Fashioned Girls* merely fluttered a white-gloved hand.

In her state of besottedness she denied him nothing. Her Premium Platinum was kept at the same sizzling temperature as her unremitting ardour. Nothing was too much for him, nothing too dear.

Except for one thing: she steadfastly refused to take him back with her to the Winter Palace guesthouse.

'I don't understand you, Lil,' he said, bringing the subject up for the umpteenth time. They were in a cocktail bar in Covent Garden. 'You're game for anything, so what's the big problem with going back to yours?'

'It's just —'

'I mean, to be honest, I've put all my cards on the table with you. My home's been yours, just about. I've even cleared space in the bathroom for your makeup. Too generous by half, that's me – my mates always say it —'

'Tom!' This was too much. There were limits which even Tom could exceed. 'Are you saying I'm not *generous*?'

He shrugged, moodily self-righteous.

'Is *that* what you're saying?' Her anger was rising, spilling over. Only two days before, she'd received her credit card statement which, at last count, showed a debt of £4,878.32. Thanks to her, they'd frequented London's most lauded and fashionable restaurants and bars. Thanks to her, instead of chain store tat, he was now nattily attired in Paul Smith and Diesel. And thanks to her, he'd been equipped with the most up-to-date iPad, gold cuff-links and at least seven executive toys. Not generous? Lily? What a cheek. 'I – well, I think you're being very unfair.'

She saw him squirming, fiddling uncomfortably with his entry-level Hugo Boss Chronograph watch (not yet accounted for) and shifting in his seat. One of the little things she'd noticed about Tom was that, when uneasy, he jerked his left knee back and forth. He was doing that now. Her glance travelled from the said knee and along his left thigh, which was barely visible behind the bar stool on which he perched. The rest of him, concealed, she found hard to think about without her throat constricting. Against her will, she found her hand edging across the table and touching his. What did it matter if, like a spoilt child, his demands seemed insatiable? She adored him and would give him anything he wanted, within or beyond her commonsense or means. Except this.

'Tom —' she began.

And, simultaneously, 'Lily,' he said, 'it's not important, it doesn't matter —'

'It is. It's important. It matters. I just want you to understand that my aunt – the Contessa, with whom I'm staying – is *very* strict about gentleman callers.'

'Gentleman callers,' he scoffed.

'Well, yes. Not that you're such a gentleman.' She squeezed his fingers playfully. 'Anyway, it's important that I remain in Aunt Anastasia's good books – she's the one in charge of the family coffers. All being well, it won't be long now before contracts are exchanged on the Chelsea flat – then you can stay over to your heart's content. Won't that be wonderful?'

There was silence. He tipped the last of his Bloody Mary down his throat and wiped his mouth with the heel of his hand. 'That's another thing,' he said.

She looked at him enquiringly.

'That flat of yours. What's up with it?'

'Why? Nothing. These things take time. I wish you'd stop asking.'

'Hmm.'

'What do you mean, *hmm*?' she demanded, her indignation fired by guilt. So what if the flat was a fantasy? She needed to believe in it, she needed *him* to believe in it. In her. Surely he had all the material evidence he wanted? 'Tom, you must have patience. It's all happened – happening – so fast. Can you believe that two months ago we didn't know one another? And now, here we are.' She shook her head in wonderment.

'Here we are,' he echoed, but his tone and expression had softened. 'Shall I put another couple of drinks on the tab so we can drink to that?'

She nodded happily. Crisis averted.

But a niggle of unease seemed to linger, despite the rampant sex with which they ended the evening and the exhausted entwinement in which they spent the night. Unlike the previous dips which had been obliterated by the euphoria that followed, this one left a small dark shadow that wouldn't go away.

He suspected her. No, he didn't – but he certainly had reason to. And if *she* wasn't the person she claimed to be, not exactly, then who on earth was *he*? She was aware that, trying to be subtle, he was probing her veracity. And, while she competently fielded his queries about her job and her family and her great lost love, she in turn started questioning him.

One morning, for instance, she was looking for a teaspoon in a kitchen drawer when she came upon a business card bearing the name *James Henderson – Mercenary Consultant*. 'Who and what is that?' she asked lightly, expecting him to dismiss its presence with a joke.

But he didn't. 'Would you mind,' he said icily, 'not snooping in my personal space?'

'Oh. Sorry.' His reaction was so startling that she almost lost her balance. Leaning on a chair, she said weakly, 'I thought we were beyond "personal space".'

'Oh, yeah?' He sounded belligerent.

'I thought,' she went on, trying to regain her moral ground, 'that when two people are as intimate as we've been – are – then the concept doesn't apply. And anyway, I wasn't snooping. The card just happened to be there. Who's James Henderson?'

'My old mate, Jimmy,' he answered grudgingly. 'Remember? The bloke who left me the flat.'

'Oh, yes, of course. And – gosh – I've never heard of mercenary consultants? What does mercenary mean?'

'Lily, stop prying.'

'*Prying*? I find a card in your kitch —'

'It's to do with the army, all right? Soldiers and stuff. How would you, with your cosy sheltered life, have heard of it?'

She shrugged. There was something guarded about his response and his unduly aggressive behaviour. He was simply out of sorts, she told herself. Hadn't Carla Devine stressed more than once that although males didn't menstruate, they definitely had their periods? She would put his mood down to hormonal flux and nonchalantly let this go.

It wouldn't leave her, though. Not the incident itself, which was minor, but a more pervasive anxiety which worsened when, a few days later, she noticed that his dictionary had disappeared.

'Tom,' she said.

'What's that?' He was mixing vodka tonics in the kitchen.

When he returned to the sitting room she pointed to the rather large gap on the shelf. 'That big fat dictionary – what happened to it?'

'Oh, that.' Quickly he adjusted the remaining books to fill the space. 'As *you* put it, big and fat – and past its sell-by date. Decided to get rid of it.'

'Really?' she joked. 'Is that what's in store for me when I get old and fat?'

He didn't laugh. With his back to her, he continued to reposition his books.

'Well, I hope you didn't just dispose of it,' she persisted. 'I think you should have kept it – *I'd* have taken it if you'd offered it to me. A dictionary like that isn't something one throws away.'

He swung round angrily. 'Let it go, Lily. It's none of your fucking business.'

'My – *what*?'

'Sorry, didn't mean to swear. But fucking hell, it's not your job to check on what I decide to do with my stuff. You're turning into a right bloody nag.'

For an hour there was silence between them. It was unbearable. Several times Lily was on the brink of breaking it, then couldn't do it. Who knew what other touchy subjects she might unwittingly broach? He, meanwhile, drank moodily, his right knee doing its involuntary jig.

The following day her unease hadn't shifted. She was monosyllabic at work, pleading a headache, and afterwards, instead of meeting Tom at the pub, went back to the Winter Palace where Madame Plotnikova, naturally, lay in wait.

'Miss Green,' she said, with heavy emphasis. 'A stranger! Look, Mavis – Jocelyn – Elizabeth. Look who is here. So? An entire week, not a sign of our Miss Green. Nothing. So? Tell us where you have been?'

'Brussels.' It was the first place that came to mind. She hoped her landlady wouldn't question her further for all she could remember about it was the Manneken Pis.

'Ah, Brussels.' Madame Plotnikova shut her eyes and seemed on the brink of reminiscence. '*Brussels* —'

'Yes,' Lily cut in swiftly. 'And now I'm afraid I can't talk – there's a breakfast meeting at the crack of dawn tomorrow. I have a huge amount to prepare.' She tried to slide past Madame Plotnikova towards her room.

'Hold your horses for a second – you are always in such a rush. I have something for you.'

Lily stopped. Madame Plotnikova was blocking her path.

'Here. Came for you.' She held out three envelopes. 'Letters. Gut to know people still send letters. In old days all news, mostly bad news, was in letters – I remember my late husband's sister Olga caught the cholera in Vladivostok; she sent us letter and Igor, without even opening envelope, struck a match and burnt it. His own flesh and blood —'

'Thank you, Madame Plotnikova.' Lily reached out.

But the landlady moved the envelopes out of her reach. '— A warning, Miss Green.'

'Why?' Lily asked. 'What do you mean?' It was bad enough suffering from free-floating anxiety without having this Transcaspian Cassandra bearing down on her with portents of doom.

'Did I ever tell you,' she was saying, 'how much of a famous man was Igor in Minsk?'

'No,' answered Lily, distracted. 'I mean, yes – may I have my mail now please?'

'All right, all right – such a hurry you are always in. A lesson you need from fate of my husband. In Minsk known as Borsht Tsar. In London – feh! – Mister Nobody. Mister *Dead* Nobody. A cheating man, I hate cheating in a man. I hate all men and my nose is telling me to *warn* you. That is all. Here.' As though they were putrid, she dropped the envelopes into Lily's hands.

'Thank you.' Warily she glanced at them. Two looked official, with windows and printed text; the third was handwritten. Conscious of the landlady's disapproval-laden curiosity boring through her, she stuffed them into her handbag and headed to her room.

Once inside she sat down, caught her breath and tried to swallow down her apprehension which, if anything, had intensified with the arrival of the mail and Madame Plotnikova's ominous burbling. How fragile it suddenly felt, this life she'd created, the fine-looking man she had found. Cautiously, she examined the three envelopes and placed them on her dressing table. Then, as though it were alive, she grabbed the one that looked least offensive and ripped it open.

It was from the Hatch End branch of Barclays, pointing out that the current account in her name was overdrawn by the sum of £3,982.56. *What*? In *addition* to the credit card debt that was tickling the £5,000 ceiling? How could that be? Was it possible that someone as prudent and level-headed as the erstwhile but reliable employee of Eagleton and Co had allowed her fiscal state to get so out of hand? Surely the Manager of Barclays would take into consideration her previously unblemished track record and her connection with the late-but-famously-frugal Max Green?

Not in the least. The message was unequivocal. 'Unless this arrears, with accruing interest, is repaid within a month, we regret to inform you that we will close your account and place the debt in the hands of an appropriate agency.'

Dazed, she wondered whether she should risk applying for another card, given how easily she'd been granted the Premium Platinum. At the time, though, her credit rating had been untarnished. Now, her accountancy background told her, she'd be seen as an unacceptable risk. She would have to persuade Premium Platinum, with its exorbitant interest rate, to extend her loan.

But this possibility was dispelled by the contents of the second official envelope, which informed her – with effusive regret and fulsome good wishes for the future – that the credit card company had gone into liquidation and all outstanding moneys were to be settled forthwith.

Her hands shook. This was called galloping debt, a dreaded malaise that happened to other hapless people, not her. Ordering herself to be calm, she decided she'd have to prevail upon Barclays for an extension and rely on the fact that months would elapse before Premium Platinum's demands became impossible to disregard. Meanwhile, she had her salary from Global Perspectives – and it would be just as well to consolidate her relationship with Tom on less material and more spiritual grounds. No need for panic, then. Deep breaths.

Warily, she took hold of envelope number three, the one with the handwritten address. Not from Eva, clearly; Lily was familiar with her mother's idiosyncratic gothic script. But who else could have sent it? No one knew where she was living and no one else cared. Mystified, she opened it and the florid signature at the bottom of the sheet of Basildon Bond jumped out at her.

Elsie Kramer.

Her mother's most scandalmongering crony had tracked her down.

'*My dear Lily,*' she wrote. *My* dear Lily. Who'd given her the right to the possessive pronoun? Suppressing her resentment, Lily read on:

I believe you are having a wonderful time in London and your dear Mum says <u>wedding bells</u> will be ringing any day now. I hate to be the bearer of bad tidings, knowing how long you have waited for your happiness, and Eva said on no account were you to be disturbed. But there are times when <u>friendship</u> is more important than anything else and we talked this over (me and Matty and Sylvia) and decided we had to let you know. It has all been very sudden, such a shock and we are beside ourselves with worry.

What happened was, Lily dear, that your Mum fell over on the last evening of our trip. On the deck, after *our final rubber. She broke her arm and they put it in a cast and we all joked about how lucky she was that it hadn't happened earlier as it was her shuffling arm. But it was no joke, really. When she got home she collapsed and they did these tests on her – all very complicated and I'm not sure I understand the medical terms. To call a spade a spade, she has <u>cancer</u>. Her bones are really bad, they say. Like honeycomb, imagine that! The doctors are not yet sure where it started. Maybe in a breast or an ovary or (most likely, they are saying) a lung. Anyway, I will spare you more details as I do not want to alarm you unnecessarily. Your Mum is in <u>hospital</u> at the moment, by the way. Please telephone me when you receive this. I am sorry to be the bearer of such unfortunate news.*

Lily read the letter three times before its significance sank in. The heavily underlined words melodramatically shouted for attention. Wedding bells. Friendship. Cancer. Hospital. The bells were a lie and the friendship was false, but cancer and hospital had the ring of authenticity.

Her immediate impulse was to blame the messenger. Who'd authorised nosy Elsie Kramer to intrude on Lily's long-awaited contentment? Hideous cow. Financial embarrassment was one thing – she'd borrow more money, tell Tom they had to cut back for a while, ask for a pay rise. She would manage somehow. But *this* – this was different. She couldn't ignore it.

She could, though.

She could shred the letter and pretend not to have received it. She could shut her mind to the image of her mother with her hollow bones alone in some hospital. She could run away with Tom to somewhere lush and subtropical, where they could live in peace and harmony on sunshine and sweetmeats and love. She could do all that. Yes. She. Could.

But despite these defiant thoughts, tears coursed down Lily's cheeks. From the moment she had told Eva her first lie, the challenge of giving it authenticity had kept her going.

But something even more powerful had sustained her: her determination that her mother would ultimately *witness* this authenticity. With Jeremy at her side (and she hadn't yet worked out how Tom would transmogrify into Mister Impeccable, but she would), she'd make her triumphant appearance and *prove* she had told the truth.

Now it seemed that Eva had grabbed the lie and run away with it. And the lie would become irrelevant if her mother died. Which wouldn't necessarily happen immediately but Elsie's tone suggested it might be imminent. Her state of insolvency, though, was a certainty. At least, she consoled herself, she still had Tom. Or did she? Might his devotion falter if he knew she was broke?

'You're very solemn this evening,' he remarked a few hours later. As usual, they'd met in the Crown and Anchor, which had indeed become *their* pub. But tonight this cosy familiarity failed to give Lily a thrill. 'Not quite yourself, huh?' he asked.

'I'm fine,' she said, averting her face from his scrutiny. Her puffy eyes had defied a ten-minute cucumber face mask and lashings of Miracle Concealer and, despite her resolute attempts at composure, she felt on the edge of tears.

'Good.' He didn't sound quite convinced. '*Excellent*,' he said determinedly. 'Anyway, you'll soon cheer up when you hear what I have in store for us tonight. We're going partying, me and you!'

She tried her best to look animated. 'Oh?'

'Oh, yes, indeed!' He downed his pint and automatically she produced the wherewithal for him to get another. 'Hang on a sec – I'll sort us out with refills.'

How blithely he tripped to the bar, how oblivious to the fact that the ten-pound-note he flourished was her second last. She'd have to prepare him – to test his response to her impending penury. When he returned with brimming glasses, she took hers, drank deeply and drew a breath. 'Tom,' she said. 'There's a slight —'

The Audacious Mendacity of Lily Green

'A nice supper first,' he interrupted, resolutely cheerful. 'There's a new Argentinean steakhouse opened near the station – I could strangle a nice slab of rump. And then afterwards I was thinking —'

She put a restraining hand on his arm. 'Tom, listen to me!' she said sharply. 'I'm trying to talk to you.'

He placed his hands, palms innocently upwards, on the table. 'So? Have I been stopping you?'

'No – I mean, yes,' she answered, and was all at once unclear about how she was going to put it or where to begin. 'It's just – well —'

'Don't tell me,' he broke in. 'The flat. It's fallen through. Am I right? *That's* what's bugging you, isn't it?'

She found herself nodding. In a way, it had. With everything else.

'Too bad.' He took a swig of lager. 'I thought you were a bit funny about it when the subject popped up last night. Happens all the time, though. When Jimmy bought the Shepherd's Hill place he was gazumped and gazundered seventeen times. Got to keep going, Lil – it's a good market for buyers. Plenty more where that came from. Cheers.' He raised his glass.

'Cheers,' she said doubtfully.

'Unless,' he went on, his expression growing serious, 'there's a problem with the funding?' Then, seeing her puzzlement, 'The dough? The big bucks?'

'No,' she said quickly, even though sympathy and compassion were written all over his face. Now would be the perfect chance to come clean. He'd be supportive, understanding. They would laugh together over Lily's folly and he'd declare how much he loved her for herself, for richer and for poorer.

Or would he? Could she risk the possibility that it was her money he cared for and not Lily herself? She couldn't. As lily-livered as her name. 'It's not the money,' she said with as much certitude as she could manage. Was her talent for deceit deserting her now, when it seemed she was going to need it more than ever? 'The money's all there,' she stressed, perhaps too hard, but he didn't seem to notice. 'It's just a little disappointing, after so many weeks, to have to start again from scratch.'

'I'll help,' he said enthusiastically.

'That's sweet of you. I'll hold you to that.' She toyed with her drink. This was wrong. She wouldn't be able to keep it up. She'd be bankrupt within the year. 'Tom,' she began, weakly.

'What? What's up?' He looked genuinely alarmed. 'What is it then, if not money? You're not ill, are you? You're not – er – seeing someone else?'

'No,' she managed, trying to smile. 'Don't be ridiculous. It's work. My job. It's been very stressful for the last while. Can we – do you think we could – call off tonight? I'm not really up to partying.'

'Sure thing,' he said obligingly. 'Tell you what, Lily – let's go back to mine. I thought *bugger it* and went and bought that Sony Vaio today. Remember you said I should go for it, that you'd pay me back. How about we get ourselves online and start searching for another property?'

'No!' It came out much more sharply than intended.

His jaw dropped.

'Sorry, Tom. I didn't mean to snap. I'm not feeling great. And I'm not yet ready to look at flats – I need time to get over this one. I need space to – um – think.'

'I see,' he said, with a shrug. Then he smiled. 'To *think*, eh? It's not often I find myself with someone who thinks. Want to know what my dad taught me about thinkers?'

'Tell me.' Relief made her light-headed. The pall of gravity seemed to have lifted. He was joking. They were telling stories again. How happy it made her when they told stories.

Tom puffed himself up. 'He said to me, "Son, thinkers are a danger to themselves and to others. A doer rather a thinker be. He who thinks, stinks." That's what the late great Hector Kennedy believed.' He chuckled.

'Hector,' she repeated. 'You've never mentioned his name before. Did he really teach you that?'

He paused, staring down at his glass. 'No. He didn't. I made it up. There was only one thing – a single memorable word – that he taught me. Want to hear it? '

'Yes.'

'*Omnipotent*,' he said with heavy emphasis.

'Omnipotent?'

'Having *infinite* power.'

'I see.' For some reason the word made her nervous. Her anxiety returned. Instinctively she reached across the table and ran her hand, ever so gently, from his forehead down the side of his face to his neck. 'I'll remember that.' She stood up to leave.

'Don't go yet,' he said, leaping to his feet as well. 'I didn't mean to scare you off.'

'Sit, Tom. You didn't. Here's some cash to settle up for the drinks. See you – tomorrow.'

She caught a glimpse of him watching her as she left. Had he noticed her hesitation? Was he eyeing her suspiciously or watching her fondly? Did he, could he possibly, *care*?

9

That night she slept very little. Her mind was a kaleidoscopic jumble, images swirling round in disjointed montage. Elsie prattling and Eva crumbling and Gordon insinuating and Madame Plotnikova interrogating. And Tom undergoing a makeover – acquiring well-groomed hair and a smoothly-shaven face and saying 'How do you do?' in a cut-glass voice. No longer called Tom but Jeremy, newly-divorced from his wife and still working for the Foreign Office in a classified capacity. A perfect gentleman. An ideal fiancé.

But the next morning, still exhausted, she awoke to inescapable reality. Jeremy was a phantom. And so in a way was Tom, who might vanish in a cloud of alcoholic vapour if, when, her funds expired. But that wasn't her only problem. There was also her mortally ill mother. For confirmation (or maybe denial) of the last, she'd have to grit her teeth and confront the source.

Before she could change her mind she dialled Elsie Kramer's number.

'Lily, you phoned! You must be beside yourself, poor girl!'

She took a deep breath. 'Jeremy and I,' she said, 'were up all night, worrying. He's doing his best to comfort me.' That sounded as contrived as it was. No matter. 'How is she?'

'Your mum? Don't ask. It's a terrible tragedy. She's not even old – not for these days. I've had a feeling about her for a long time, though. We all have.'

'Does – she know?' Lily ventured.

There was a pause. 'Well, dear,' Elsie answered, emotion or bad phone reception inducing a wobble in her voice. 'She doesn't know that I made contact with you. After she was taken to hospital, I came across the postcard you'd sent her with your London address. As for the cancer – she knows she

The Audacious Mendacity of Lily Green

has it, and we *all* know what that means, sooner or later. In Eva's case, the consultant says she's so far gone that things are likely to give in quite soon. One after the other. Hips. Back. Brain. The lot.'

'What you're trying to say,' said Lily, doing her best not to visualise this rapid and relentless decomposition, 'is that I should come and see her – quite soon?'

'Up to you, dear. I know how busy you are with your job – and, of course, with your Jeremy. Eva tells us you're both doing so *terribly* well! All I can say, Lily dear, is that I've known people who make the wrong choice and afterwards, when it's too late, they're *devoured* by regret.'

'Well, thank you,' she said after a moment, aiming for courtesy but unable to mask her irony. What delightful alternatives she was being offered: her mother being consumed by cancer and/or Lily eaten up by remorse.

'Well, don't blame *me*, dear,' said Elsie self-righteously, picking up on her tone. 'It's not *easy* to be the one to deliver unhappy news. I'll give you the details of the hospital and you can make up your mind.'

Hastily dressing for work, Lily shelved her decision-making. With bankruptcy imminent, she couldn't afford to lose her job. She was aware, when she scuttled into the office seven minutes late, that her grooming lacked its usual lustre and that Gordon, who seemed to observe these things, would notice. No matter. A girl was allowed an off-day.

Steadfastly she typed through the morning, trying to suppress rogue thoughts about the choices that faced her and conscious of Gordon's curious glances in her direction. Several times she suppressed the urge to confide in him until, at last, the compulsion grew too strong to resist.

'Uh – Gordon,' she began in a deliberately casual manner. 'What would you say to a person who found herself – or maybe himself – in a bit of bother with a bank? Overdraft, I mean. Nothing larcenous.'

He shook his head sagely. 'A bit of bother,' he repeated. 'That's a good one. Covers a multitude of —'

'Gordon, this isn't a joke.'

'Who's laughing? Tell me, Lily my sweet – are you addressing this dilemma to Marge Scott, Madame Katinka, Pete Preston or Gordon McCloud?'

She considered. Was it an emotional problem? Maybe. Were there answers in the stars? Please God. Was there a phallic connection? Perhaps. 'Could be all of them,' she said. 'Or maybe I'm just asking *you*?'

'I'm honoured.' He dipped his head, then raised it to study her. 'Am I correct in supposing that the handsome young flautist is proving expensive to maintain? Without going into personal details, ducky, I know about such things.'

She neither confirmed nor contradicted this. As a story, it was as good as any.

'Well, then,' he said, taking her silence as assent, 'ditch him. It's the only thing to do when they become a serious drain. Katinka, Marge and Pete are in complete accord on the matter.'

'What does Gordon think?' she asked.

His smile was rueful. 'I'm less sensible than my counsellors, I'm afraid. Heart tends to rule the head, which could be why I turned out to be a drunk churning out lies for a crook instead of the toast of the national press.'

There wasn't much she could say to this. He also lapsed into silence. She tried to return to her work, miserably contemplating life without Tom. It *was* the most sensible course and would alleviate at least one of her problems. Perhaps after she'd attended to her mother and somehow replenished her capital —

'There's another thing,' she found herself saying.

'What's that?' He looked up enquiringly.

'What advice would you give to someone who hasn't seen her mother for – well, several months – and then discovers that she's very ill?'

He put his pen down and gave her his attention. 'When you say "she's very ill", are you referring to this someone or to her mother?'

It struck her that, the way she'd put it, the identity of the victim wasn't clear. 'Oh, no. Not me,' she assured him, touched by his concern.

'Well, then,' he said, visibly relieved, 'it seems that – after all the gin-swelling and the fortune-squandering you've told me about – the old bat's got her come-uppance.'

'I didn't —' she began, all at once remorseful about the unflattering pictures she'd painted of her nearest if not dearest relation. But lies were lies, and if she started refuting them now who knew where the unravelling would end? 'I suppose she has,' she conceded.

'The question,' he went on, 'is whether or not you're fond of her.'

'She's my mother.'

'That's biological. We're talking emotions here. *Are* you fond of her?'

Lily considered. She'd never been asked the question before. It was as alien to her as the concept of a God who was supposed to have made things bright and beautiful for children with the kind of mothers who baked apple pie and crooned lullabies. Lily's world until now had been neither bright nor beautiful and Eva had never baked or sang. She'd just been Eva. And fondness hadn't been within the range of possible responses to her, as far as Lily had ever been aware. 'There's duty,' she said cautiously. 'A daughter has certain obligations.'

'No question then,' he said definitively. 'Katinka, Marge and Pete all agree that you should set off for mother's bedside right away and do the dutiful thing.'

He made it seem simple. But he'd left someone out. 'And what does Gordon think?' she asked.

'Gordon,' he answered, 'is a self-destructive idiot who avoided his awful mama like the plague. So she didn't leave him a bean and he ended up poor and unhappy and full of remorse about almost everything except not seeing the witch before she expired. It was about the most honest gesture he'd ever made.'

She considered for a moment. 'You think honesty's worth all that?'

'Could be.' He gave a bitter-sad laugh. Then his face grew serious. 'Do you want to know what Gordon really thinks? On balance, I mean?'

She nodded.

'That you should take tomorrow off. I'll invent something to placate Eddie while you get yourself over to – where was it?'

'Hatch End. That's where we – she – lives. She's in a hospital nearby.'

'There you go. Bracing country air. Get all that obligation out of your system and you'll come back nicely refreshed.'

She pondered for a moment. He made it sound so simple. 'And then?' she asked.

'Then, of course, there'll be your flautist and funds-deficit to deal with.'

In despair, Lily covered her face with her hands. 'It's all a bit much for me,' she said. 'I don't know how I got myself into this mess.'

'Would you like to borrow a few quid?' he offered. 'You can pay me back, whenever.'

'No – no, thank you,' she said immediately. 'That's really kind of you, Gordon. I can't take money from you. In any case,' she added valiantly, 'my problem's minor, a temporary one – it will sort itself out.'

Bravely spoken, she thought, when she'd returned home and considered again her mother's plight and her own destitution. Brave, but stupid, for she could have done with a small loan. Wasn't there a refuge somewhere for the indigent working girl? If so, she could check into it, thus avoiding Tom, Eva, *and* destitution in one fell swoop?

Listlessly she pulled out her cuttings file, which no longer seemed adequate to the predicaments of real life. She vaguely remembered having created a section called 'Coping with a Cash Crisis'. But the only practical advice it contained was a *Hello* interview with a Serbo-Croat stripper who'd been rescued from insolvency by the unspecified services of a twenty-four-hour pawnshop on the Finchley Road. Despondently, Lily examined the baubles she'd accumulated in her making-the-most-of-herself days. A string of cheap pearls, a trying-to-be-ruby ring and a diamanté brooch. Even if they were worth something, she felt that surrendering them meant abandoning all hope.

She couldn't do that. Tom and her new life were, through practical necessity, being put on hold. *Temporary* hold. She'd tasted freedom and nothing would persuade her to relinquish it. Meanwhile, she would scrape together whatever it took to make an appearance at Eva's bedside as the dutiful daughter.

Appearance being the key element here – far superseding duty and any filial bond. She was determined to astound her mother, incurably sick or not, with her own dramatic transformation.

The next morning, having rehearsed her reunion with Eva through much of a sleepless night, she rose early to attend to her toilette. With expert precision she applied make-up to enhance her eyes and define her mouth and maximise her cheek bones. She tried on four outfits before she settled on an understated but perfectly-cut taupe shift dress that would boost her endowments and minimise any excess curves. At last, smiling at herself in the mirror as she knotted her silk Pucci scarf, she bade her London self a temporary farewell and set off to catch the train.

And far too soon she was in Hatch End. Home, dreary home. 'Northwick Park Hospital,' she directed the morose-looking driver of the taxi she impulsively entered. Hoping she had the means for the journey. Praying she didn't, which meant he'd either call the cops or kidnap her, thus delaying or preventing her arrival.

En route they passed the Public Library, where she'd first been inspired by heroines who had emerged from a chrysalis of dullness into full-blown splendour. Cinderella. Sleeping Beauty. Snow White. Not Lily, though. As everyone, including Eva, *especially* Eva, seemed to have agreed: Lily had not only missed the boat, she'd never booked a passage on it in the first place. She'd lied her way out of imprisonment – but now, like her mother's bones, her fibs seemed to be crumbling away. What insanity, then, was pulling her back to expose this terrible disintegration? She could abort this mission, even now.

But even as this thought took hold, the taxi was pulling up. 'Here we are, miss. Hospital,' announced the driver.

Lily fumbled in her purse. It contained the exact change for the journey; not a penny remained for the return. Her fate was sealed.

'Eva *Green*, you said? Could you spell that for me please?' asked the receptionist. 'Ah! Here we are. She's in Oncology.'

'Oncology,' repeated Lily, bemusedly.

'That's cancer,' the receptionist explained.

'Where is it?' Lily asked.

'Well, it depends, dear. You'll have to talk to her consultant about that. I can't really discuss particular cases. The trouble with cancer is that it can strike anywhere.'

Lily sighed. 'Where is *she*?' she persisted, wondering if she were hallucinating.

But the directions, finally issued, were specific. Eva Green was in O'Connell Ward on the fourth floor. 'Turn left out of the lift, then first on the right, third on the left, straight through two sets of double doors. You'll have to check with the nurse in charge before you enter. They're very strict about visiting in O'Connell, as they have all the terminal cases.'

'Fourth floor,' she muttered to herself, trying to repeat the complex instructions. But all the while the word 'terminal' pulsated through her head. Terminal, terminus. The end of the line. No cure. No treatment. Surely this must be a mistake? Could it be that she was the victim of the sickest kind of joke – that Elsie and the girls had cooked this up to surprise her and when she arrived they would all spring out in party hats, Eva included, and cry out, 'Gotcha!'?

Nothing like it. When she finally found herself at the ward, a large ebony-skinned nurse with a name-badge identifying her as Staff Nurse Delphina Martin looked at her with mournful sympathy and confirmed that her mother was 'very, very ill'.

'*How* ill?' Lily ventured.

'Doctor Snow will explain everything to you. He is very understanding. We were talking about you just this morning.'

'Really? About me?'

'You are her next of kin, aren't you? And soon to be married, I believe. Your mother is a lovely lady and extremely proud of you, Miss Green. She's told us everything about you.'

'She has?' Lily asked cautiously.

'Oh, yes. She did say, though, that we were not to get in touch with you. Not yet. She ordered that you *must* not be disturbed until absolutely necessary. I see she changed her mind?'

'She didn't,' Lily pointed out. 'Her friend Elsie contacted me.'

'Elsie,' the nurse repeated in a tone of distaste that endeared itself to Lily. 'Don't talk to me about that lot. Go in and see your mother. For a little while only. And try not to be too shocked at the way she looks – I can imagine you'll find she has changed.'

Lily, at the door, inhaled deeply and braced herself: not for the altered appearance of her ailing mother, though, but for Eva's first sight of *her*. She was a diva in the wings, about to storm the opera house in her greatest role. Breathe yourself beautiful, she told herself. You're elegant, successful and suitably betrothed. Magnanimous too. Didn't you drop everything, cancelling several important meetings, in order to be at your poor mother's side? She took the powder compact out of her handbag for a final dusting and, inspecting herself in the mirror, added a final touch: a graciously compassionate smile.

Then she pulled the curtain aside and stepped forward.

No applause. Silence. Slowly Lily's gaze travelled from the small mound made by her mother's feet to the flattened bit round the middle, to the pink floral night-dress, to the chicken-thin neck. The chin, the mouth, the eyes, the lank grey-brown hair. And during the course of her scrutiny it felt like all her elegance and success was melting away, fiancé, job, the lot. She became weary and docile.

'Well, well,' Eva said.

But it came from far away. In her mother's presence she was immediately plain awkward Lily again. 'Hello,' she managed. 'I heard. From Elsie.'

'*I* didn't tell her to contact you.'

'Didn't you want me here?'

'Not really. But I suppose now you've come I'm quite glad.'

Did she mean that? Lily studied her suspiciously, then decided that her mother's paper-pale face with its drawn cheeks and sunken eyes was beyond dissimulation. Maybe she would reach out now and take Lily's hand and say *why* she was glad?

No. Eva lay quite still, eyelids drooping, desiccated hands resting on the sheet. Lily touched her gently but her mother didn't respond, not at first. After a long moment, though, she murmured, 'I've been thinking about you.'

'Have you?' Lily tried not to sound over-eager. She waited for more, but nothing came. 'I'm sorry,' she said, breaking the silence, unsure what she was apologising for. Eva's illness, her own lies, everything.

'Don't be sorry. It couldn't be helped. Your father was like that too. I *hate* apologies.' The ferocity of this eruption seemed to exhaust her. 'You're making me tired, Lily. I'm not very well, as you know.'

'Of course I know.' She took hold of her mother's arm, forgetting its frailty. 'That's why I'm here. Look at me. Talk to me,' she pleaded, very close to tears.

Eva opened her eyes. They widened. 'My goodness,' she said, in a complete switch of tone. 'You *are* looking glamorous. Your new life seems to suit you.'

Pleasure coursed through Lily, despite herself. 'You think so?'

'A changed person,' her mother confirmed. 'I'd never have predicted this a few years ago. Shows you.' Her eyelids sagged again. Lily watched her slipping into a shallow sleep, every shift of expression magnified on her transparent features. A frown, a twitch, a tremor of the mouth, a sigh that seemed to spring from the depths of her soul. What stranger inhabited that shrunken form?

Then her eyes sprang open and the alien became Eva again, devoid of mystery and petulant about her plight. 'Elsie and the girls pretend to be kind,' she said. 'But mostly they're just glad that this happened to me and not to them.'

'I'm sure they're not glad.' Lily wondered why she was defending them instead of applauding her mother's astuteness. Could it be that she had been aware of their hypocrisy all along?

'People are very strange when it comes to illness,' she was saying. Then a stab of pain made her face contort. She clenched her fists.

'Shall I call someone?' Lily asked in alarm.

'No. Don't. Please. It will pass. I hate the drugs they give me, they make me so tired.'

'But they'll help the pain. Let me call the nurse?'

'No.' Gradually her expression relaxed. 'There. It's passing. That's better.' She looked at Lily, new urgency in her gaze. 'Please take me home, Lily. Will you? Please.'

Lily looked back in horror and disbelief. 'Me? Take you home? I can't – *you* can't.'

'I can't stay here.'

'But you *must*. You're too ill —'

'They can't do anything for me. The drugs make me feel worse. I can't bear to be in this place any longer.' Her hands lay still on either side of her inert body. Only her eyes moved, communing with Lily's, burning into them.

She had to turn away. 'I don't know what to say,' she managed at last. 'You can't be at home on your own – you know that. And surely you don't expect me to drop everything in London, just like that? I can't. There's – Jeremy. And my job. I have a life in London. I've *made* a life.' She dared to meet Eva's gaze again. It hadn't wavered.

'I know,' Eva said.

'So, I'm afraid that will have to be that, then,' continued Lily, with gathering conviction. 'I'll visit you, of course. And the nurse is very nice, she *seems* nice. And your friends – whatever you say, you do have friends. I'll come often, I promise. And anyway, it's not as though you aren't going to recover. You have to believe you'll get better —'

'I won't.'

'Don't say that. There have been *loads* of people who have beaten cancer. You must try and think positively. After all, there's the wedding to look forward to – Jeremy's divorce has come through at last and we're finally talking dates. He's *so* looking forward to meeting you. I'll try and persuade him to come along next time I visit – shall I?'

Lily knew her voice was becoming increasingly breathless and uncontrollably high. Her mother's gaze, meanwhile, remained unfaltering. A small smile had begun to play on her lips as, with arduous deliberation, she extended her hand and crooked a skinny finger. Lily stopped speaking and, mesmerised, leaned forward into the smell of stale Yardley's Lavender – or maybe the stench of decay, for it was nauseatingly sweet.

'There's no Jeremy, is there?' her mother whispered.

Caught in her scrutiny and in the sickly odour, she shrugged helplessly.

'Don't worry. I haven't told anyone. I've always known, though. I knew from the start.'

'So why —?' Lily began.

'I was amused. I enjoyed the joke. I thought you'd still be there in the house when I got back from my trip. I looked forward to your embarrassment.'

A gust of anger made Lily tremble. She pulled away sharply from her mother's hypnotic orbit. 'Well, I *wasn't* there,' she said defiantly. 'I'd gone. And even if I'd *starved* out there in the big city, nothing would have induced me to return.'

Despite her condition, Eva managed a small acerbic laugh. 'As I can see, you didn't starve,' she said. 'Another couple of pounds off and you'll be perfect.'

'Thanks for that,' said Lily indignantly.

But her mother ignored her. She was still studying her closely. 'I can also see,' she said, 'that you are no longer a virgin. You must have found someone. You've changed. In fact, Lily, we're much more alike that I'd imagined, you and me.'

Lily shook her head slowly, finding no adequate response.

But Eva wasn't waiting for one. 'Who is he?' she asked. 'Is he rich?'

How she wished should could say 'yes' with conviction, that he was a millionaire – a *multi*-millionaire – who kept her in furs and diamonds and opera boxes and limousines. But what would be the point? Eva saw through her lies – she saw through everything. 'No,' she said. 'He's not. I'm the one who's supposed to be rich.'

'I see,' Eva said knowingly. 'Supposed to be rich,' she mimicked. 'Can you afford him?'

Again Lily wanted to lie, but couldn't. 'No,' she said.

Eva motioned for her to come closer and Lily wearily dipped her head. 'I can,' she whispered. 'As it happens, *I* am rich. Very rich. *Extremely* rich.'

'Mother, what are you talking about?' Lily stood back, puzzled. How rich was *extremely* rich? Max, she understood, had been adequately insured and left his widow comfortably able to afford coastal cruises, household improvements and the best leisurewear money could buy. But the way Eva had put it implied something more. Something secret and, the way she was saying it, possibly larcenous? 'When you say rich —'

'When I say rich, I mean *stinking* rich,' Eva said with the old abruptness. 'I also mean that I don't want to remain here, decaying in this goddamn hospital.'

Lily considered. 'If you're as wealthy as you say you are,' she said, 'then why don't you hire yourself a top-class nurse and go home? You don't need me.'

'Good point,' Eva answered. 'You're right – I don't need you. I want you.'

'I'm not for sale,' Lily retorted. Then, softening, it occurred to her that perhaps her mother had experienced some kind of terminal epiphany – a realisation that Lily meant something to her after all? Could it be that she wanted to use what remained of her time to make amends for her previous lack of maternal attention? '*Why* do you want me all of a sudden?' she asked. 'I'm not sure I understand.'

Eva gave another of her small, throaty and slightly malevolent laughs. 'Because I'm curious,' she said.

'Curious?' Disappointment drained through Lily. 'Is that all?'

'It's everything.' Eva took a deep breath which seemed to revive her. She sat up, unsupported by pillows. Her eyes had brightened and her colour had improved. 'I haven't been so curious in years.'

'Why?' Lily asked. She wanted to howl out her indignation, but all that came out was, '*Why*? Why now?'

'Because at last, at long last, you've reached an interesting age.'

Then the nurse approached, splintering the icy silence in which she was contemplating her mother, furious that even now, almost on her deathbed, she retained the upper hand.

'I'm sorry – I have to ask you to leave now,' the nurse said to Lily. 'We don't want to tire your Mum out. Oh, Mrs G, you are looking a hundred percent better! I had a feeling your daughter's visit would be just the tonic you needed. See? It wasn't the end of the world about your friends going, was it?'

'What's that?' asked Lily. 'Who's gone? Where?'

'Didn't you tell her, Mrs G? Honestly, you are too protective of her.'

'The girls went back to rejoin the ship for another leg of the cruise,' Eva said in a flat voice. 'They left this morning.'

'Elsie didn't say.' Lily shook her head. 'She might have told me.'

'She probably felt bad,' said the nurse. 'Your Mum was meant to have gone along with them, you see, but as you see —'

'— I missed the boat,' Eva put in.

And she said it with such mocking irony that Lily didn't know whether to laugh or to cry. She bent down and brushed her lip against Eva's parchment cheek.

'Think about it,' her mother whispered.

Without replying, Lily drew herself up to her full height and departed.

Part Four

10

Thoughtfully she watched Lily disappearing through the door.

'What a *lovely* daughter you have,' remarked the nurse as she plumped the pillows. 'I can see why she's done so well.'

'You wouldn't have said so a few months ago,' Eva snapped. How she detested Delphina Martin's indefatigable goodwill. It had a rubbery quality that resisted all Eva's efforts to dent it. 'No one would have called her lovely then.'

'Oh?' The nurse tucked in her blanket with a little too much vigour. 'I thought you told me she had always been exceptional – outstanding in every way.'

'Hmm.'

'Well, Mrs G – that *is* what you said.'

'Exceptionally and outstandingly dull,' Eva muttered.

'You can be very nasty,' reprimanded the nurse self-righteously. 'I thought you would have been in excellent spirits after a nice surprise like that. Some of my patients don't have *any* visitors.'

Eva fixed her with her severest stare and waited for the sermon to end. In her present condition there was not a lot she could do to put down this woman's irrepressible and maddening benevolence. She was helpless, dependent on assistance for her every need. There was nothing, however, to stop her cogitating on what, if able-bodied, she *might* have done to stem the compassion. There was, for instance, the possibility of applying something soporific to the nurse's tea. Or if not soporific, something deeply and embarrassingly emetic —

'There we go. All comfortable now. I will come around with your tablets in a little while. Twenty minutes or so. How is the pain, Mrs G? Do you think you are able to wait?'

'I'll wait.'

'Are you sure?'

'I said I'd wait.' She shut her eyes. She'd do more than wait; she had made up her mind to resist those awful mind-numbing pills altogether and endure the agony in order to be able to think. She wanted to process the impact of Lily's visit. A nice surprise, the nurse had called it. Talk about understatements; Eva was in shock. If her daughter's arrival had been unexpected, her transformation was nothing less than astounding. It had roused Eva out of her apathy and revived her interest in being alive. After all her arid years, she was curious again and – as she'd pointed out to Lily – curiosity was everything. The only god she'd ever worshipped. Until today she'd believed her life's measure of it had run out; until she'd seen Lily she hadn't cared whether she lived or died. No longer.

'Nurse,' she called to the departing figure, who obligingly turned round. 'May I have a cup of coffee, please? Strong, no milk.'

'Black coffee?' The nurse looked appalled. 'Can't I tempt you to some delicious milky tea, Mrs G? Or hot chocolate? Coffee isn't really advisable for someone in your condition.'

'In my condition,' said Eva, 'I can afford to live dangerously. Doctor Snow said I could eat or drink anything I fancied.'

'He didn't mean —'

'It's what he said.'

She observed the nurse bustling off to do her bidding and thought what fun it was going to be to exercise her manipulative skills once again. How dull and pointless it had been to lie here being depressed when, at the very least, she might have maximised her compensation from Elsie and the girls for their blatant desertion. The delicacies she could have demanded, the attentions she could have received. Beluga caviar, specialist laundering, celebrity hairdressing.

'Your coffee, Mrs G.'

'Thank you. You're an angel.' No harm in a bit of ingratiation as a deposit for future support.

'I'm no angel,' the nurse demurred with predictable humility. 'Just doing my job. And I must repeat, Mrs G, that I'm not happy about the coffee. Next thing you'll be asking me to supply you with – oh, I don't know – cigarettes.'

Which made Eva, who hadn't smoked for three decades, absolutely long for a fag. 'Oh, no, nurse,' she said. 'I'd never expect you to do something like that.'

She sipped the coffee. It was instant, the cheapest kind, but its bitterness aroused her taste buds from their extended dormancy.

Eyes shut, she sipped again.

And now the taste was nudging her memory into terrain it hadn't traversed for more than six decades. She tried to halt this nostalgic tide but it was more powerful than she was. A girl. She was a girl again, in a drawing room that gleamed with burnished oak and silverware and cut-glass chandeliers. Bone china cups were clinking and voices murmuring. Huge shadowy figures, long since excised from her recollections, were making sounds of doom and exile, rumblings about terrible things to come. And all the while she was listening but not listening, almost choking on the aroma of coffee and fear and impotence. It hung in her nostrils even when she'd boarded the train that tore her from the glittering rooms and the large fragrant people.

'You're lucky, Eva,' they said, when the journey had ended and she had stepped, bewildered, off the train and looked around and sniffed the air and recognised nothing. Not even the coffee-smell had accompanied her to this alien place with its incomprehensible clattering language. Even her name seemed to have mutated en route.

Lucky. Her first English word.

Just as the smell of coffee would always be associated with loss, that word would evoke forever a state of miserable and mute invisibility. It was years later before Eva understood the concept of good fortune, but never remotely believed that it had anything to do with her. Her own life quota of luck, she'd decided, had been depleted by the time she was fourteen. By then she'd been smuggled into England and, through various connections, placed as a housemaid with a decent family in a picturesque Devonshire cottage. By then she had become fluent in English and adept at all manner of housekeeping skills.

All of which, she'd been widely assured, was exceptionally lucky. Slightly less lucky, perhaps, was the fact that her parents and relatives had been forcibly consigned into oblivion. And that the master of the Devonshire house, Gerald Pemberton, treated her even worse that he did his own two daughters, beating and mercilessly taunting her. And that, while cooking and cleaning were useful in their way, she was never formally educated. And that, on the rare occasions when confusion and grief surfaced in that now-forgotten enemy tongue, she was silenced and called 'foreign slut'.

Until the day it came to her that she could take matters into her own hands. Literally. She'd accompanied the Pembertons on a family picnic to a favourite cliff-top clearing near Exmouth. It was windy and the sea beneath them wildly churned, while Gerald – even crosser and more demanding than usual – snarled and carped about the weather and the limp sandwiches and the meagre supplies of ale. As usual, he blamed the 'clumsy stupid foreign slut' for all adversity.

'Well, it wasn't *my* idea to take her in, Gerald,' Martha Pemberton pointed out. 'You're the one who said we should do our bit —'

'I thought she'd be useful,' retorted Gerald, immediately redirecting his resentment to his wife. 'We needed *someone* to be useful round the house since you're such a damned waste of time. As for those daughters of ours…'

Eva tried not to listen, she tried not to react. The words were confusing but the hatred was unmistakeable. She couldn't bear the proximity of such vitriol; it was like a sharp stick pressing against the membrane in which her worst memories were sealed. Grabbing the discarded sandwiches, she made for the cliff edge and tossed crusts to the swooping gulls.

'A bird lover, eh?' Gerald had followed her. He had drawn up behind her and was cupping her breasts with his rough farmer's hands. She felt sick. 'So,' he mocked, 'the alien has a tender little heart.'

'Go – away,' she managed. Those were the next two words she'd mastered, after 'lucky'.

'Nicely said.' He pressed harder against her.

'Go away,' she repeated. He was squeezing her, his breath in short gasps against the back of her neck. She stepped sideways, trying to evade him. He was gripping her forcefully. 'Leave me alone!' she cried.

'You're enjoying this, aren't you?' he said. 'Don't worry, no one can see us – or hear us. We're perfectly safe.'

She lurched backwards, a rush of fury giving her the strength to push him aside. He staggered, frowned at her and was about to retreat.

Which was when, with another dizzying surge of strength, she swung round to face him. There was a din in her head that was composed of all the vileness she'd ever heard, a cacophony of power and submission and rage. She stepped forward. He stepped back. Again she stepped forward and again he stepped back, terror in his eyes. When he stepped back once more, his third fatal footfall, she watched grimly as he tumbled into the foaming sea.

And the noise in her head abated. The silence was triumphant bliss.

From far away she heard Mrs Pemberton calling: 'Gerald, where are you?'

The waves crashed in answer.

Eva, coming to, rushed to Mrs Pemberton's side and feigned concern. She took part in the search and helped pack up the leftovers from the picnic. It wouldn't be long, she thought, before Gerald's twisted, bloated body would be washed onto a beach. For days afterwards, she was braced for retribution.

But it never happened. His remains were never found. Gerald seemed to have dissipated into the deep. She had a feeling that Martha Pemberton suspected she had something to do with his disappearance but was so relieved to be free of him that she refrained from pressing charges. Eva, however, was summarily dismissed.

'I never want to see you again, piece of scum,' Martha Pemberton told her. 'As you know, I never wanted you in the first place.'

At Taunton station, alone with her small suitcase and with nowhere to go, she defiantly applauded herself for securing her liberation. She ignored the tears that, despite her, trickled down her cheeks and the sick feeling inside her. Such loneliness. Such indefinable, unattainable longing.

But she didn't allow herself to wallow for longer than it took to find another position. In her luggage was a list of potential new hosts and Eva, who'd now discovered her own ruthless pragmatism, examined it carefully. Lord Monkton of Crowshanks Manor seemed to offer the most promising compound of aristocracy, widowhood and a well-placed estate. She would give him a try.

It turned out he liked her. A lot. Eva was aware that, with her new steely expediency, she had recently acquired a stunning embonpoint. And she could see the moment she presented herself at the door of his crumbling Cotswolds country house that Edward Monkton was agog.

Enthusiastically he steered her round the dilapidated facilities, clearly bent on convincing her to stay. Crowshanks, he told her, was once celebrated for its seasonal parties and exotic greenhouses and comprehensive library.

'And now?' she asked, wondering if the house and its owner were perhaps a little on the antediluvian side for a thrusting young maid like her.

'Now – well, it's rather peaceful,' he said, leading the way past a rickety staircase into a dusty book-lined annex, which was apparently all that remained of the once-lauded library.

'And here,' he announced, 'is the famous Crippen Collection of Forensic Toxicology. My pride and joy.'

She pondered. Her knowledge of English was mostly confined to the domestic and the defamatory. 'Forensic Toxicology' sounded way over her head.

'Poisons,' he explained.

'Ah, poisons.' The Pembertons, she recalled, had kept whole arsenals of substances to counter regular infestations by rats and other undesirables. It might be interesting, perhaps even useful, to acquire knowledge in this field.

He laughed apologetically. 'Yes, I know,' he said. 'Most people think it's a terribly dull subject.'

'No,' she assured him. 'Not at all.'

He looked delighted. 'This collection's been in the family for yonks. It's said to be the most comprehensive of its kind in England. If you like, I'll take you through it and give you some background.'

And so he did. In painstaking detail and with no demands for imbursement other than her engrossed attention and the proximity of her tantalising chest. Under his enthusiastic tutelage, Eva soon became an expert on the concoction, development and identification of poisonous substances. She read about them in the library, grew them in the greenhouses and mixed them in the bathrooms. After a few months she'd become sufficiently knowledgeable to focus on particular areas of expertise. She knew everything there was to know about the destructive capabilities of wisteria and oleander, not to mention climbing bitter-sweet and hellebore.

But a year later, the joy of talking toxins with Lord Monkton began to pall. They seemed to have covered all possible poisonous permutations and it was becoming clear that his interest in her breasts was as abstract and theoretical as his love of forensic toxicology. She tried to amuse herself by devising fieldwork for all her hypothetical knowledge, but that became frustrating.

In truth, Eva was bored.

Shelley Weiner

So when the doorbell chimed to announce an unexpected visitor, she sprang to answer it. A distraction! Someone new! After more than a year as Edward's sole companion, another human being – at last.

'It's Irving!' cried Lord Monkton, who seemed as overjoyed as she was with this break in their routine. 'Eva,' he said, urging their white-haired caller into the hallway. 'I'd like you to meet the famous Irving Magnus. A legend. A music hall star.'

A musical celebrity was so far outside her life's range of acquaintances that Eva was immediately intrigued. With the aid of two walking sticks Irving settled down by the fire and, within minutes, he and Edward had launched into a series of croakily-rendered popular tunes. His days of dance and song were clearly long over, but it seemed to Eva that his life in Hampstead remained fascinatingly bohemian and packed with arty friends.

And he liked her. Blatantly. The covetous way he gazed at her reduced Lord Monkton's gawping to mere passing fancy.

So when Magnus pulled her aside and wheezily offered her a job as his live-in help, she immediately said yes. As a gesture of fond farewell, Edward gave her some prime toxic samples and she happily swapped the isolation of rural Oxfordshire for the anticipated stimulation of Irving's much-vaunted thespian circle in Hampstead.

A big mistake but, in the long term, quite a lucrative one.

The flat was squalid, the creative friends mostly dead, and Irving turned out to be a self-obsessed bore. For interminable hours she sat listening to his anecdotes or accompanying him on slow perambulations round Hempstead Heath, his anecdotes drumming in her ears. One night he took her into his confidence and showed her his bank statement, which revealed him to be a multi-millionaire. He also disclosed to her his priceless collection of fascist memorabilia. He was not a nice man.

'Goodness gracious me,' Eva said, for her mastery of English was now comfortably colloquial.

The collection was bewildering, but she had no doubts about her response to his wealth: tenacity. She'd listen to his stories till Kingdom Come if there was a chance of becoming his beneficiary. More than a chance. Doctors had pronounced his heart as susceptible to failure and advised his devoted carer to keep a watchful eye. The same watchful eye had surreptitiously checked that, in the event of his passing, a substantial legacy would come her way.

Four years later, however, Irving was still going strong. Eva had begun to think that her own death by boredom would precede that of the garrulous eighty-seven-year-old. How much longer would she have to submit to his droning voice and increasingly cantankerous moods?

One day she decided she could endure it no more. With the help of Lord Monkton's parting gift and drawing on her expertise, she would assist Irving Magnus into the Eternal Music Hall. She prepared an untraceable compound of belladonna titrated with a little of this and a little of that, and no one suspected a thing.

He'd *had* his life, she told herself afterwards. Now young, orphaned, dispossessed Eva deserved a chance to live hers.

As she still deserved it now, cancer or no cancer. They said her condition was 'terminal'. But then, life was terminal, crossing a street could be terminal. Beds were often terminal. On the plus side – see, even here, there was one – her daughter had come to see her. Dull galumphing Lily had miraculously metamorphosed and managed to pull Eva back from the brink.

'All done?' asked Nurse Martin, who'd reappeared to collect the empty coffee cup. She was wheeling the medicine trolley.

Not quite,' said Eva. She wasn't. They *thought* she was; they'd written her off. But she'd show them. 'And you can keep those tablets. I'm not taking them.'

The nurse sighed. 'You're being very difficult this evening. There are other patients who are as sick as you are, a couple even sicker. Your doctor has prescribed this medicine to ease the pain.'

'There is no pain,' Eva stubbornly lied. 'And if you force these drugs into me I'll sue you afterwards for setting me on the road to morphine addiction.'

'You're being ridiculous.' The nurse's equilibrium was now pleasingly off-kilter. 'Suit yourself then. I wash my hands of you. I shall have to report you to Doctor Snow.'

'Why?' Eva affected puzzled innocence. 'What for?'

'Non-compliance. You are making my job very difficult.' Moodily the nurse turned away.

'Oh, dear,' said Eva with false sympathy. 'You know what *I* think a person should do when a job gets difficult?'

'What?'

'Take the money and run,' she said, only half joking. She heard the nurse's snort of impatience and her heavy footsteps clumping away. Take the money and run, she thought, and it became a tune that repeated in her head. *Take the money and run*. She had. She'd run and run until at last, aged almost thirty-nine, she had bumped headlong into a forty-something bachelor called Max.

Maximilian Green.

'Eva. Eva!'

'Not now, Max. Please. Leave me alone.'

'Wake up, Eva – it's me.'

She stirred from her reminiscent reverie and saw it wasn't lugubrious Max wanting what he'd called a 'special cuddle'. How could it be? Max had been dead for twenty-four years. 'Doctor Snow,' she murmured, wondering how much she might have inadvertently given away. 'I nodded off.'

'Sorry to disturb you. I was on my way out when Nurse Martin collared me. She's concerned. What's this I hear about you refusing medication?'

He placed a gentle hand on her counterpane which irritated and tantalised her. Silly man. Dr Kildare he wasn't.

'I'm entitled,' she said huffily.

'You are indeed. I must point out, however, that it's taken an entire team of specialists to attain optimum analgesic control. You might have forgotten the state you were in when you reached us.'

'No, I haven't,' she retorted. 'I may be ill and in my seventies but my mind is as clear as a bell. Or it was, before those pills. Didn't *you* tell me how important it is for me to be strong and positive?'

'I did. Certainly. But you'll find it harder be optimistic when the drug levels drop.' He was considering her with such pity that Eva, who'd been hesitating (after all, she wasn't *looking* for martyrdom), decided that she'd rather die than comply. If she had to choose between sacrificing her dignity or accepting the agony – there was no question.

'I do not want the tablets,' she said slowly and deliberately. 'And by the way,' she added, struggling a little to sustain the even tone, 'I've made arrangements to go home.'

'Home?' He looked astonished. 'How will you manage at home?'

She adored his stupefaction. 'My daughter,' she said nonchalantly. 'I mentioned that I had a daughter, didn't I? As it happened, she came to see me today and said she couldn't bear to be so far away from me at such a time. "Mother," she said, "let me take care of you – I have a lovely flat in London and we'll get in help when necessary – what do you say?" What *could* I say?'

'Stop – stop here, Eva.' Doctor Snow was frowning and rubbing his head. 'God, I'm tired. Nurse Martin said nothing about this. Does your daughter know what she'll be taking on? I know you think highly of her, but I thought she was very committed to her career. And didn't you say she was about to get married?'

'It's off.' Eva set her expression in a way that brooked no further interrogation. 'He let Lily down.'

'I'm sorry.' He sounded sympathetic but weary. 'Extremely sorry. She must be very upset. Would it be fair, though, to make emotional demands on her at this stage?'

'That's what I asked her. But she insisted, and there's no arguing with Lily when she makes up her mind. So, Doctor Snow —'

'No. I'm not agreeing to any of this. Can we talk about it tomorrow? And – please, Eva – won't you take your medication?' He was pleading with her. This was gratifying.

She smiled and shook her head. 'No, on both counts,' she said. 'There's nothing further to discuss.' She closed her eyes and kept them squeezed shut as she heard his receding footsteps, until there was silence.

Then she relaxed and tried to catch the thread of her reverie again. Max, she remembered. She'd been musing about Max. About how, after everything, she had fallen for his ordinariness.

11

It was in a spa hotel in Hertfordshire that they collided. Eva was by now extremely wealthy, for she'd discovered that her talent for investing and augmenting her inherited fortune was even greater than her gift for Forensic Toxicology. Over the years there had been men in her life, all passing amusements, but much of the time she was quite lonely, and the high spirits she was known for (along with her financial acumen) were often rather forced. Perhaps – she'd decided on booking herself into the hotel – a few massage treatments, seaweed wraps and extended immersion in the super-jet Jacuzzi would cheer her up. But the relentless pampering quite soon became tedious and she decided to head to the hotel bar for a recuperative gin and tonic.

Which was precisely the same time as a portly and flustered man in golfing gear was making an urgent exit through the narrow doorway.

'Oh – oh, dear,' he said and, in a clumsy attempt to move out of her path, knocked her sprawling onto the floor. 'I am sorry – extremely sorry.' He shook his head helplessly.

'So?' She managed to gather her dignity and wits, and extended her hand. 'Aren't you going to offer to help me up?'

'Of course. I didn't mean —' He reached down, sighing. 'I can't tell you how I wish I weren't such an —'

'Idiot,' she said and then, back on her feet, looked him full in the face. And there was something so guileless about his expression, so nakedly regretful and embarrassed, that she didn't have the heart for the derision which was her usual response to awkward situations. Instead, she laughed – a warm, throaty chuckle she rarely unleashed. 'These things happen. You seem in a bit of rush.'

Even as she spoke, he was edging away. 'Yes – sorry – yes,' he was mumbling.

'Wait!' Someone who wanted to get away never failed to stimulate Eva's instinct for pursuit.

'Wait?' he repeated, for her tone was peremptory.

'Yes.' She grasped his shoulder, which felt more muscular than suggested by his ill-fitting jacket, and spun him round to face her. Fully conscious of the mesmeric effect of her eyes, she held him in her gaze – wondering what had got into her. Why on earth did she want to detain such a dull and ungainly little man? She did, though. She couldn't help herself. 'I'd say that the least you can do,' she said, 'is to offer me a drink to make up for knocking me over.'

They drove to Rickmansworth in his spotless Ford Escort and found a booth in the local Berni Inn. Cautiously he suggested that, since it was well past cocktail hour, they should opt for a Surf 'n' Turf Combi-Meal instead of a drink.

'An excellent idea,' Eva said, marvelling at how ravenous she'd suddenly become. Enthusiastically she followed him to the All-You-Can-Eat Salad Bar and when they'd settled back, plates piled high, she asked him why he'd taken off from the hotel so fast.

He chewed and swallowed a mouthful of coleslaw which, for some reason, made him seem more attractive than ever.

'Teambuilding,' he said at last.

'Teambuilding?' she prompted. She wanted him. It was lunacy, she knew it, but she wanted him so badly that she was happy to offer herself up to him on the Formica table, then and there.

But his explanation, his confessional, was extended and intense. She didn't have the heart to cut him short. Max, it seemed, was a misfit in a large City firm where, for the past five miserable years, he'd worked as an accountant. The Teambuilding Awayday, enshrined in the corporate calendar, was an annual reminder of his inadequacy. His golf was appalling, he hardly drank and he completely failed to understand his colleagues' bawdy humour.

'I hate it – all of it,' he confided. 'Shall I tell what I really want – my dream?'

She didn't answer, but he told her anyway.

'I would *love* to find a nice, safe position in a family practice in somewhere like, say, Hatch End. And a house with a garden. And a wife of course. And finally settle down.'

He looked so wistful that she wanted to take him in her arms. 'I understand, Max,' she said. 'Of all people, I totally understand.'

Which was exactly what she repeated to him two hours later when he'd accepted her invitation to a nightcap in her hotel room and, after a preliminary fumble or two, made swift and inept love to her and climaxed far too soon. He apologised and she reassured, inwardly fuming and regretful that she'd succumbed to such an obviously-doomed onslaught of lust.

And when, early next morning, he whispered that he was on his way, she thought with relief that the episode was over. Nothing lost. Just an ill-judged fling.

'Thank you,' he said. 'You've given me the courage to take my future into my own hands and live out my dream.'

'That's good.' She was half asleep.

'Au revoir, Eva. Here – here's my card.'

Quietly he left. And when she heard the door click shut, she turned over and dozed off again. Farewell, Maximilian Green, she thought. A sweet man. It had been an ill-conceived coupling, but no harm done. The chances were high – more than high, enormous – that she'd never see him again.

How wrong she was. Max's ejaculation was hasty but supremely potent. While Eva slumbered, luxuriating in the comfort of her five-star bed and consigning her encounter to oblivion, one seed – even speedier than the rest – was settling into a thirty-nine-year-old but still-fairly-fertile egg.

Lily had been conceived.

This was a disaster. When Eva, eight weeks later, suspected then confirmed she was pregnant, it was a nightmare come true. There was no rational explanation for the horror of her reaction.

She had to get rid of it. People did that sort of thing all the time. Surely someone with her record of elimination shouldn't be daunted by an early termination? Early one morning, a few days after the discovery, she went as far as calling an abortion clinic and holding the line.

But she couldn't do it. She dropped the receiver and collapsed on her bed in a paroxysm of desperate tears. The invasion of her body by this creature, this *thing*, was terrifying beyond her endurance. How could she bear it? What would she do? Part of her was aware of the absurdity of her fear. How ludicrous it was that she, who prided herself on being devoid of guilt or superstition or religious conviction of any sort, had got it into her head that if she ended this pregnancy, she would suffer for all her sins. For Gerald, for Irving, for her ill-gotten gains, her lost parents, for everyone. It was mad. Primitive. She tried to dismiss the thought, making several more attempts to call the family planning centre (an ironic misnomer), but aborting (another irony) each time. Eva was convinced that the obliteration of this miniscule life would be a murder too far.

Well, then – she'd ignore it. She would pretend it had never happened. Defiantly squeezing her waist into her belt, she booked a room in the Savoy and slept all day and gambled all night. But as much as she slept, she was always fatigued – and as much as she won (for Eva always won), she received no pleasure from it, none at all. Instead she became increasingly nauseous and miserable.

There was no doubt about it, she acknowledged one night when she dared to confront her rotund belly in the mirror, this thing was stronger than her. Until now she had believed that she had acquired mastery over her own destiny. But a relentlessly-growing intruder was proving her wrong.

One evening by chance (or was it destiny again?) she came upon the card that Max had left behind and, on impulse, rang his number.

He greeted her with such delight that she, in her nausea and misery, burst into tears. 'I'm so happy to hear from you. I knew you would call, eventually. Guess what?'

'What?'

With a sinking heart she heard him say that, thanks to her encouragement, he'd left the City and found a job and acquired a top-notch bungalow in Hatch End. She agreed to visit him the following Sunday and fell into his comforting arms, and before she had left, five hours later, had agreed to be his wife. She would, she promised herself, be a *good* wife – conscientious and considerate, even if it wasn't her nature to be kind. She would keep her personal fortune strictly hush-hush and live modestly and traditionally on her husband's earnings. That would serve his ego and her conscience and leave her an emergency nest egg, just in case.

'I'm so happy,' he said rapturously. 'And you look happy too! More – content, somehow. More – substantial?'

Her determined smile vanished at this reference to her thickened waist. Eva's vanity wouldn't allow her to be seen as merely fat. 'I'm pregnant, Max,' she blurted out. 'I'm expecting our – your – child.'

'Ours? Mine?' he asked in wonderment. 'Are you sure?'

She nodded, doing her best to feign delight that almost replicated his.

'My dream has come true,' he kept repeating. 'This is the most wonderful thing that's ever happened to me...'

Before his lyrical flow became unbearable, she marched him into the local registry office, then into Mothercare. She would divert herself, and him, with domesticity. Having agreed to this extended sentence of suburban connubiality, all she could do was hope that good behaviour might shorten the term.

Lily came into the world sluggishly, three weeks late. Max, in high excitement, arrived at the hospital to visit his wife and daughter. He was garrulously enthusiastic, bearing a vast bouquet and an excited account of how he'd popped into the office to announce his good news and been showered with congratulations.

'Pipe down now Max. Please,' Eva said. 'You have your baby now. There – she's yours.'

Enthralled, he stroked the newborn's cheek.

Eva, meanwhile, refused to clap eyes on the life form they said was her daughter. There had been an unbearably intense moment of tenderness when the child had been placed in her arms, but she had resolutely suppressed it, and in its place had come aversion and fear. And then – nothing. It was as though love and hate had cancelled each other out in a mathematically-perfect equation, and a vacuum remained

'What are we going to call her?' Max asked, breaking the long silence. 'I was thinking Lily might be nice. I had an aunt called that – my late mother's sister, actually. She was known for her amateur dramatics —'

'That's fine,' interrupted Eva. 'We may as well call her that.'

'Wonderful!' Max's expression brightened. He placed a hand on Eva's and squeezed it. 'You care, I can see you do. It's a huge thing to happen, for both of us. But a wonderful one, such a blessing – don't you agree?'

She didn't answer. Nodding, she forced herself to give him a smile.

He returned it joyfully. 'See?' he said. 'I knew you'd come round to her – to us, as a family.' He bent over the crib. 'Look at her. Isn't she gorgeous? Our Lily – our little Lily Dreamboat.'

She wasn't gorgeous at all. She managed to be both lethargic and petulant and induced in Eva the deepest, most soul-destroying lassitude. Sometimes, late at night, she crept into the baby's bedroom and examined her carefully for any signs of the retribution which had feared her child might carry. But all she saw was an extremely subdued and apparently normal mortal, who was growing to resemble her unexciting but decidedly unwicked dad. In the old days, thought Eva, she might have considered giving Max a shot of something for his part in her current ensnarement. Max and his Lily Dreamboat, both. As a test, she began to run through her mental catalogue of poisons and tried to imagine Max and their daughter writhing and churning and burning in response to a particularly noxious administration.

But it didn't work. The magic was gone. Homicide held no interest for her any more. After three years of maternal labour, Eva had totally reformed. No prison sentence could have been more punitive or corrective than her incarceration with Max and Lily who – far from showing any signs of embryonic evil – was growing more lacklustre with each passing month. Eva sometimes wondered whether she'd got it wrong and this infuriating *dullness* was the monstrous legacy she'd bequeathed to her child. It drove her crazy sometimes – to distraction – almost to the point of throttling her.

But she held back, always, congratulating herself on her restraint. It was remarkable. And surely it was as a reward for her long stint of servitude that Max's heart packed in of its own accord? No toxic intervention whatsoever, thought Eva, trying to overlook the instant of searing pain that had cut through her with the solemn announcement, 'I'm sorry, Mrs Green —'. For a second, she had wanted to scream out in rage and despair.

Then she'd caught herself, steeled herself, nodded shortly and in a flat voice broken the news to ten-year-old Lily, who was distraught. At least someone would sincerely grieve for Max, thought Eva, as she defiantly rejected the trappings of mourning that her daughter suggested.

'*You* can wear black,' she snapped. 'I don't have anything to prove.'

Lily frowned, awaiting an explanation. But Eva wasn't about to share with the kid her triumph at having finally attained the status of what she liked to think of as a Bona Fide Widow. This long-desired standing absolved her from draping herself in widow's weeds. Murderesses, she knew, did that.

'But don't you miss him?' Lily asked.

'Course I do,' answered Eva, without elaborating on the emotional range of the verb 'to miss'. She wasn't pining for him; she was merely aware of his absence. The untended collections of miniature liqueurs and boats-in-bottles and cigar cutters spoke of it. As did the unregulated meal patterns that she and Lily had fallen into. As, too, did the space alongside her in the double bed and the empty Parker Knoll reclining armchair in front of the telly and the absence of his tuneless humming.

But not for long. Eva couldn't wait to mark her liberation by erasing traces of Max. She'd get some colour into her hair, her clothes, her walls, her shoes, her collection of Tupperware, her co-ordinated household furnishings – her life! This legitimate graduation into Merry Widowhood was what she'd been waiting for. She'd served her sentence as dutiful wife, fully earning her new state of grace. Flinging herself into finger suppers and shopping sprees and gossiping sessions with a coterie of new purpose-made friends, Eva did her best to ignore the depressing presence of her glum daughter. In her spiky sandals and round-the-clock leisurewear, she became the life and soul of every bridge afternoon in Hertfordshire.

But Lily hovered like a chronic dark cloud. Her brooding company was a constant reminder to Eva of everything she wanted to forget. Surely, any year now, she would leave the cuckoo's nest? Short of throwing her out (which was what cuckoos did for the good of their chicks) or murdering her, there was little she could do. She watched Lily's transition from awkward schoolgirl through ungainly adolescence into lumbering womanhood and, honestly, if not for their identical eyes, she would never have believed in their genetic connection.

'She's not like you at all,' Eva's friends remarked. Not in a good way. Matty Morris's daughter Diana, for instance, was a brilliant trainee solicitor and Matty pretended to be at her 'wit's end' with worry over Diana's hectic popularity. 'You're so lucky with Lily,' she'd effuse. 'She's so *wonderfully* quiet.'

'She certainly is,' Eva would agree. Quiet was an understatement. She hardly saw her. Like a shadow, Lily would slip past her and into that infantile bedroom that she wouldn't allow Eva to enter, never mind to renovate. What did she do there? How could she endure so many hours there, a grown woman in a grotto designed for a Disney Princess?

One day while Lily was at work she hesitated outside her room. Whatever her iniquities, Eva drew the line at prying. Or she had, until then. Finding the door unlocked, she couldn't refrain from entering. It was Lily's fault for not securing it, she told herself, feeling guilty nevertheless to be invading her daughter's sanctuary. Not guilty enough, though, to resist opening the cardboard box peeping out from under the bed.

It was crammed with papers. Cuttings from magazines. Eva pulled them out, one after the other and, as she grasped the overall theme, was seized by a terrible ache. What yearning she picked up in this repository of artifice, of superficial self-improvement. Futile yearning. Could any woman be further from fulfilment of the ideals of beauty, romance and success laid out in these articles than plain, plodding Lily? The pain of her daughter's birth had once brought uncontrollable tears to Eva's eyes. Now, more than thirty years later, she almost cried again.

But she pulled herself up sharply. This wouldn't do. Her daughter was a grown woman. It was time she took responsibility for her own life, or patent lack of it. If she wanted to hole up in her room with this ridiculous anthology of false aspiration, it was nothing to do with Eva.

Yet the ache wouldn't go away. It was a dull but persistent pain that lingered long after she had carefully replaced the cuttings in the box and the box beneath the bed.

Then Lily announced her 'engagement' and, as though she'd been delivered a bumper shot of pethidine, Eva's ache lifted. The declaration wasn't plausible and not for an instant did she believe her, but Eva grasped immediately that if she played along with the story then Lily would have no choice but to leave. At long, long last. This was her chance to get her daughter off her hands.

Jeremy, though – for goodness sake. How typical of Lily. Couldn't she have come up with a more exciting name? Quite a job she'd allotted to him, though. In a classified section of the Foreign Office, no less. And Jewish, as though that were feasible, as though Eva cared. How ironic, though. How supremely ironic. At least her dull daughter had finally shown a bit of her mother's spirit. Maybe she and Lily had something more in common than the flecks of gold in their eyes.

It was rather wonderful to see Lily's eyes shimmering as she elaborated on her lie. And Eva – caught up in the amazement of this make-believe – began to act along, playing the part of potential mother-of-the-bride. In the high chatty voice she'd acquired with her Bona Fide Widowhood and perfected down the years, she burbled on about the wedding and the reception and how wonderfully exciting it all was.

'I can't wait,' she said breathlessly, 'to tell the girls!'

By the time she prevailed on Lily to share her news, Eva had almost convinced herself that Jeremy was a fact. It boosted her own social standing for a son-in-law-to-be to exist. 'Jeremy' gave her credibility and proved she had reared a *normal* daughter, after all. A dear, darling daughter with whom she shared secrets. And, most importantly, if carried to its ultimate conclusion, it would remove Lily's depressing presence from the house.

Throughout their protracted bridge cruise Eva sustained this illusion. Jeremy featured prominently in her conversations; she crowed about his successes and Lily's achievements and their circle of glittering friends. Whenever

The Audacious Mendacity of Lily Green

Matty Morris boasted about something Diana had done, Eva topped it. Same with Elsie, endlessly on about Miriam and Michael. Same with Sylvia, whose own daughter Rachel was, alas, getting divorced. Eva gloated triumphantly – while suspecting that 'the girls' harboured as much covert ill-will to her as she did to them. Meanwhile, all was vivacious bonhomie.

Until the last night of the cruise when she slipped and fell on deck.

'Damn,' she said, not sure if agony or humiliation were harder to bear. 'I'm fine,' she snapped at Elsie, who'd immediately bent down to help her up. She brushed her aside, trying to ignore the pain that radiated from her elbow down to her hand and up to her shoulder. It was excruciating.

'Oh, poor, poor Eva – that looks sore,' Elsie commiserated.

'It certainly does,' agreed Matty.

'On the other hand,' put in Sylvia, who had an annoying tendency towards sermonization (her late father had been a rabbi), 'you should count yourself lucky that you didn't slide further and land in the drink.'

'Oh, piss off,' exploded Eva, her inhibitions released by throbbing pain.

Silently the four – all nervous to say any more – proceeded to the medical room where an x-ray confirmed that Eva's humerus, radius and ulna had all been shattered by the fall. 'Very serious fractures, given the fact that you didn't fall very far,' commented the doctor. 'On the other hand, you should count yourself lucky —'

'I'm *not* lucky,' interrupted Eva, while friends looked on in trepidation. 'Will everyone please stop telling me I'm lucky?' She could have flung out a few more epithets, but couldn't be bothered; she was too tired and in too much pain. Later, lying awake in her narrow bunk bed, she thought about the bungalow off the Uxbridge Road and wished she were there. Then her thoughts drifted to Lily, and she wondered where and how she was. The exultant little card from London was so clearly fictitious that Eva had not bothered to answer it.

But now – ironic, in view of how desperately she'd wanted to be rid of her – she hoped that she'd find her sad liar of a daughter still stuck in Hatch End.

12

When she got there, however, the house was silent and deserted. Eva, having been assisted to the door by the taxi driver, waited grimly for her luggage to be brought inside. Then she wandered slowly – *extremely* slowly, in view of the state of feebleness engendered by her broken arm – from room to empty room and, with each faltering footstep, her misery increased. Until at last she came to her bedroom, the prison she'd shared with Max for more than a decade, and fell down in a heap on the bed.

What was the matter with her? She'd endured far worse than this and come out – well, not exactly smiling, for Eva didn't smile much. But undaunted. If there was one thing she prided herself on, apart from her instinctive ability to invest and augment her capital, it was her resilience. She would not give in now. With a defiant surge of vigour, she succeeded in undressing and preparing for the night and finally lost consciousness in a temazepam-induced sleep.

For three nights and three days she remained mostly asleep. She couldn't believe how exhausted she was and how little she cared about feeding herself, washing herself or engaging with the world outside. The post collected in the hallway, the phone rang unanswered and dust gathered everywhere. All the while – apart from occasional faltering forays to the kitchen, where she pushed into her mouth dry cereal and crackers until she'd run her basic supplies to the ground – she remained curled in bed.

Until the fourth afternoon around teatime. She was making her way downstairs, tentatively, step by step, when she stumbled and everything went black. Blacker than black. She had no knowledge of falling, no sense of hurting herself. It was as though she was slipping into a murky pool and sinking.

When she came to she was vaguely aware that her limbs were peculiarly aligned, but she felt no pain, not at first. She was numb – dead. *Dead*? Was this what it was like being dead? Sylvia would say, 'You're so lucky, Eva, to slip from one state of being into another with such ease'. From within bubbled up her throaty laugh and, as it did, she was overwhelmed by a surge of pain so intense that it took her breath away. This wasn't being dead, it was far, far worse. She tried to move but found she couldn't. It was torture. She was in agony and stranded.

From far away the telephone began to ring. Until now the sound had been a piercing intrusion. Now she wanted to reach it, every fibre taut with desperation for someone to rescue her from the unbearable darkness and the crashing waves of pain and the gut-wrenching sensation that was undiluted terror.

By the time the front door was broken down and deliverance came, a sedative buffer had settled round her. She heard repeated peals of the bell, then violent hammering and finally the crash. Her pain by now had dulled and fear had turned to calm acceptance.

'You're remarkably brave, Mrs Green,' the paramedic encouraged, as they lifted her out of the house and into an ambulance. 'Really, really brave.'

She didn't make a sound.

'This is one plucky lady,' he commented to the driver as they sped, sirens squealing and lights flashing, to the hospital.

Still she didn't make a sound.

Nor did she react, beyond the involuntary responses of her vital organs, to the emergency surgery in which her previously-broken arm was reset and various other skeletal fractures were attended to. During the days that followed they prodded and pricked and tested every part of her anatomy and, at last, drew the curtain round her bed and solemnly announced she had cancer. Cancer with multiple secondary lesions. Terminal cancer.

'She's taking this amazingly well,' the nurse remarked to the doctors gathered round her bed. As though she wasn't there. As though the 'plucky lady' was some kind of phantom figure. Which it was, being so far removed from the sarcastic opportunist she'd always believed herself to be. 'She's either in complete denial or exceptionally courageous.'

Denial? What rubbish. Had anyone bothered to *ask* her whether or not she'd consented to her predicament? As for the mythical bravery they said she possessed – what nonsense. Bravery was active and Eva had slipped into extreme passivity. She had ceased to care.

Until the day Elsie Kramer arrived at the hospital and announced she'd made contact with Lily. *Then* she cared, she cared terribly; emotion flooded through her broken body with such force that she almost erupted in tears. Such a mix of emotion – but all she could express was fury. 'And who,' she demanded, as icily as she could, 'gave you permission to do something like that?'

Elsie looked stunned. She had clearly anticipated a different response from the 'gutsy little lady' her pal had become. Gratitude, relief, something like that. 'I thought —' she began.

'You had no right to think,' Eva snapped, and it felt as though *she* were snapping. Her protective cloud of apathy was dispersing into icy particles that were dissolving around her and all she could see was this big smug face looming over her, swollen with false concern. 'You should have asked.'

'*Asked*?' Elsie repeated in a self-righteously offended way. 'If I'd have waited one more moment to *ask* whether or not to get the police to check on you, dear Eva, you would – let's face it – have been dead. *I* made the decision – we did, the three of us – we were deeply concerned about you. And now I took it upon myself, with the best intention in the world, to be the one —'

'Come off it. I may be sick but I haven't lost my mind. I believe I'm still capable of deciding for myself whether or not to send for my daughter. Anyway, how did you know where to get hold of her?' In the silence that followed, she remembered Lily's ebullient little card saying how well and happy she was and providing an address in West Hampstead, should Eva want to contact her. It had been in the hand luggage she'd left in the hallway on her return from the cruise. 'You snooped through my bag,' she accused.

'Not as such. I was only trying to help. I have – *we* have – been so worried about you and know how close you are to Lily and what a comfort she would be. Despite whatever happened between the two of you —'

'Nothing happened,' Eva cut in. 'Who told you anything had happened?'

'Just a *feeling* we had. Don't be so angry, Eva – please. I wasn't expecting this. I thought you'd appreciate —'

'Oh, sod off,' she said, about to launch into a torrent of furious invective. But it occurred to her that her friends might abandon her if she was too offensive; she needed them to help her find her way out of this jungle of tubes and tethers and plasters and pills. 'It's the stress,' she said apologetically.

Elsie snorted with relief. 'That's perfectly understandable. We'd been wondering when you'd start *dealing* with your situation. I was chatting to one of your doctors the other day and he said how important it was —'

'What did *Lily* say?' asked Eva through her clenched jaw. She was determined to maintain iron control over her language and frustration. 'It's a real pity you had to worry her. She's got so much on her plate already, poor pet.'

'I know.' Elsie happily settled into their familiar conversational groove. 'I thought about that – but, honestly Eva, there's a time when a mother's need *has* to take precedence. Anyway, after long deliberation, I sent her a note and she called me almost as soon as she received it. Such a sweet person. Truly. You did a wonderful job with her —'

'*And?*' Eva interrupted.

'And – well – she'll probably come and see you quite soon. She couldn't say exactly when, being so busy, as you know —'

'Of course.'

'— but I'll let you know immediately I hear from her again.'

'*If* you hear from her again.'

'Of course I will! Now stop being an old misery-guts and think on the bright side.'

She launched into her self-designated hospital-visiting tasks – tweaking the flowers, topping up the water jug, clucking and fussing and chattering away. Then Matty arrived, closely followed by Sylvia, but which time Eva had recovered her equanimity and was able to participate in the familiar round of jocular gossip. Finally they gathered at the foot of her bed to take their leave.

'Eva, dear,' Elsie began, in a way that didn't augur well. She glanced for support at Sylvia and Matty on either side of her. 'There's something —'

'What now?'

'Well, one of the reasons why we contacted Lily was – um – you remember the night before you broke your arm we all agreed to return for the final leg of the cruise? And then after it happened we immediately – *naturally* – decided that we'd postpone our departure until you were well enough —? But now, of course —'

'I'm not going to be well, am I?' Eva said bitterly.

Elsie ignored her. 'Anyway,' she went on, 'there's been a slight hitch, insurance-wise, and – well, we're being forced to take up our booking. Aren't we, girls?'

Fuming inside, Eva managed to maintain her calm, if frosty, demeanour. 'Goodbye and good luck,' she said.

'Oh, *thank* you,' Elsie sang. 'It's wonderful that you're taking it like this – so generous! Didn't I tell you, girls? Eva is one of the most unselfish people in the world. The travel agency absolutely *refused* to postpone our booking – we tried, we really did. It's tomorrow we leave – gosh, doesn't time fly? But it will work out fine, I promise you, Eva. Lily will take care of you while we're away and — I know it seems like ages now, but eight weeks will pass and —'

'Stop — please.' Eva's impulse was to repeat her earlier expletive but, even though she had nothing to lose by offending them now, she suppressed it. She couldn't be bothered. They could go and drown themselves for all she cared. 'I'm very tired suddenly. All the best and thanks for everything.'

There was a pause. They hovered indecisively.

Then Elsie gave the signal and they embraced her, each in turn, and left.

At which point she let rip. Her fury erupted in a torrent of blasphemy, all the effing and blinding that she'd ever assimilated in every language she'd encountered. The nurses tried to calm her and Eva heard the saintly Delphina Martin remarking to her colleague how amazed she was that the stoic Mrs Green had it in her.

'Mind you,' she added, 'in her state of health, it's surprising that the outburst hasn't come sooner. At least she's getting it out of her system now — but she'll be shattered, poor creature.'

Eva knew there was a long way to go before her complex and guilt-ridden system was purged. Nurse Martin was correct, however, about her being shattered. Once her tantrum had subsided and with the help of a double dose of morphine, readily supplied, she was very soon out for the count.

The following day Lily arrived.

From the moment of her drugged awakening Eva had been dreading this. Her daughter's appearance would, she feared, be her final humiliation. After all the bragging about her brilliantly successful and soon-to-be-married child, in would waddle the ungainly embodiment of failure, futility and false aspiration. Eva had resolved to ignore her. She would fail to recognise her and freeze her out of existence. She would keep her eyes tightly shut and the graceless creature would go away.

Then she heard approaching footsteps and the sound of the curtain being pushed aside, and couldn't resist taking a peek. She opened one eye, then the other. 'Well, well,' was all she could say.

'Hello,' Lily said in a voice that was most definitely hers but sounded older and more assured. 'I heard – from Elsie.'

For at least ten seconds, Eva couldn't answer. She was dumbfounded. Could this elegant woman be Lily, her ugly duckling? Everything about her was transformed – her hair, her bearing, her new sophistication. Eva didn't believe in miracles, but this vision at her bedside was nothing less. If Lily had pulled this off with such panache, could it be that there really *was* a fiancé? Maybe she *had* landed herself some executive job? '*I* didn't tell her to contact you,' she said petulantly.

'Didn't you want me here?' Lily asked.

A few minutes before, Eva would have said she no, she didn't, in no uncertain terms. Now she wasn't sure. 'I suppose now you've come,' she said grudgingly, 'I'm quite glad.'

Lily's expression brightened and Eva thought – my God, she's beautiful! 'You *are* looking glamorous,' she said. 'Your new life seems to suit you. A changed person. I'd never have predicted this a few years ago.'

There was no ulterior motive in her approbation, none at all. Eva was simply relieved to be able regard her without embarrassment. It was only after a spasm of pain so severe she almost passed out that it occurred to her that her daughter could be more than a mere accessory. Now that her friends had deserted her, maybe Lily could help her out of this hideous place?

'Please take me home,' she demanded impulsively, desperately, hardly knowing what she was saying. How could she ask this of her? And where on earth *was* home? 'Will you?' she begged, for it had become a sudden, urgent necessity. '*Please?*'

Lily clearly vacillated for a second or so, then refused point blank. There was Jeremy and her job. She had her own life in London. 'I've *made* a life,' she declared.

At which Eva, now sensing that she was hanging onto the thread of that momentary hesitation, drew on her long-dormant poker genius and showed her hand. Beckoning Lily to come closer, she called her bluff: 'There's no Jeremy, is there?'

The shock and shame paraded all over Lily's countenance were confirmation, if she needed any, that she was correct. Of *course* there wasn't a Jeremy, how could there have been? But there certainly was *someone* now. Lily's sheen was beyond the orbit of even the most rigid course of magazine-inspired self-improvement. Eva's nose for these things told her that her daughter had discovered sex.

'Who is he?' she dared to ask. And then, over Lily's confusion, 'Is he rich?'

And when, uncomfortably, she confessed that it was *she* who was meant to be rich, Eva knew she had her. The combination of filial guilt and the temptation of her own substantial wealth would be fatal. Lily might baulk and try to stand firm but Eva was certain she'd eventually give in. It wasn't fair but, in her state, was Eva obliged to be fair? Bloody hell, no. She was sick and – as she with commendable candour admitted to Lily – curious.

'Curious?' Lily asked, crestfallen. 'Is that all?'

All, Eva had thought. What meagre life experience the girl possessed, despite her new aura. One day she'd find this out for herself. 'It's everything,' she had said.

Which was why, immediately after Lily had been hustled out, she'd made the resolve to opt for lucidity over analgesia. If curiosity was to be her driving force, then Eva was determined to have a mind clear enough to satisfy it. No tablets.

Grimly she'd resisted Doctor Snow's entreaties and battled all night long against huge boulders of pain, adamant that she wouldn't succumb. Not only would she prevail over the lure of medication, she would also do her utmost to get out of this hellhole with its stink of bodily decomposition. They couldn't keep her here against her will. Lily would take her, she had to; Eva would *make* her...

At last dawn broke and with it came Nurse Martin and her clattering trolley full of pills. Eva pursed her lips.

'Good morning, Mrs G,' the nurse trilled, clearly restored to her default joviality. 'How are we this morning?'

If anything was designed to entrench Eva's sedition, it was this patronising use of the first person plural. She didn't deign to answer.

'Good!' exclaimed the nurse, as though she had. 'Medicine time now.'

'No.'

'You're *still* being stubborn? It's up to you, Mrs Green – we can't force you. But I must warn you that if you keep this up things won't end well.'

As though her compliance would offer a happier conclusion. Not the way they were putting it, with their 'terminal' talk. Did this woman think Eva was a fool? 'So be it,' she said, a calm sense of power sweeping over her. She could say no and mean it. At least she could do that.

Doctor Snow came to see her in the late afternoon and listened to her chest.

'And so?' she asked after he'd completed the examination and was contemplating her silently. 'What's the latest? How am I doing?'

He sighed.

'You mean there's been no change,' she said.

'There has,' he admitted. 'For the worse I'm afraid. But the deterioration is slightly slower than we'd anticipated, which is good news in a way.'

'Brilliant news,' she said dryly, trying to swallow down her disappointment and fear. 'Tell me more, Doctor Snow. I think it's time to tell me everything. How much time have I got?' She looked at him squarely.

He scratched his head and evaded her gaze. 'It's hard to say,' he hedged.

'Forget it.'

She shut her eyes, shut him out. What did it matter anyway? Weeks, months, what was the difference? All she knew was that any more of her allotted span spent here would not be worth living. She had to organise her exit, fast.

'When I get to London,' she said coolly – empowered again by this control over her voice, 'my daughter will arrange for me to see a few more specialists. You're not the only doctor in this field.'

'No, I'm not.' He produced one of his soulful sighs again. 'You must understand that no one would be more delighted than I would if someone were to offer you an avenue of hope. But it's very important that your daughter is fully au fait with the situation before she takes you on.'

'So what exactly *is* the situation?' She was aware that it was unjust to vent her fury on him, but who else could she take it out on? Nurse Martin seemed impermeable.

'Oh, Eva,' he said despairingly, 'I believe I have made myself clear.'

And I, she thought, glaring at him, haven't. The arrogant sod assumed that because she was small and old and fatally ill, she was beneath his proper regard. He had no right to talk down to her. Would he do so if he knew how rich she was or how ruthless she could be? He'd been given access to all her organs but that gave him no insight into her soul.

'You don't know me, Doctor Snow,' she said ominously.

'I don't claim to,' he answered. 'I know only the workings of your body. But without them, I'm afraid —'

'How can you be so sure?' Desperation had gripped her and entered her voice. She tried to hold down her rising panic. 'Lily understands how much I need to be out of this place. She'll take care of me. She'll take care of everything.'

When he'd gone Eva amused herself with the notion of her Lily as a liberating angel. How wonderful if this were to become true – as true as Eva was plucky and Elsie was faithful and Lily was stupid and Jeremy existed. Lies, all of them – yet somehow the truth, *a* truth. Would the lie she'd just told about her daughter sweeping her away to London also come true? She prayed for Lily not to turn her back on her. She'd do anything, anything, to make up for her sins.

Her eyes were closed and her lips moving in supplication, when someone tapped on her shoulder. It was a nurse holding a telephone.

'Call for you, Mrs Green,' she said. 'I think it's your daughter.'

Eva shook her head in awe at this indisputable evidence of her interventional power. She accepted the phone and hesitated for a moment before speaking. When she said hello, her voice – even to herself – sounded small and uncertain.

Part Five

13

'How are you feeling?' she asked, disturbed by the tentativeness of her mother's 'hello'. This sounded neither like the chit-chatting reveller of old nor the witch who'd sniffed out her lie and was holding her spellbound. It was the tone of an old frightened woman.

'Top of the world,' Eva answered with heavy sarcasm. 'How *should* I be feeling?'

That was more like the mother Lily recognised from the day before. 'And what else should I be asking?' she retorted, angry and disappointed and slightly scared. She couldn't understand why she was bothering with this nasty creature. What masochistic force was drawing her back into the range of her mother's disparagement? Was she seeking a return to her childhood mortification – to be stripped bare again and pulled down?

'Well, if you must know,' said Eva, rather wearily now, 'the doctor says I'm as sick as ever. Looking on the bright side, though, it seems I'm not quite as sick as I might have been. And you?'

'Me?' asked Lily in surprise. Compared with her mother's woes her own seemed trivial. 'Not too bad.'

'I know it's a shock when someone lets you down like that, but you'll get over it, take it from me.'

'What are you talking about?' Had the malignancy begun to nibble at Eva's brain?

'That Jeremy – I could kill him! It was obvious to me from the moment I clapped eyes on him that he wasn't to be trusted. Extremely attractive, I must admit. But trouble, clearly trouble. You wouldn't have listened to me at the time – you were completely besotted. But I could have told you it would end in tears.'

'Oh.' Lily didn't know what else to say. Everything she'd planned to tell her mother had been wiped from her mind. It struck her that the woman was delusional. She was completely off her head.

'Anyway,' Eva went on, 'you'll find someone else in two tics, I'm sure of it. Everyone here thinks you're gorgeous – Nurse Martin remarked that it was pretty obvious to her why you'd done so well!'

'Really?' She had to put a stop to this. If it went on much longer she'd go crazy too. 'Mother, listen – you know what you said yesterday about going home? I've been thinking about it and – well, certain things have happened. If you're still so keen on it —?'

'Lily, my *angel*,' Eva exclaimed in high-pitched delight. Never before had she used the endearment. 'I *knew* I could count on you! When? Please come and get me soon – I don't want to waste another moment here, not with my prognosis. It's always been my *dream* to end my days in London.'

'London?' Lily was aghast. 'I didn't mean London. I thought I'd bring you back to Hatch End, to our house —'

'No, no, *no*,' interrupted her mother. 'Definitely not. I could never do that to you. I'm perfectly aware how much your job means to you. There isn't the remotest chance that I'd expect you to give up everything and rush back to Hatch End for me!'

'Mother —' she tried.

But Eva rushed on regardless. She seemed high as a kite. 'Do you imagine I could exploit your good nature like that? It's kind enough for you to have offered to put me up in your flat, never mind uprooting yourself again. We'll get in help if necessary —'

'Mother, *please* —'

'Doctor Snow, by the way, seems to think it all sounds quite feasible. In principle, of course —'

'Stop. Please. You don't understand,' she broke in, aware of the inadequacy of her response to this hallucinatory drivel. 'I *have* no flat.'

'Well, *buy* one then! *Rent* one, if you will. Even better, go the whole way and hire a suite for us in the Dorchester. You don't seem to have grasped, Lily dear, that I am exceedingly rich.'

Lily, dumbfounded, tried to decide whether this was delirium or deliberate falsification. Could it be a kind of counter-counter-lie? Maybe there was a medical or psychological condition in which a person lost all ability to distinguish between truth and untruth, reality and dream. If so, could there be a genetic predisposition to such a malaise?

It was unlikely, of course, but there was the teeniest chance that her mother really *was* as wealthy as she claimed to be – and, if so, where had the money come from? Oh, God – her head hurt.

'It's no good trying to discuss this over the phone,' she said at last. 'I'll have to come and see you again. Or call you later. I don't know what on earth to do.'

Dejectedly she pocketed her mobile and joined the throng along High Holborn, barely restraining herself from walking straight into the traffic. She saw little reason not to. Insolvency was unfortunate. Being an insolvent with an insane mother who had terminal cancer was sad. Being a *jobless* insolvent with a mad dying mother was tragic. This last desperate predicament had been revealed to her when, promptly at nine, she had arrived at work to find the entrance to Global Perspectives sealed with yellow tape and a policeman guarding the door. The night before she had returned from the hospital in a state of confusion and apprehension. Her head pounding, she had arrived at the guesthouse and managed to sneak into her room without interception. There had been fleeting thoughts about Tom and how he might be waiting for and wondering about her, but she'd been too tired and disturbed to do anything but crawl into bed. Tomorrow, she'd decided, falling into an uneasy sleep. She'd be less exhausted and all would become clearer.

And then fate had dealt her its final chastisement. Confronted by the yellow tape, it had seemed to her she had nothing left, nothing more to lose. 'Sorry, lady – no entry here.' The officious policeman had barred her way. 'Office shut down. Under investigation.' What option was there now but to retreat to Hatch End? And since she was being forced to return home, perhaps doing so under the cover of a mercy mission would take the edge off her embarrassment. Which was why'd she rung her mother. It had seemed a logical if demoralising solution which would provide a role for her and temporary salvation for Eva.

So she'd imagined, until confronted by her mother's absurd insistence on being brought to London.

Deep in thought, she thought she heard her name being called but ignored it. This was the heart of the West End. The chances of being recognised were minimal.

Then, 'Lily!' and, more clearly and urgently, 'Wait! Lily Green!'

She stopped, turned round and saw it was Gordon McCloud looking more dishevelled than ever. She'd never encountered him outside the office and, against the backdrop of the crowded street, he appeared slight and defenceless.

'I waited for you in the coffee shop downstairs,' he was saying, out of breath. 'Saw you going up to the office but you slipped away before I could get hold of you. What a dreadful business. And what luck that I spotted you!'

She nodded agreement on both counts. 'It was more than luck,' she said, realising how ridiculously relieved she was to see him. 'It was in the stars, Madame Katinka.'

He pulled her into a quieter side-alley and gave her a stubbly kiss on each cheek. 'Madame Katinka,' he repeated ironically. 'I'm afraid, dear Lily, that Katinka and Marge Scott, not to mention the astute Pete Preston, have gone the way of Global Perspectives – down the drain. All that remains is yours truly.' He lowered his head in a rueful little bow.

'What happened, Gordon? I couldn't believe what I saw. For me, it's the last straw. Truly it is.'

'I wouldn't have chosen it either,' he said quietly, and she felt suitably rebuked for her selfishness. She was about to apologise when he patted her arm and said, 'Oh, God, Lily – what a night. I'd say a top-up's now urgently required – there's a pub round the corner.'

She allowed herself to be steered there, meanwhile hearing his account of how all hell had broken loose in the office while she'd been tending to Eva. Ed Paterson, it seemed, had fallen drastically behind with a consignment for Singapore and a couple of heavy-set gentlemen had forced their way in to get things moving. They'd started dismantling the place, accompanied by the unremitting yelps and moans from the antechamber, where Bernadette and Vince proceeded imperturbably on the job at hand.

'Their commitment to their work was amazing.' Gordon shook his head in admiration. 'If those two had decided to take up ice-dancing instead of professional pornography, the world title would have been theirs.'

'And what were you doing while all this was going on?' she asked.

'Keeping my nose down, scribbling away and pretending not to notice that every page I filled was immediately being ripped to pieces by one of the thugs. But as you know — ' He smiled wryly. '— I've never over-rated my prose.'

'And *then* what happened?'

'Eddie arrived.' He paused for dramatic effect. 'And when *he* walked in, there were no holds barred. The way they laid into him, he didn't stand a chance. Arms and legs flying all over the place, blood gushing. Enough noise to distract even the diligent Bernadette, who burst into the room wearing nothing but a feather boa with Vince hanging onto the end of it.'

Lily couldn't help laughing. 'I kind of wish I'd been there.'

'No you don't. Not when the cops arrived and took down all our details. I can't tell you how many crimes Ed's being charged with. Assault, fraud, indecent exposure, narcotics, pornography, tax evasion. And, to clinch it, his car was illegally parked on a double yellow line and towed away. Not that he'll be needing it for some while. We were all been hauled in for questioning, but everyone except Eddie was released after a couple of hours. Naturally I celebrated my freedom and joblessness by making sure that I got paralytically drunk.'

By this time they had found a seat in the pub. 'What would you like?' he offered.

She considered. 'I think,' she said, 'that in view of the extreme tribulations I'm facing, I'd better make it a snakebite and black.'

'A what?'

'It's a mixture of cider, lager and blackcurrant – a friend introduced me to it. Really hits the spot.'

'Hmm.' He studied her with amusement. 'You mean the penniless musician?'

'No,' she said. Then, 'Well, yes. Thomas.'

He smiled. 'You're an enigma, Lily Green,' he said as he went off to collect their drinks.

They sipped in silence at first. Then she asked, 'So what happens now?'

'I don't know about you, ducky, but I'm planning to retire to the country to grow roses.'

'Oh?' she said, surprised. 'You? The country? You're a bit of an enigma too, Gordon.'

'Yup,' he said. 'From tomorrow I'm going to be a reformed character. I also had this crazy idea that I'd try my hand at a novel, but I don't think I'll put that one to the test.'

'Why not,? You should —'

'No, Lily dear. I'd rather hold on to the dream.'

She thought about this for a moment. 'Maybe you're right,' she said. 'I blew all of mine in one shot, and look at me.'

He took a deep swig of his Scotch. 'I'm looking.' He contemplated her intently. 'And I see a surprisingly interesting young woman – there are not many of those about, I can assure you. Things will work out for you, I'm sure they will. Katinka and her pals are also optimistic. One of the last things they said to me before they left for Cloud

Cuckoo Land was to tell Lily to stop worrying and to make hay with her flautist, and the future would take care of itself.'

She sighed deeply. 'He's not a flautist,' she confessed. 'He sells tickets at West Hampstead tube station, and I've spent all my money and borrowed even more to keep him thinking I'm rich.'

He spluttered over his drink. 'This gets better and better. And you like this fellow? Better than all the others you've told me about?'

'There haven't been any others. Tom's the first. And, yes, I do like him very much. I simply can't afford him any longer. And then there's my mother —'

'Ah, yes. The dying dowager. Don't tell me you invented her along with the flautist?'

'Partly. She isn't a dowager. But she *is* dying, the doctors have confirmed it, and I don't really know who or what she is. I thought until yesterday that she was the ultimate card-playing widow who was splurging her retirement fund on round-the-world cruises. And until a few months ago I lived at home with her and worked as a book-keeper for a local firm of accountants.'

He nodded encouragingly.

'Then one day – I don't know what got into me, some kind of delirium – I blurted out that I was going to be married to an imaginary boyfriend called Jeremy. So I left home, I had to after that, and came here —'

'— and landed Tom!' He raised his glass unsteadily. 'Great stuff, Lily.'

She glared at him. '*That's* not a story, I'll have you know. It's what happened. It's the truth. Tom exists, he has a flat in Shepherd's Bush.'

'Ok, ok – I believe you.'

'Thank you. But now *I* don't know what to believe.' The alcohol was making her thick-headed and maudlin. A sense of unreality was settling over her. 'Um – where had I got to?' she asked.

'Your mother?' he prompted. 'The merry widow?'

'Oh – yes. Well, the merriment's all over now. As I said, she's been diagnosed with terminal cancer, very advanced. And this morning I decided that – what with my money crisis and now no job – I'd have to go back to Hatch End and take care of her. But now, would you believe, she's got it into her head to come to London instead.'

'To stay with you and the so-called Jeremy?'

'No.' She gave a bitter little laugh. 'She guessed about Jeremy. She only *pretended* to swallow my story. And now she's pretending that he ditched me.'

'Wait.' He scratched his head. 'I don't get it. What's *her* case then?'

'No idea. I suspect she's mad. Seriously. Out of the blue she's now claiming she has so much money that she can afford a suite in the Dorchester Hotel.'

'And has she?' he asked. 'Might she have?'

Lily pondered for a moment. 'I don't know why,' she said, 'but I have a sneaking feeling that, yes, she might.'

'Well, ducky,' he said after a while. '*I* don't know why, but my feeling is that you should take her up on it.'

'And do what?'

'Install her in the Dorchester if it's what she wants. It would impress that Thomas of yours no end.'

'Tom?' She was aware of a surge of joy at the mention of his name. 'I suppose it would,' she acknowledged. 'Funny – I'd written him off as an unaffordable indulgence.'

'Never do that, unless of course the passion's burnt itself out. You think it might have done?'

She remembered her twinges of doubt about Tom's mysterious origins and aspirations – but now, with a pint and a half of snakebite and black inside her, all she wanted was to be with him in bed. 'The passion's still there,' she said.

'Well then, sweetie, I'd say you should go for it.' He yawned and stretched his arms and hauled himself to his feet. 'If your mother's that determined to come to London and really does have the means, she'll have to advance the deposit for the hotel. After that – I trust you're resourceful enough to know exactly what to do. By the way, you're more than welcome to come back with me to my flat – you can even stay the night if you wish. I can't offer you lover-boy's brand of services but I have an excellent spare sofa.'

She was too tipsy and befuddled to say no and, in a daze, accompanied him home. At eleven the next morning when she surfaced, she had no idea where she was and how she'd got there. Then she saw Gordon – and with his appearance came a mortifying half-memory of being drunk and emotional. What had she told him? What must he think of her?

'Good afternoon, Sleeping Beauty,' he said.

She smiled despite her embarrassment. 'Tom sometimes calls me that.'

'You mentioned that yesterday. And a lot else.' He spoke teasingly but without rancour. 'Men will say anything to have their way. Actually,' he went on, 'on closer inspection I take back the *Beauty* bit. I'd say you need some urgent renovation to get back into the fairytale heroine league. Booze plays havoc with the complexion – I speak from experience.'

'Thanks for the advice,' she said haughtily.

'My pleasure. And my next suggestion is for you to get yourself up out of bed and prepare to do battle. God knows why, but I'm feeling so much more cheerful this morning! Come and have some breakfast.'

Two hours later, with an omelette and coffee inside her, she was ready for action. She would make the Winter Palace her first call and placate Madame Plotnikova. Then she'd check the availability of suites in the Dorchester, inform her mother that the deal was on, beautify herself, and finally seek out Tom. A logical operation and seemingly infallible – but thwarted at its inception by Madame Plotnikova, who would not be appeased.

'Miss Green. At last!' In perfect timing with Lily's entry, the landlady had taken up position to obstruct her passage upstairs. 'So?' she demanded, and Lily immediately noted the absence of her usual conviviality. 'You have something to say for yourself?'

'I don't know what you mean —' she began in confusion. The speech she had so carefully rehearsed, purposely designed to tickle Madame's snobbishness and schadenfreude, had been forgotten. It was a story of temporary hardship induced by the tragic and mortal illness of her rich patrician mother and would, she'd been sure, have moved her. Now all she could do was mumble incoherently. 'Madame Plotnikova,' she tried. 'Anastasia. *Ana* —'

'I have trusted you,' the landlady said accusingly. 'You still have cheek to call me *Ana*? Ha? You still have nerve?'

'Madame,' she protested. 'Listen to me, please —?'

'No.' She stood there, expressionless and implacable. 'You listen to me.'

Lily, cornered and silenced, had no option. She waited resignedly for a tirade, still unsure of what in particular could have instigated this fury. Surely it wasn't just the fact that she'd been absent, or even the late payment of her rent?

'When you sign up to stay here, what is number one condition?' demanded Madame Plotnikova.

'Oh – um – I'm not sure.'

'Exactly. Such a clever career-woman, you agree something and then pretend you forget? That is what I am talking and that is what I am meaning.'

'What, Madame Plotnikova?' asked Lily, growing desperate. 'I agreed to pay my rent, and I'm sorry it's late but I promise —'

'You agreed to tell me straightaway if you change status from single person to not single. Huh? A deal. A done deal. And, between us, if it was a *decent* young man you been seeing, someone that fits in with respectable status of Winter Palace, I'd overlook. But last night a riffraff, a no-goodnik, comes ringing on my doorbell and guess?'

Lily had guessed but wasn't letting on. Tom. He'd tracked her down. She tried to keep her expression blank and shrugged noncommittally.

'When I open up, he is asking for *you*!' Madame Plotnikova was narrow-eyed and accusing.

'Are you sure?'

'Unless it is *other* Lily Green he is visiting?'

'There must be some mistake,' she tried. 'I certainly don't know anyone who looks like a – the way you describe him.'

'Exactly,' agreed Madame Plotnikova emphatically. 'My thinking too. So I politely tell him just that. But then Mavis Fishburn is coming in at same time and she screams and says *that* is man who has been watching Winter Palace. A stalker. She has seen him at least two-three times in our street. And so, Miss Green, do you know what I did? What did I *have* to do?'

'I – er —'

'Of course. Naturally. I call police. And no sooner I put down phone, come two officers here. Such speed, I think, is too good to be true in this lazy city. And it *is* too good to be true! *Why*, I'm asking you? Why too good?'

This time Lily didn't even try to guess.

'Because,' Madame Plotnikova continued, 'these policemen are not for the no-goodnik. They are coming for *you*. Yes, do not look so shocked. They are looking for *Miss Lily Green* to help with enquiries. You, Miss Green, must report urgently to Scotland Yard and ask for Detective Superintendent Mike Brown, a top-cop policeman, if you don't mind. And please to take all your belongings with you when you go.'

'My belongings? You mean —'

'I mean: you must leave. *Now*. I will *not* have such troubles here. Was quiet after Igor died and I now have beautiful, decent establishment. I believed you to be a quiet lady with a steady job, a proper lady —'

'But I am,' Lily cried. 'You're jumping to conclusions. I can explain.'

'Explain to police. I am sorry. Such things I cannot tolerate.'

She shook her head weakly. 'What happened to *him*, then? The man? Did another officer come and arrest him?'

'See!' Madame Plotnikova pointed an condemnatory finger at her. 'You *do* know him. When I'm right, I am right. As happens, Miss Green, police have not enough evidence to press charges, but now they know what he looks like, they are going to keep an eye. A warning he is given, a very serious warning.'

'But —'

'No buts. I was saying to Mavis how I have nothing against you personally. We are upset, all of us.'

'Madame Plotnikova,' Lily implored, sensing a softening and hating to grovel, but what else could she do? 'Please can I stay for a few nights – a week – I know I'm a little behind with the rent, but I paid you in advance so there must be something —?'

'I am sorry. You must be out of here by tonight.'

It was clearly futile to plead further. Lily nodded and, with as much dignity as she could muster, ascended to her room. Once inside, though, she was struck by the unfair humiliation of her plight and burst into tears. Which, she knew, was inflicting further damage on her beleaguered facial appearance, but what did that matter when the war was all but lost? At least Tom had come looking for her. That was something. Maybe he really cared? Maybe it was still possible that all this would end happily?

Lily heaved a sigh and looked around the tiny room. She'd been living here for four months but made little impact on the ornate faux-Victorian clutter. Her belongings were concealed in gilt-embossed drawers and behind cupboard doors and, immediately she'd packed and departed, there would be no trace of her occupation. From underneath the bed, she pulled out her matching pair of Vuitton-style suitcases and remembered the hope with which she'd bought them and the certitude with which they had been recommended. Maisie Fitzherbert had sworn that this was *the* luggage for the go-getting woman on the move. Or had it been Gina Woods? Or Megan McCloud?

How familiar all those names had been, how sage their advice. Even now, when all seemed lost, she didn't entirely

The Audacious Mendacity of Lily Green

disbelieve them. After all, even Eva had remarked on how glamorous she was looking. And Gordon had said she was 'interesting' and Tom had been searching for her. Someone so glamorous and interesting and elusively alluring surely deserved better than this vulgar little room? A suite in the Dorchester, at the very least.

Madame Plotnikova had done her a favour, she decided, as she searched through her cuttings file for advice on Emergency Repairs to the Complexion. By chance she came upon a *Harper's* piece by Margery Levenkind. 'There are four prime requisites for Big Success,' she wrote. 'Spontaneity, Adaptability, Improvisational Skills, and Good Fortune.' Lily, looking back, decided that she had a proven track record in the first three. Surely it was time for Good Fortune to come her way?

Not long after, her bags were packed and her appearance and resolve were restored. With a refund on her deposit of £28.74 and Madame Plotnikova's chilly good wishes, she made her way to West Hampstead Station. She would approach the ticket office with unassailable aplomb and there he would be, looking very forlorn, and she would gaze into his eyes and smile and —

'Can I help you?'

She started. It wasn't Tom's voice. Not his face either. 'I'm not sure,' she said.

'Make up your mind, please, miss. There's a queue behind you. People are in a hurry.'

'Is Tom Kennedy at work today?' she asked.

'Tom? Tom's been — oh, it's *you*.' He regarded her knowingly and Lily, disconcerted, wondered what he meant. 'His *lady*,' he went on. 'More trouble than you're worth, is what *I* think. Thanks to you he got the push this morning. And if I were you, I wouldn't go running after him – he's had a gutful of you. Next please,' he called to the person behind her in the queue.

But Lily didn't move. How dare he talk to her like that. 'Excuse me,' she said firmly. 'You haven't dealt with my

193

transaction yet. I'd like a single ticket to Shepherd's Bush, please.'

'I'm warning you —' he began.

'And I'm warning you,' she interrupted. 'You have no right to be rude to me and, if I could be bothered, I'd report you. What's your name anyway?'

'Joe Perkins.'

'Oh, *Joe*.' She said it in a way that implied she knew as much about him as he knew about her. She did, in fact, recall Tom mentioning his name. 'See you around.'

She walked away with proud, determined strides, a suitcase in each hand and her head held high. Inside, though, she was in turmoil. 'He's had a gutful of you,' his workmate had inelegantly said and Lily, despite her appearance of resolute confidence, was full of apprehension.

14

Shepherd's Bush Green looked seedier than ever and the entrance to Tom's block as dingy. At night the area had seemed romantic and adventurous, but now it appeared merely squalid. Hardly the destination for a stylish executive with matching luggage and Marc Jacobs shoes – but then, who the hell was she kidding? Beneath her elegant exterior beat a tremulous heart and in the smart leather purse was her entire worldly fortune of £24.74. She had never walked these pavements alone and, as she pressed the button marked '435 – Kennedy', felt vulnerable and conspicuous. It seemed that a hundred eyes were leering at her and nobody cared.

Including Tom who – if he was at home – was ignoring her. This was awful. It was the worst possible scenario. She tried to stay calm and examined her options. She could while away the time and examine two-man tents in the camping shop or the wines in the off-license until he returned. If he returned. Or she could seek asylum once again with Gordon. *Or*, of course, there was Hatch End. Eva could be forced into choosing between remaining in hospital and going back to a perfectly adequate, unoccupied and fully-paid-up house. She'd have to relinquish that ridiculous notion of coming to London but, in her state, what right did *she* have to dictate?

As she hovered in uncertain deliberation with her suitcases parked next to her feet, someone tapped on her shoulder. 'Sorry – I need to get past,' said a harassed mum at the helm of a double buggy, the concerted screaming of two infants emanating from within. Lily stepped aside and then, on impulse, followed the buggy into the building, mumbling something about having lost her keys. She took the rasping lift to the fourth floor, found her way along the corridor with its soiled mattresses and seatless chairs, paused at Tom's front door and knocked three times. And waited, and knocked again much harder. Nothing happened. He could be disregarding her, or he could be out. Or in prison. Or unconscious in a ditch somewhere. Or dead.

She perched on a suitcase, breathed deeply, and told herself not to be melodramatic. It was pointless exploring alternative scenarios for Tom's fate when she herself had no option but to wait.

At least an hour passed before she heard the creak of the lift and his approaching footsteps. Not dead then. 'Lily! How the fuck did you get inside?'

He was alive but did not sound glad. She gave him a tremulous smile. 'Hi?' she said.

He didn't smile back. Instead, he looked from her to the suitcases and back to her again. 'What's this?' he asked.

'What does it look like?' she answered indignantly. 'Can we discuss it inside?'

He didn't move. She decided that this was going to be more difficult than she'd anticipated. He seemed seriously annoyed with her. 'Please?' she said, trying not to sound too distressed. She had to hold on to her dignity, even now.

Grudgingly he unlocked the door and picked up her suitcases, public schoolboy that he claimed himself to be. 'What have you got in here? Bloody concrete,' he muttered.

She followed him inside. 'You don't have to worry,' she said as lightly as she could. 'I'm not planning to settle here.'

'Who's worried?' He set the luggage down rather aggressively and then turned round to face her. 'And so?' he demanded. 'What do you have to say for yourself?'

What could she say? That subsidising his extravagance had brought her to insolvency? That she had no faith in his continuing interest in a mature woman without funds? Her turmoil expressed itself as indignation. 'What a nerve you have,' she said. 'I don't have to explain myself to you. I owe you nothing. I thought we understood that.'

He indicated her belongings. 'What's this about, then?'

'I told you – I'm only passing through. On my way to the Dorchester, as it happens.'

He exploded with laughter. 'The Dorchester. What are you on about, woman? From that White Palace dump to the Dorchester. Do you honestly expect me to believe that? Didn't you tell me the last time we were together that things were a bit tight? What happened since then? Robbery? Embezzlement? A lottery bonanza? Maybe your old lady pegged and left you a fortune?'

'Stop bombarding me,' she pleaded. 'Please?' Then looked him squarely in the eye. He was as attractive as he'd ever been. She wished they could stop arguing and get into bed. 'It's the last. The old lady. Well – um – more or less.' She studied his expression, which was softening. There was something very persuasive about the truth.

'What do you mean, more or less?' he asked. '*Is* it your old lady and *did* she peg? The size of a fortune, I suppose, is open to interpretation, but – will you please explain?'

She subsided onto his sofa which squeaked in protest, and patted the space at her side. He shrugged resignedly and sat down.

'Did you miss me?' she risked asking.

'I missed the good life.'

'Is that all?' She couldn't hide her disappointment. 'That's all you care – cared – about?'

'Come off it, Lily,' he said harshly. 'You were only gone for two days. I have stuff to do, you know. There's work – my mates. As you so nicely put it, we owe one another nothing – we never had any exclusive arrangement.'

Her anger rose again. Talk about rubbing it in. 'Work,' she mocked. 'I've heard whispers about your work. Apparently it's being said that you're no longer in the running for Managing Director of Transport for London.'

He was silent for a moment and looked gratifyingly uncomfortable. 'Who told you? Joe, the blabbermouth? Did you come looking for me at the station?'

She didn't deign to answer.

'Anyway,' he went on. 'You've got room to talk, Miss High-Powered Executive. I took a little stroll down Panton

Street earlier today and – guess what? Global Perspectives, *was* it? Hmm.'

Furiously she glared at him. Touché. She was about to retort about how strange it was for someone who claimed he hadn't missed her to have spent so much time lurking outside the White Palace Guesthouse. But as she opened her mouth to speak, she felt his lips pressed against hers, kissing her urgently.

He cared. He did. His cool insouciance seemed to have dissolved, and her anger with it.

'I did miss you, Lily Green,' he confessed. 'I've been searching for you everywhere.' And, with all the passion of their first encounter, they discarded a trail of garments from the sitting room to Tom's bedroom and set to on his king sized bed.

'That was *shit*-hot,' he proclaimed afterwards.

'Delicately put,' she objected.

'Sorry – I'd forgotten I was addressing a lady bound for the Dorchester. So? Time to tell me all about it.'

She sat up and breathed in deeply, about to begin. Then a thought struck her. Madame Plotnikova had stressed that she should report to Scotland Yard urgently. With things the way they were, she couldn't risk any delay. 'Oh, God,' she said. 'I've just remembered something? How do I get to Scotland Yard?'

'Scotland Yard?' he repeated, and lay back as though defeated. 'Lily, you mystify me. I can't keep up with you —'

'You don't have to.' Rapidly she gathered her clothing and got herself dressed. 'Give me directions and I'll be as quick as I possibly can.' She tidied her hair and hastily restored her make-up.

'Shall I come with you?' he offered.

'No – keep the bed warm and take good care of my worldly possessions. If all goes well I'll bring back oysters and champagne.'

'And the story about your mother?' he reminded her.

'The full story,' she confirmed.

Which was more or less what earnest-looking Detective Superintendent Mike Brown of Scotland Yard Police Station was after. He offered Lily a seat in an austere interview room and grilled her about everything she could recall about her period of employment at Global Perspectives.

Having haltingly provided him with her version of events, she asked what had happened.

'Well,' he said cagily. 'All I can say at this point is that Mr Paterson faces a number of serious charges. And there are question marks hanging over some of the employees, including your friend Gordon McCloud.'

'But he's a journalist, not a criminal,' she cried, horrified. 'He was only doing his job.'

'That's what they all say,' Brown muttered grimly. 'Anyway, Miss Green, at this stage it seems you're in the clear. There's general agreement that you were merely a typist supplied by a temp agency.'

'I suppose so,' she acknowledged, wishing for at least a shadow of suspicion to dapple the bland dullness of his label but not quite bold enough to claim any culpability. When asked for a contact address, though, she boldly announced it to be care of the Dorchester.

'The Dorchester Hotel?' The Detective Superintendent was clearly taken aback. 'I see. You live there? It's your permanent place of residence?'

'Not quite yet,' Lily admitted. 'I'm temporarily staying with a friend in Shepherd's Bush. But I'll be moving into the Dorchester quite soon.'

'Ah.' He deliberated, frowning. 'Can I take it then that you're currently without a fixed abode?'

'Yes – that's correct,' she said, elated by this enlivening of her circumstances. How intrepidly footloose being homeless made her seem. She gave him Tom's address in Shepherd's Bush and watched him writing it down – and saw that he affixed to it a large question mark and 'query Dorchester Hotel'.

'We'll be in touch, Miss Green,' he said, looking up and studying her properly for the first time.

Cheered by this new interest in her, she nodded eagerly and suppressed a niggle of unease. There was nothing to worry about. She'd done nothing wrong. Hadn't he assured her that she was completely in the clear?

'Is there anything else?' he asked, for she was hesitating at the door.

'Well, maybe,' she said, about to ask whether she could make a telephone call to her gravely-ill mother. But instinct told her that she shouldn't provide this cop with more personal information than he already had. 'No, it's nothing. Good luck with your enquiries.'

She stepped into the street to find she'd run out of credit on her mobile. No choice, then, but to seek out a public phone and feed it with her remaining cash.

She dialled the hospital, asked to be put through to O'Connell Ward and then, recognising Nurse Martin's voice, asked whether she could have a brief word with her mother. During the long pause that followed, which involved much mumbling and shuffling and swallowing of her fast-dwindling coins, she composed herself for a compassionate speech. It would climax with the offer to indulge Eva's every last whim. Dying children were carted to Disneyland and if her mother's wish was to be in London – well, then, Lily would make it come true.

At last Eva took the phone. 'So?' she snapped.

'So?' echoed Lily, taken aback, for she hadn't banked on being barked at and nor would she tolerate it. If her mother behaved like a grumpy hound, she could stay chained to her hospital bed. 'Feeling any better?' she asked coolly.

'When are you coming to get me?' Eva demanded, ignoring the question.

'That's *if* I come and get you.'

'You will – won't you?' Her stridency had melted and a pitiful note of appeal had entered her voice. 'Please get me out of this prison, Lily. Please?'

Lily's impulse was to soften immediately and to say, yes, of course she would, she wouldn't leave her to suffer there a moment longer than necessary. But she steeled herself. Impassively, she asked whether Eva had meant what she'd said about the suite in the Dorchester. If not, unfortunately, Lily wasn't in a position to —

'Of course I meant it,' Eva broke in. 'Do you take me for a liar? I hold back, maybe, but I certainly don't mislead. Not like some people I know.'

Paying no attention to the insinuation, Lily went on to state her terms. She would reserve the accommodation and then come to Hatch End to regulate the move. Naturally, she'd expect to have access to some (if not all) of Eva's supposed wealth, for the set-up she had demanded didn't come cheap. There were also certain debts she'd need settling – credit card, bank overdraft, that sort of thing. Finally, she'd need Eva to compensate her for the loss of her earnings, for she couldn't possibly manage a job at her level in *addition* to caring for an invalid.

'My, my,' Eva said eventually. 'I'm impressed. Who put you up to this, Lily? The boyfriend?'

'The *boyfriend*? Tom, you mean? Of course not. He's not like that – he isn't the scheming sort at all.'

'Calm down. I'm not criticising. I said I was impressed. When will I see you?'

Lily ordered herself to remain calm despite the nausea that was rising and the vertigo that made the booth start to spin. She was trapped in a snare of her own setting, trapped by someone who'd cried *she* was trapped. Eva was ill, she was dying – yet it felt to Lily that *she* was the victim, however assertively she tried to act. If she cared about her own salvation she would extricate herself now. Every ounce of good sense urged caution, retreat.

Yet she heard herself saying with utter composure, 'I'll be with you tomorrow or the next day. There's an enormous amount to organise. When I'm ready I will let you know.'

She telephoned the Dorchester after that and was encouraged by the ease with which she achieved a provisional reservation for a Mayfair suite with a sitting room, dining room and two well-appointed bathrooms. This was fun. It could be enormous fun. How many people moved into rooms freshly vacated by the Sultan of Brunei? How many daughters arranged for their mothers to expire in such opulent surrounds? Tom, with his leanings towards luxury, would be charmed by the tale.

She emptied her purse to count her remaining assets. Not nearly enough, alas, for oysters and champagne. For now, peanuts and plonk would have to do.

15

He was waiting for her, his face a picture of puppy-dog anticipation. If he'd had a tail it would be thumping on the floor. Lily, suddenly seeing him through her mother's hypercritical eyes, worried about this unbridled enthusiasm. She wanted Eva to be impressed. 'The bubbly as promised,' she said, drawing the bottle out of its bag and handing it over. 'Not quite champagne, I'm afraid, but just as alcoholic. And here, to accompany it, are some extra-giant peanuts. I know I said oysters, but it so happens that peanuts are aphrodisiac as well. As if we needed any chemical help —'

He grabbed her and spun her round in an exuberant waltz.

'Stop,' she cried. 'Stop!' She tried to pull away, but he held her fast. 'Tom, if you don't let me go this instant, I'll ... I'll —'

'You'll do nothing at all,' he said. 'Why would you want to go and spoil such a perfect partnership?'

'I'm not. I'm just tired.' Her head was reeling and her body had begun to ache. The rush of elation triggered by the call to the Dorchester had dissipated, and she was suddenly worn out. 'Why don't you pour the drinks and then I'll answer your questions.'

Eagerly he made for the kitchen to dispense the wine while she sat back and waited. Glancing at his bookshelf, she noticed that the OED had returned to its place. 'I see,' she called, 'that you've got your big dictionary back. Or is it a new one?'

He wheeled round to face her, then seemed to take a grip on himself. 'Oh, that!' he said. '*That* old thing. Yeah, well, it's the same one, as it happens. I lent it to Joe and he gave it back.'

There was something odd about his forced breeziness. Hadn't he told her that he'd thrown it away? She was sure he had and, as far as she recalled, they'd even disagreed about it. Anyway, why would Joe have required the long-term loan of a cumbersome dictionary? It seemed a minor issue, though; hardly worth quibbling about.

He handed her a brimming crystal goblet. 'Cheers,' he said, sitting down alongside her. Then, draining the glass quickly, he said, 'Right. Tell me what's been happening. One minute you're a rich careerwoman negotiating to buy a Chelsea flat. Then suddenly there's a cash crisis and the company you work for has folded and you disappear, who-the-fuck knows where. And now, suddenly, your mother comes into the picture.'

'Well, yes.' Put like that, it all sounded a bit florid.

'She's on her last legs, you're saying.'

'Well, yes! I told you —'

'So why don't you stick her into one of those hospice places where you're given a really good death? As a matter of fact, I saw a TV programme the other evening —'

'She's determined to come to London, Tom. She has made up her mind.'

He shook his head. 'All I can say is that it's fucking ridiculous. If someone's that sick, they shouldn't *have* a mind. As for the Dorchester – that's completely bonkers. Big-deal businessmen stay there, royalty, movie stars, oil barons. Not dying old ladies. You know what, Lily? I think you're making this all up. And what about your urgent mission to Scotland Yard? How did *that* come about?'

She tried to brush it aside. It was nothing, she told him. A mere inconvenience. All to do with Global Perspectives which, as he knew, was now defunct. They were investigating various charges of drug-dealing and soliciting and illegal trade in pornography, crimes of that nature —

'You?' he gasped. 'You've been involved in heavy stuff like that?'

'Peripherally,' she said airily, then saw his sceptical face. 'Don't you believe me? Do you think I'm inventing this? Do you honestly think that with things at such a crisis point I'd be telling you lies? Well, check up on me then. Ring

Northwick Park Hospital or have a word with Detective Superintendent Mike Brown. Or, best of all, phone the Dorchester.'

'Ok, I will.' He jumped up purposefully. 'I'll buzz the Dorchester right now. In whose name did you say the booking was?'

'Eva Green,' she said, offended that he should be taking her up on the offer. Did he really not trust her? Had he reason to? Or, for that matter, had she any real reason to trust *him*? 'It's a provisional reservation for one of the Mayfair suites in the name of Mrs Eva Green.'

Moments later he came bursting back into the sitting room. 'Well,' he said, 'I'd never have believed it if I hadn't heard it with my very own ears. "Yes indeed, sir," says this poncy fellow. "We do have a booking for a Mrs Eva Green – we're awaiting confirmation." I was so gobsmacked that I almost dropped the phone. So you *were* telling the truth!'

'You shouldn't have doubted me,' she said coldly.

'Lily, please don't be pissed off,' he said. 'I'm sorry – maybe it was wrong to have rushed off and checked up on you. But, well, you know how it is?'

She nodded.

'Come on,' he pleaded. 'Are you trying to make me grovel? Here – have some more booze.' He refilled their glasses. 'To the future,' he said, holding his aloft. 'To your mother. To her very good health.'

'Not such good health,' Lily reminded him.

'Well, then – to her improving health.'

'Even that's a bit over-optimistic.'

'Ok – to her *declining* health —' He stopped, clearly not wanting to offend her. 'Not that I wish the old bat any harm, but you're telling me it's kind of inevitable, aren't you? What's the timetable?'

'How do I know? They haven't said *exactly* —'

'I mean the transfer to the Dorchester, the – um – patient care?'

'Oh,' she said. 'I'll go out there tomorrow and arrange stuff with the hospital. There's the money to sort out as well. She wants it all to happen immediately, but I'd say it'll take at least a week.'

'And in the meantime?' he asked, indicating her luggage.

She remembered she'd said nothing to him about having been evicted. 'Oh, yes – I've checked out of the Winter Palace,' she told him. 'With everything that's been going on, I couldn't bear it there a moment longer.'

'I don't blame you. The woman's a cow. So, I suppose you're wanting to hunker down here with Kennedy while you get your show on the road?'

'Well, yes. Only for a few days.'

Very gently he took the glass from her hand and set it down on the table.

He gathered her in his arms and pressed her head against his. 'I – um – like you very much,' he whispered into her ear.

'You do?' This was the closest he'd ever come to any kind of declaration, beyond wonder at her eyes and ineffable elegance. She took his ardent kiss as confirmation and, as ardently, kissed him back. And it was no time at all before they were journeying along the well-trodden path from his sitting room to the Orthopaedic mattress and beyond.

But despite the exhilaration of their reunion and the depth of the exhausted slumber into which she dropped, she arose at dawn in a sweat of anxiety. Gingerly she crept out of bed. He didn't stir. Nor had he woken an hour later when, bathed and perfectly groomed for another encounter with her mother, she deposited a note at his bedside, saying, 'See you later – I'll meet you in the pub at seven.'

With almost the last of her cash she topped up her Oyster card to cover public transport to the hospital. A solitary five-pence piece and two useless pennies were all that remained. When she faced Eva this time she'd be broke as well as stripped of her camouflage of lies.

But the game wasn't over yet, she resolved. If her mother thought she was dealing with the compliant daughter of old, she could think again. Lily would see to it that her terminal care did not come cheap.

'Thank goodness you're here,' exhaled Nurse Martin when she appeared in the ward at noon. 'Your mother's been agitating for *hours* about whether you were coming and when.' Gone were the empathetic niceties of their previous encounter; she seemed thoroughly fed up. 'It might have been considerate of you to let us know what time you'd be getting here.'

Lily apologised. She hadn't thought. She'd been so busy that she hadn't known until the very last minute whether she could make it that day at all.

'I have to tell you, Miss Green,' the nurse interrupted, 'your mother has been *extremely* difficult since you were here last. Impossible's the word. We ordered a brain scan to give her the benefit of the doubt but found no sign of metastases. I wouldn't say the same for her other organs, but so far her brain is miraculously clear.'

'I appreciate your frankness,' Lily said, empathising for the first time with the urgency of Eva's desire to leave this place. 'May I go in and see her now?'

'If you can find her.'

'Oh – has she been moved?'

'No, she insists on moving herself. *And* dressing herself every morning. She shuffles round with a Zimmer frame, practising for when she's in London. So she says. She's a determined woman, your mother – I'll grant her that.'

Lily tried to replicate the compassionate smile with which she had greeted Eva when she'd first turned up as triumphant executive visiting her poor expiring mama. But her bed was empty. Then, from the corridor, came a series of advancing bumps and squeaks and, a moment later, her mother and her Zimmer frame appeared.

'I kept telling them you'd be coming here today,' Eva said in a high aggrieved voice. 'They don't take the slightest notice of me, none at all.'

'Nurse Martin implied you were being a little – well, *challenging*,' Lily pointed out.

Eva gave a little snort and tossed her head, and Lily took in her dramatically altered appearance. A few days before she had been helplessly bedridden. Now her pallor was covered by a frosting of make-up and her emaciated limbs concealed by a leisure suit in turquoise velour.

'So?' Eva faced her challengingly. 'Looking better, aren't I? It's only skin deep, of course. They tell me I'm riddled inside, not a hope in hell. But I'm sick to death of talking about my health. We have other matters to discuss.' With considerable effort but remarkable efficiency, she was making her way towards the bed. 'See?' she said when she finally reached it. 'I'll be ready for the marathon in no time at all.'

'Which – um – marathon?' Lily asked, for the situation had become unnervingly surreal.

'Don't be ridiculous,' Eva snapped. 'You always were too literal-minded.' Frowning, she levered herself onto the bed.

Watching her, Lily was torn between admiration of her feistiness and fury at being subjected to her caustic tongue. Anger presided. 'I will *not* be spoken to like that any longer,' she said, softly and ominously. 'You're the patient. I can walk away – and I'll do it if you don't treat me with respect.'

Eva eyed her narrowly. 'I believe you. You've done it before. Well, then, Lily – let's talk business.'

'Right.' Lily drew up her chair, confident of her advantage in whatever negotiations were about to ensue. Her mother was helpless. She had no option but to agree to every proposal, not matter how extravagant. 'I've reserved a suite at the Dorchester, but they're asking for a deposit. A large one. Something in the region of – well, several thousand pounds. I also need an advance against my own expenses. Apart from anything else, I'm going to have to buy you some appropriate clothing – you couldn't possibly go within a mile of the Dorchester wearing something like this.' She addressed to Eva's leisure suit an expression of disdain.

Her mother shrugged and smiled. 'You're right. I'm no longer a Hatch End widow. I've graduated. But tell me, Lily – drawing on your expertise with makeovers and how to attract men – what's the latest look for the Cosmopolitan with Cancer? Hmm?'

Lily eyed her suspiciously. Her mother wasn't exactly saying she knew about the cuttings file, but there was an edge there, an undeniable edge. 'I'm serious,' she said.

'Me too,' Eva agreed. 'In my condition, how could I not be? Surprisingly, though, I'm still perfectly capable of attending to my own appearance and have excellent taste. How much do you need for yourself, then? Five, six thousand? For the sundry expenses, I mean'

'That sounds about right.' She did her best to sound offhand. Five, six thousand for *sundries*? She could barely think on that scale.

Her mother, meanwhile, had that conspiratorial look on her face and was summoning her closer. Lily acquiesced and was aware once again of the cloying scent of dead lavender. She shuddered. 'Have a look inside my handbag,' Eva was whispering. 'It's in my locker. See if you can find my keys.'

Lily did so, handing the bunch to her mother, who picked out one.

'This is the one to my safe,' she said. 'It's built into the back of my wardrobe – you'll see it if you look carefully behind my winter coats. It's directly opposite the mock ermine.'

'What's in the safe?' Lily wanted to know.

'Property deeds, share certificates, premium bonds, cheque books, credit cards – you name it. And cash, of course. Seven thousand, eight hundred and sixty pounds at the last count. Plus a bit of change. Help yourself.'

'You're not serious.'

'Absolutely serious.'

'Where does it all come from?'

'Here and there.' She paused, considering. 'Thinking about it,' she said, 'there are a couple of things *I* need to sort out. What I'd like you to do is to put the entire contents of the safe into one of my overnight bags – you'll find plenty of those in the storage lockers above the wardrobe – and bring it to me. Here's some cash for a taxi. See you back very soon.'

Unable to articulate a response, she looked at the two twenty-pound notes stuffed into her hands and, nodding dazedly, left Eva's bedside and went out to find a taxi. There was something not right about all this. *Not right*? It stank. How on earth had dowdy Eva Green accumulated all this supposed wealth? Being a shrieking, cruising, card-playing harpy was tasteless enough, but having half an oil well behind your mock-ermine mantle was obscene. Lily was tempted to call the whole thing off but knew she wouldn't. It was too late and she was too deeply entrenched. And – *now* she understood what Eva had meant when she'd said it – she was curious.

When they reached the house she asked the driver to wait, she wouldn't be long, and – with some trepidation, for it had been months since she'd left here – she went inside. It was dark and silent and creepily unchanged. As quickly as she could she went upstairs and in her mother's wardrobe, exactly as directed, found what she was looking for.

She also found, among the scattering of mail on the doormat, a postcard depicting a sleek white cruise-ship on a cobalt sea. 'Darling Eva, We wish you were here,' was scrawled on the back. Angrily she tore it up.

Eva was in bed when she returned with the brimming overnight bag.

'Good girl,' she said to Lily, as though she were a dog who'd retrieved a ball. 'Clever girl.' Her skinny hands immediately began rummaging, extracting papers which she swiftly scanned and either cast aside or returned to the bag. From the depths she pulled out a small leather-trimmed box, which she quickly put back. 'Not that,' she muttered, and kept poking around. 'Ah!' she said, extricating a larger box. 'The cash. Now how much did you say you needed?'

Lily had been watching in astonishment. There was a brisk efficiency about her mother that she half recognised from her household ministrations but seemed incongruous when applied to this evidence of high finance. Questions buzzed in her head but she couldn't articulate them. Eva's fingers, meanwhile, were inside the box and, by touch alone, she was verifying its contents.

'On second thoughts,' she was saying in her throaty whisper, 'you'd better take all of this. You won't believe how much gets stolen in this hospital.'

'I can't,' Lily protested. 'How can I walk around London with all that? What do you want me to do with it? Deposit it in a bank?'

'Spend it,' Eva said with relish. 'Here's a security pouch – stick that round your waist. Might spoil the svelte effect you've worked so hard to achieve, but if anyone tried to separate you from the cash they'd have to kill you first.'

'I don't know about all this.' She was frightened. She didn't want the money or anything else that made her worth killing. The quiet life she'd once spurned now seemed rather cosily attractive.

'Lily,' her mother said reproachfully, 'you're not going to disappoint me again, are you? Don't tell me you're *afraid*?'

'I'm not,' she said quickly and defiantly. And as she uttered the denial it became true. A sense of inevitability had overtaken her, vaporising any illusion she'd ever had about being in control of her life.

'Good.' Eva handed her the cash-filled pouch. 'You'd better go to the Ladies and discreetly sort yourself out. There's one at the end of the corridor. Come back as soon as you have that thing in place we can talk about what to do next.'

'What about the hotel?' Lily asked.

'What *about* the hotel?' echoed her mother imperiously.

'I can't go in there with wads of notes.'

'You can. Easily. But I'll spare you the embarrassment. I'll ring them – I'm sure I have a couple of enticing credit cards among this lot. I don't think you *quite* understand the power of money, dear, but in the time I have left to me I'll do my best to teach you.'

She had fallen asleep when Lily reappeared at her bedside. In repose, she'd reacquired her look of paper-thin fragility. The make-up that flaked away at the sides of her face was grotesque; her breathing was shallow and the hands that twitched on the counterpane were impossibly frail. Lily regarded her fearfully. The idea of transporting her to a luxury hotel seemed crazy and cruel. How could she have allowed this unsubstantial being to dictate to her? It was the power of money, Eva had said. Which certainly was a factor, but there was also something else...

'That took you a long time,' her mother was saying as she opened an eye. 'I thought you'd got lost or decapitated. Or decamped with the liquid assets, which I might have done in your position, I must confess.'

'Doctor Snow stopped me in the passage. He wanted to have a word.'

'Oh? And did he fill you in? Did he warn you about me? Did he tell me how mad you were to take me on?'

'Something like that,' Lily admitted. 'Although he implied that the madness was more on your side than mine.'

'Do *you* think I'm mad?' she asked seriously, now fully alert. When her eyes were open they seemed to animate her being. Even her hands appeared more solid, her chicken neck less scrawny. Suddenly the venture seemed, if not the apex of sanity, at least possible.

'Perhaps not in the clinical sense of the word,' Lily answered. 'Only perhaps.'

Eva seemed about to pursue this avenue, then stopped. Her mouth tightened. 'So where do we go from here?' she asked. 'Or perhaps the question should be *when*? Bring me the telephone.'

The power of money. In less than a minute, Eva had secured the hotel suite for immediate occupation. Luxury accommodation overlooking the rooftops of Mayfair at a rate, including sales tax, of more than three thousand pounds a night. Lily was appalled.

'Don't worry,' Eva whispered, seeing the horror on her face. 'It's well within my means. I thought we may as well stretch to that second adjoining bedroom – it will be much more fun with the boyfriend there as well. He's still around, isn't he?'

Lily nodded. Tom in the Dorchester with them? He'd be over the moon.

'Well, then,' said Eva, 'get out there, the two of you, and enjoy a night together in the suite. You may as well, once it's being paid for. Go and have fun.'

'And tomorrow?' asked Lily. This was happening a little too quickly. She couldn't quite take it in.

'Tomorrow you'll come and get me and off we'll go.'

'Are you sure you can leave, just like that?'

'They'll rejoice at my departure.'

'What about drugs, pain relief?'

'Stop *worrying*, Lily. They'll give me everything I need. We can hire a private nurse, a team of nurses if necessary. I can buy anything, anything.'

Almost anything, thought Lily. It was a qualification that must have struck Eve too, even as she gloated. For she shut her eyes again and in a voice that was small and tired said she'd be ready for collection by taxi early the following afternoon. Lily hadn't yet left the room before she lapsed back into sleep.

Part Six

16

By seven-fifteen Tom was uneasy and half an hour later he'd become anxious. By eight he was furious and, with a couple of pints inside him, well on the way to being sozzled. It was *twenty-five-past-fucking-eight* when she finally appeared.

'I'm sorry,' she gasped, sinking into a vacant chair. 'It's been quite a day.'

'Do you know what time it is?' He jabbed a finger at his watch.

'I know. As I said —'

He looked at her and, for Lily, she was dishevelled. Endearingly so. He'd kept telling himself that their relationship was purely commercial, she was his meal ticket and he was her toy-boy. No strings either way. But that sudden disappearance of hers had distressed him in a way he hadn't expected and seeing her again the night before had thrilled him more than he could say. Even now, when he was meant to be furious with her, he could feel his anger melting away. 'Want a drink?' he asked abruptly.

In response, she caught his hand and pressed it to her lips, an unfamiliar (perhaps over-familiar) gesture. Awkwardly, he edged it away.

'Tom, darling,' she said – again an unusual endearment. He wondered why she was looking so pleased with herself, a bloody Cheshire cat about to scoff a pot of double cream.

'What?' he asked as gruffly as he could.

But she saw through him immediately. 'Relax,' she said, smiling. 'I know I'm late. But wait till you hear this! There's a suite awaiting us in the Dorchester – just me and you. Would you believe it? Come – let's get moving.' She tried to pull him to his feet. 'We may as well head off there straight away.'

'Wait,' he said, resisting. There was something a tad over-bossy about her. No way, not even for the frigging Dorchester, was he going to allow her to order him around. 'Hang on a sec. A suite for *us*?' He couldn't take it in. 'I thought you said your *mother* —'

'My mother arrives tomorrow. Tonight is our night.'

He allowed her to lead him outside. Dazed. Surely it wasn't real, what was happening? Ever since he'd got mixed up with Lily Green, his life had begun to take on a dream-like quality. From the start he hadn't been able to believe that this strange child-woman, the embodiment of all Jimmy had ever taught him about gullible, rich, mature females, had popped into his life. In the beginning he'd swallowed everything: all the stuff about her wealthy family and that mysteriously go-getting career of hers, even the elusive and illusory Chelsea flat. Even when he'd decided her stories were just fucking stories, he had carried on listening. Hooked, he'd become. Line, sinker, plus the odd pair of Diesel jeans and Hugo Boss Chronograph Watch. And now this new twist…

'Lily,' he said, for it was happening a bit fast for him. 'I need a little more info here. A bit of time to prepare.'

She'd stepped into the street and was hailing a taxi. Not that they hadn't caught cabs before; they did it all the time. But there was new confidence in her gesture, self-assurance that seemed to come from within. 'We'll pop into your flat to collect our stuff and for you to shower and change. I'll need to sort myself out as well.'

'Sure thing,' he said obediently. Why resist? Why argue? Here she was, taking him on a Big Night Out that even in his wildest dreams he couldn't have envisaged. And even if they ended up in a fleapit somewhere, it would be something to boast about to the lads.

But the edifice outside which the taxi drew up bore as much relation to a fleapit as a donkey cart to a Rolls Royce Phantom Coupe. Following the uniformed doorman through the Dorchester's opulent lobby, he did his best to look as though he was born to it. And in a sense – on his mother's side anyway – he *had* been. Beatrice Courtney-Upminster had been a classy dame until she'd got herself mixed up with a lowlife like Hector. Tom drew himself taller, telling himself that being pampered and deferred to was his genetic due.

But it was hard to look cool when his excitement kept threatening to spill into manic, gleeful laughter. When they were ushered into their suite and he saw the champagne in a bucket and the pile of posh fruit and the size, the sheer *size* of it – well, all he could think was that not very long before he'd have been thrilled by a night in the Milton Keynes Travel Lodge and the complimentary custard creams on the hospitality tray. He'd come a long way.

'Lily Green,' he said. 'I don't know how you've managed this. You're a marvel.' He looked around. She seemed to have disappeared. 'Lily!' he called.

'I'm coming. One moment. Please.' She couldn't keep the annoyance out of her voice. Which was highly inappropriate, given the astounding thing that was happening to her, the splendiferous suite that was theirs. (Eat your hearts out, Angela Manning and Megan McCloud.) If only she could wrench open this ridiculously discreet safe deposit box and transfer into it the wads of money from that uncomfortable pouch. And get her waistline back. It was a burden dragging round so much cash.

'What's up?' He'd appeared in the master bedroom, where she was on her knees fiddling with the panelling behind the four-poster bed.

'Nothing,' she said hastily, springing to her feet. 'Just making sure that the thermostat's working – we have an invalid coming to join us, in case you've forgotten.'

'Not tonight though, Tiger Lil.' He spread out his arms and advanced to embrace her but she smartly ducked beneath them. Not friendly, she knew. But she couldn't help herself. The exhilaration with which she'd swept him from the pub and into the taxi and into the hotel seemed to have abated and in its place there was a dead weight of apprehension. As much as she tried not to, she felt like an imposter – a fake with stolen money and a phoney boyfriend, who was bound to get found out soon.

The phoney boyfriend wasn't deterred, though. He was jumping up and down like a kid at a fairground. Tiger Lil – since when had he ever called her that? It made her feel like a busty saloon-bar waitress; she wasn't sure if she liked it.

But she didn't have time or the heart to protest. He was urging her back into the sitting room and plying her with champagne. 'Come on,' he implored. 'Don't be a spoilsport.'

He was right. She was a complete party pooper. She'd put aside her ridiculous anxieties and luxuriate in their night. 'Shall we go down for some supper?' she suggested.

'*Yesss*!' He grinned delightedly. 'Brilliant idea!'

In the maroon-and-cream magnificence of the softly-lit dining-room, with their small talk augmenting the genteel hubbub around them, Lily tried her best to immerse herself in the splendour of the experience. She almost succeeded, animatedly asking after Tom's Denham Castle lamb with fennel risotto and enthusing over her own Dover sole.

'Isn't this lovely?' she asked, perhaps one time too many, for he – in response to her excessive fervour – had grown increasingly subdued.

'Lil,' he said at last, chasing the last of his lamb with the dregs of fine wine that had been especially selected by the head Sommelier. 'You're not really enjoying yourself, are you?'

'I am, I am,' she insisted, but had to blink away tears at the softening of his tone. 'It's just – I don't know what it is. Probably exhaustion, that's all. Everything seemed to have fallen apart this week. My job. The – er – flat in Chelsea. And now this thing with my mother —'

'But look.' He indicated the sumptuousness around them. 'There's the *here*. There's the *now*. And there's *this*! Can't you try and forget about all your troubles? Come – let's seize the moment and make whoopee, Tiger Lil.'

What the fuck was *wrong* with the woman? He could understand she was a little drained; there were good reasons for it and, after all, she was no spring chicken. But one thing he'd learnt to count on with Lily was her gusto for sex. Even when they'd been out of sorts with one another, even when they'd had far too much to drink, there'd been no stopping her. She was up for it, rain or shine.

And now, when they could be dangling from the chandeliers and doing unmentionable things with designer bath-bubbles, here they were in this monster sized bed lying side by side like two flipping corpses. She'd made a little effort over dinner then subsided into her own world. It wasn't sexual frustration that was bothering him as much as the way she was blocking him from engaging with her predicament. There'd been a moment, which he'd blown; a moment when she'd mentioned her mother —

'Lily.' He reached across and touched her. At least she didn't flinch.

'Hmm?'

'Lil, I understand about your mother.'

There was silence. 'She *is* dying, Tom,' she said, as though he were disputing it, or perhaps she still needed to convince herself of it.

'I believe you.' He had a sudden vivid image of a large white bed with his own mother Beatrice upon it, as shrunken and still as a skeleton, and felt again the terror that had overtaken him. Lily knew nothing about this, nothing about him. 'My mother died when I was a kid,' he said softly. It was an offering, an opening. 'She'd been ill for some time and then died in hospital. No-one in the family seemed to mind much, except me.'

For a long while she lay very still.

'I went to boarding school after that,' he went on. 'Then my – er – my old man died as well.'

'Hector,' she said.

'Hector,' he affirmed.

But she didn't ask him anything else; nor did he volunteer further information. Sharing details about the life that had predated their meeting in West Hampstead Station wasn't in the nature of their relationship.

'I'm afraid, Tom,' she said at last, a rare show of vulnerability that was admissible. Just. '*She* frightens me. My mother. The whole situation frightens me – I feel like I've agreed to some Faustian pact. You can leave, though, if you like. You don't have to go through with this. I thought the glamour would make it exciting, but I don't think there's any way of dressing up – you know —'

'I'll stay,' he found himself saying without a moment's hesitation.

'You will?' She turned to look at him and, for the first time since they'd arrived there, gave him a proper smile.

'Yup. In for a penny,' he said lightly. It was thrilling to be here and understandable that he should be grabbing the experience with both hands, but it wasn't the entire reason he was sticking around. She needed him and – bugger it – it made a pleasant change to be needed.

'I'm glad,' she murmured and he felt quite protective of her as he watched her relax into sleep.

The next morning she opened her eyes to opulent chintz and elegant mouldings, the rose-tinged scent of affluence and the expensively-muffled sounds of London. She remembered where she was and what the day would bring and wanted to retreat beneath the soft cotton sheets. 'Tom,' she called, for the space alongside her was cold and empty.

'I'm here. In our – ahem – drawing room. And if you know what's good for you, you'll get here fast. Bloody hell.'

Sighing, she climbed out of bed. Then she remembered how kind he'd been the previous night and how outspoken, for him, about the loss of his parents. She would stop analysing and dreading; try to enjoy being with him, here and now. Entering the room, she saw him poised before a breakfast trolley that was bedecked with silver domes like some ornate Byzantine monastery, and her anxiety dissolved in the face of his unrestrained delight. 'Stupendous,' she said with as much eagerness as she could muster. 'This should set us up for the day ahead.'

But not even the lavish helpings of scrambled eggs with smoked salmon washed down with a glass-and-a-half of champagne could bolster her against the panic that almost glued her to the seat when her taxi drew up outside the hospital a couple of hours later.

'Here we are,' the driver announced needlessly.

'I know,' she managed. 'Please wait. I'll be coming back with the – um – patient. And then we'll be returning to the hotel.'

'That'll cost,' he warned.

'I'm aware of it,' she said coldly. Could he sniff her financial insecurity the way a dog detected fear?

And could the previously-amiable-but-now-definitely-hostile Nurse Martin sense the uncertainty with which she was extracting her mother from a medical establishment to the daft indulgence of a Dorchester suite? 'Miss Green,' she said snootily, 'I very much hope you know what you're undertaking here. It's a folly, that's what it is. Almost tantamount to murder, I'd say.'

Lily hesitated at the entrance to the ward. She could abort this mission, even now.

Then she heard a rhythmic thumping which came closer and closer, until Eva appeared with her Zimmer frame. She was wearing an expensive-looking navy-blue linen trouser suit. Her hair had been elegantly styled and her make-up applied with discreet and expert precision.

'Take no notice of Nurse Martin, Lily,' she said. 'Come. I am ready to leave. I have all my medicine and a letter from Doctor Snow. Since he insisted, I have also engaged an agency nurse to help look after me in London. You won't mind, Lily, will you? She's German, very efficient according to her references, but if she gets on our nerves we can tell her to go.'

Lily nodded. She herself wouldn't have had the gumption to flaunt medical authority. Nor would she have the balls to sack the German, any German, for the offence of getting on her nerves. But then, she wasn't Eva and she wasn't dying.

Maybe the condition lent reckless audacity to a victim with little to lose.

'I like your suit,' she told her mother.

'Me too. I sent one of the young nurses off to buy it. Fortunately I'm back to a perfect size eight – one has to look at the bright side of cancer. It's not cheap, as you can tell, but there comes a time … Mind you, the way Nurse Martin carries on about my prospects, I shouldn't even risk investing in a green banana in case I die before it ripens.'

'What are you talking about?' the nurse protested. 'I said that green bananas were bad for your digestion, that's all.'

'See?' Eva said smugly. 'Stupid. That's why I'd rather be with you, Lily. Come. Let's be off.'

In the taxi Lily noticed that her mother had been fitted with a small contraption that delivered a painkiller straight into her bloodstream. She observed how Eva winced, struggling to turn the tiny tap as the vehicle bumped and roared.

'Bloody morphine,' she muttered. 'They say it works like magic but between us I've never been convinced. A stiff whisky will do it – you can order me a double as soon as we get into that hotel. Better still, a bottle. Even better, a case.'

Lily watched her in concern. She wouldn't make it. Nurse Martin was right. Even before they got to the hotel, the only magic effected by the morphine would be to transform the taxi into a hearse.

'Talk to me, Lily,' Eva was saying. 'Keep me amused so that I don't think about the pain.'

Her mind went blank. 'I don't know what to say,' she confessed.

'Nonsense,' Eva exploded. 'You have plenty to say. Your head's absolutely swarming with stories. Why don't you tell me the one about the woman who lied to her mother about getting married and how she eventually found herself a man?'

'That one?' Lily asked.

'That one,' Eva confirmed.

And once Lily had started, her mother seemed so captivated that she didn't wince again until they'd arrived at the hotel.

17

Between surges of pain Eva heard about Lily's great quest and, despite the agonising spasms, she marvelled that this most phlegmatic of daughters was now able to make her laugh. Lily had not only turned out to be satisfyingly mendacious but also developed a mordant wit. No business operation could possibly be as crooked as the one she'd landed in, nor could any landlady be so abhorrent. As for this Tom – how hilarious that she'd found him on the Tube. Couldn't she have upped it a notch and got herself someone on the overland rail network at least?

'What sort of person is he, this boyfriend of yours?' she asked. 'Is he someone to trust?'

'Oh, yes,' Lily said immediately, then seemed to waver. 'In certain ways.'

'Hmm.' She thought about this. 'That's fine as long as one is aware of those ways. The important thing is to know who you're dealing with. That's another advantage of this cancer – at least I know my enemy.' What a nauseating optimist she'd become, she thought, as the 'enemy' delivered another salvo to remind her of its might.

'Tom's not an enemy,' Lily protested. 'I didn't mean that at all.'

'We'll see,' she said. The taxi drew up outside the Dorchester. 'I'm an excellent judge of character.' She looked at her daughter and it struck her how she'd erred in her case. Maybe not erred so much as underestimated. 'Of course, one makes mistakes now and again. A person can't be perfect. But on the whole —'

Lily handed over to the taxi driver a sum that would probably fund his next family holiday. For the in-laws as well. She wouldn't think about it; money had assumed Monopoly dimensions since she'd engaged in this harebrained scheme.

Eva, meanwhile, allowed a doorman to assist her to her feet, then imperiously waved him away. Lily could hardly believe this regal being was the same person who'd gossiped with her cronies at the card table and attached china ducks to her wall. She followed her mother into the lobby and watched her striking a courtly pose with her Zimmer frame as she inhaled the rarefied air. 'Ah – it's good to be back here,' she sighed.

'You've stayed at the Dorchester before?' Lily asked.

'I've stayed *everywhere*,' Eva answered. 'Paris, Hong Kong, Dubai, Tokyo, Beirut. You name it, I've been there.'

'But *when*?' Surely her mother's jaunts with Elsie et al hadn't taken in the world's most exclusive hotels?

'Never you mind.' Eva waved her hand dismissively. 'Now, what were we saying in the cab about liquid refreshment? God, I could do with a Scotch. Or maybe, in honour of the occasion, something a teeny bit more exciting? Why don't we pop into the Bar? I remember it from way back – those martini cocktails were something —'

'Are you sure about this?' Lily began, imagining Nurse Martin's face if she discovered that, far from succumbing en route to London, her patient was settling down to martinis in a hotel bar. '*Ought* you to be drinking with the drugs you're on?'

'Definitely. As much as possible,' Eva said firmly. 'If you were as far gone as I am, would you deny yourself anything?'

The question was rhetorical. Her mother was shuffling on regardless. She managed to reach the Bar and proceeded to the far end, where she delivered herself, tight-lipped and pale with effort, onto a padded seat.

Then her head flopped back and she shut her eyes.

Was she dead? How annoying if the woman had bloody snuffed it before he'd even had a chance to meet her. Tom, who'd been occupying a discreet booth in the corner of the Bar for the past three hours or so, had seen the old biddy who was clearly Lily's mother appearing through the door. She moved like the clappers on that frame of hers, bump-shuffle, bump-shuffle; he'd almost wanted to stand up and cheer. But the truth was he'd had a few too many and it might have seemed tasteless, knowing what he did about her precarious health. Just as well he hadn't, now she was out for the count.

But look. She'd come round. A fighter, you could see it. The Mohammed Ali of Hatch End. He hiccupped and tried to get to his feet but was weighed down by the mixture of champagne, peach clafoutis, raspberry brûlée and beer in his stomach. If he wasn't careful he'd be the one out cold in a puddle of puke. Bloody mortifying.

Silence fell. And then, clear as a bell, he heard her voice. 'Lily, dear,' the old lady was proclaiming, 'will you please stop fussing over me and get me a dry martini. And something strong and exotic for yourself. Enjoy yourself, girl. This is your chance.'

Well put! *Enjoy yourself, girl*. Hadn't he been telling Lily that since the moment they'd strolled through the portals of this hotel? He'd support the old lady on that – he'd support her on anything, since she was the one who was footing the bill. 'And so say all of us,' he intoned drunkenly, and in the continuing lull it rang out loud and clear.

Lily quickly jumped to her feet. 'That's Tom,' she said, and scoured the room to locate him. He helped her by dragging himself to his feet and, like the man waving flags on an airport runway, directed her attention to him. 'Tom,' she cried. 'I didn't notice you. What are you doing here?'

He hastened towards them as well as he could. 'What am I doing? Quantum physics,' he managed, wondering why, with his inebriation, he'd latched onto an activity with quite so many consonants. He bowed as low as he could before the old lady. 'Mrs Green, I presume,' he said, with chivalrous charm. Trying not to teeter over, he knelt down beside her and planted a great smacking kiss on her mottled, bony hand. She studied him with apparent amusement. 'Bugger me,' he couldn't help saying as he met her gaze, 'you've got Lily's eyes.'

'Since I came first, I'd say that *she* has *mine*. But no matter. Yes, I'm Eva Green and you, I gather, are Tom.'

'Tom Kennedy,' he said. 'Delighted to meet you.' There. Could anyone have expressed it with more refinement? And he *was* delighted, in a peculiar way. This woman while she lasted could turn out to be a hoot. 'I totally agree that Lily should relax and enjoy herself. I'd say we get her to swallow a couple of Seven Stars – then we'll see some action!'

'Seven Stars?' Eva cocked her head to one side and eyeballed him.

'Bloody outstanding. I had several earlier today, to make sure. Vodka, peach schnapps, Campari, cassis —'

'I'll have one,' interrupted Lily. She sounded slightly desperate. Her nerves seemed shot. 'And a martini for my mother. I clearly don't need to encourage *you* to order something for yourself.'

'And a pack of cigarettes for later,' called Eva. 'Camel, if they have them. Something good and strong. I used to get through at least fifty a day. Hence the lung cancer, which they say kicked off my entire state of corporal rot. But it's too late to bother about all that now.'

He handed Eva her drink with what Lily thought was obsequious and inebriated charm. What a creep. She noted with relief that her mother took a single sip and coughed convulsively. That didn't stop her, though. She took another large swallow and smacked her lips.

'Delicious,' she said, and gulped it down.

When she was done she burped loudly, spluttering with mirth, while Lily, embarrassed and concerned, worried that she'd start vomiting next, or wetting herself, or worse. Surely she couldn't carry on ignoring her state of ill-health in this high-handed way? Couldn't she exercise some restraint?

'Would you like something to eat, mother?' she offered, hoping that food would offset the alcohol and remembering that neither she nor Eva had taken nourishment for hours. 'These nuts look good. Or maybe an olive?'

'Oh, no.' Eva dismissed the plate with an exaggerated shudder. 'I couldn't. Much too fattening.'

Tom roared with intoxicated laughter. 'Too fattening. Listen to her. Look at her. Skin and bones, and she calls them fattening. Your mum's great, Lily. What a gal!'

'Let me tell you something, Tom.' Eva extended her hand and tapped him on the shoulder. 'One of the most important rules for anyone who wants to stay in shape is: *Say No To Nibbles*. Simple.'

'Say no to nibbles.' Tom chortled as he decanted into his mouth a generous handful of nuts. 'What do you think about that, Lily?'

'What does *Lily* think?' Eva's hilarity was as noisy as Tom's. 'Lily doesn't *think*, she *knows*. My daughter, I must tell you, is a walking Health and Beauty Encyclopaedia. She is a model for what can be accomplished when someone makes up her mind. I'm extremely proud of Lily.'

'Shut up,' she said furiously. 'Both of you – shut *up*.' She wanted her mother to be proud of her, she had longed to impress her, but not like this. She hadn't undertaken this insane venture to have Eva and Tom ganging up and sniggering about her in this awful taunting way.

'Where's you sense of humour?' said Tom. 'We're joking. Aren't we, Eva?'

So it was *Eva* now. Thus were allegiances formed. Lily wondered whether she should offer to stand down and give this new partnership some space to flourish. *Then* Doctor Tom would see how he managed if, as the nurse warned might happen, Eva had a sudden collapse. She was about to excuse herself, to allow them to get on with their little party without her dampening presence, when a concierge appeared and murmured something in her mother's ear.

'Oh, my goodness,' said Eva. 'The German. She's here. I'd forgotten all about her. What a nuisance. I knew I shouldn't have agreed, but that bloody doctor used all kinds of threats.'

'Shall I go and tackle her?' Tom offered. 'I have a feeling I could handle a German.'

'Course not, you foolish boy.' Eva extended her hand and he helped her to her feet. 'You stick with handling me. Adorable, isn't he, Lily? Come, let's go and meet Fraulein Nightingale.'

They proceeded to the lobby where, awaiting them, was an immense blonde in uniform who introduced herself as Sister Hildegarde Grün.

They'd have to pull out her toenails before she admitted this, but Eva was secretly relieved to see The German. She was dog tired, her body throbbed, and she welcomed being forced into bed. Only partly, for she knew that each stolen second of normality was a victory. Not over her ultimate fate, she couldn't win that, but over the quality of her remaining life. It was bad enough to be dying, but why did everyone insist that on the way she had to be officially 'sick'? It was like she'd stepped onto an assembly line as soon as she'd been diagnosed and, from a Well Person, instantly become a Very Unwell Person. Which meant she was obliged to talk like a VUP, think like a VUP, dress like a VUP, sigh and moan like a VUP.

She wouldn't do it.

Especially now that she'd regained a bit of the old curiosity and just a hint of the vixen she'd once been. *Tom* didn't seem to mind, sweet fellow, that she was on the way out. To him she was still a woman. A person. Neither Well nor Unwell. Oh, she could tell him a thing or two.

Tomorrow.

What a day it had been. Even Lily looked drained, and she had Well Person written all over her. *Very* Well Person, judging by the frisson Eva detected between her and the lover boy, and she'd always had a nose for such things. No reason for Lily to be jealous of her ancient mama. Eva would tell her so; she'd reassure her.

Tomorrow.

'We go to bed, Mrs Green,' ordered The German. And Eva, while trying by her stance to suggest stoic resistance, allowed herself to be led to the suite. She yielded to the practised ministrations of the nurse, who undressed her and washed her and settled her for the night.

'Tell me, Mrs Green,' said the nurse, as she turned out the light, 'why are you lying with arms stretched out in zis fashion?'

'To feel the width of the bed and remind myself I'm not in hospital,' Eva answered, her words slurred by the alcohol/morphine combination washing through her veins. She wasn't sick. She was resting. Everyone rested at night. 'Don't forget to unpack my suitcases,' she managed. 'See that everything is properly put away and organise a hairdresser for tomorrow.'

The nurse announced to Lily that she had a complaint. 'I want to make very clear,' she said, when Eva had fallen asleep. 'I am not employed here to be lady's maid.'

'Definitely not,' answered Lily, who wasn't about to argue with Sister Grün. Not only was The German far too large to oppose, but her presence was also – Lily had quickly realised – fairly necessary.

'So,' she said, as if that clinched that. She handed Lily a leaflet containing her Terms and Conditions and announced she would be back at the hotel at seven-thirty sharp. When a nurse was required for the nights (it was *when*, not *if*), Sister Grün would organise it. Miss Green should realise, however, that night nurses did not come cheap. *Nor* day nurses, as it happened. But Mrs Green was clearly very well off?

'My mother has the necessary means,' said Lily loftily. Being businesslike was one thing; prying into Eva's finances was effrontery.

'I merely ask because my agency insists on a deposit for minimum two weeks. If Mrs Green dies before – unlikely, but possible – you are entitled to refund. After zat, another two weeks in advance.'

'I see,' said Lily. 'And when would you like the first payment?'

Sister Grün waved her away. 'Tomorrow is fine. By the by, your mother would like suitcases unpacked. Zis is not my duty.'

'Of course not.'

'And here is agency's emergency number should you encounter a crisis.'

She was aware that her nervous farewell to the nurse was more fulsome than necessary. 'Thank you so, so much. See you tomorrow, Sister Grün,' she said, and tiptoed into Eva's room.

Her mother was lying flat on her back, arms splayed cruciferously. Her cheeks were sunken and her mouth hung open and to Lily she looked unlikely to last the night. Poor Eva. She thought she'd averted her extinction by discharging herself from hospital but her life kept oozing out, relentlessly. In fortnightly instalments, it appeared. Lily decided that if she herself were dying as expensively as this, her innate thrift might speed her up. Not Eva. She'd be obstinate enough to spin it out till the money was exhausted and everyone was screaming for her to go.

'Has Grunhilde left yet?' asked Tom from the sitting room, where he was idly flicking through programmes on the multi-channel forty-two-inch plasma screen.

'Hildegarde,' Lily corrected. 'I'd get her name right if I were you. She doesn't take kindly to laxity. She handed me a copy of her Terms and Conditions and I must say I wouldn't mind earning a quarter of what she charges.'

'Eva is a first class lady and deserves the best,' he declared, his eyes glazing over The Top Thousand Moments in Swedish Pornography. 'Talking of which, I've just had a deck at the Room Service Menu and took the liberty of ordering us a little sustenance. Drinking is hungry work. I thought a Caesar salad would do for you and, for me, decided to go downmarket with burger and chips. At twenty-six quid, I had to try it. What do you say?'

'Great,' she said, recalling her earlier resolve to quit counting. 'I hope you ordered mineral water – I'm very thirsty.'

'*Much* better than that,' he said proudly. 'We're about to knock back a bottle of Moet et Chandon, Cuvee Dom Perignon 1990. A bargain at just under three-hundred smackers.'

'Oh, Tom,' she said. 'How could you?'

'Why not? Eva said I could. "Tom," she told me, "help yourself to anything at all that you fancy – and especially anything that *Lily* fancies. You're my guests and my home is yours."'

'Nonsense. She never said anything of the sort.'

'She would have. Definitely. She simply got too tired. I promise you, Lily, she wants us to have a good time. What's all that money for, otherwise? *She* can't enjoy it. How did she get hold of it, anyway? Was your old man some kind of magnate or something?'

Fortunately she was saved from trying to answer by the arrival of the food order. Tom grinned until it looked like his face would split, as another trolley bearing an escarpment of silver domes was wheeled inside. And the champagne, of course, which he immediately opened.

'Golly, gosh,' he marvelled, tracing the course of the overflowing bubbles. 'What d'you think each of *these* little beauties is worth?'

'Tom, it's not *all* about money,' she objected.

'Course not,' he said. 'I'm not *talking* about money here. My speculation is philosophical, an existential issue, if you like. When a bubble bursts, that's disintegration. Decomposition. Death.' He chuckled.

'Maybe let's talk money,' she said quickly.

'In that case,' he said, beaming at her and raising his glass, 'I'd say this was a fucking rip-off. But cheers anyway. To Eva. To the Dorchester.'

Their mood grew increasingly mellow as the evening drew on. The television blinked soundlessly lest Eva awake, and they lay curled together on a single armchair sharing cognac from the mini-bar. They reminisced about the history they were making and, even before it happened, were waxing nostalgic about what was to be the past.

'Imagine,' said Tom. 'One day we'll remember waking up every single morning to a full English breakfast served on a trolley with linen napkins, freshly-squeezed orange juice and a personalised omelette.'

'And a twice-daily laundry service.'

'And The Promenade for lunch.'

'And overnight shoe-shines.'

'And endless champagne.'

'Heaven,' she sighed.

'Heaven,' he agreed.

18

It took a few days more before Lily was able to properly repress her puritanical qualms and immerse herself in this life of idle contentment and hyper-indulgent luxury. West Hampstead, Shepherd's Bush, Hatch End – even Holborn, which was only a couple of miles away – began to seem part of another universe. Nothing existed beyond their hotel rooms. The Dorchester's Mayfair Suite, floating free over the soft green lawns of Hyde Park and the rooftops of posh Mayfair, had become her world. Their world. A tiny select planet inhabited solely by her and Tom and Eva.

And Sister Hildegarde Grün, of course, who marched in at seven-thirty sharp each morning to attend to her charge. When the breakfast trolley arrived an hour later, Lily would enter the sitting room to find her mother, having been washed and dressed and medicated with Teutonic efficiency, propped on an armchair near the fireplace.

But after a fortnight, the thrill of the silver domes and lavish offerings had lost its lustre, even for Tom. He and Lily helped themselves indifferently to this or that while Eva, who'd taken tiny amounts to begin with, had reduced her intake to almost nothing at all.

Her spirit, though, seemed undaunted. Lily, who'd grown sluggish through inactivity, marvelled at her mother's capacity to command and provoke, which seemed to grow inversely with her shrinking frame. Each morning after breakfast she ordered Lily to help her to the desk where she unlocked the largest drawer, withdrew her papers and settled down to work. For at least two hours she barked across the world to brokers and bankers and fiscal advisers to ensure she was getting the best rates. This mercantile activity seemed to stimulate what was left of her miniscule appetite and, when lunch was wheeled in at around one-thirty, she daintily ingested a mouthful of grilled sea bass or halibut.

Lily, meanwhile, worried that she was putting on weight. Tom, she saw, had certainly lost the muscular definition that she'd once found so thrilling. On the other hand, he'd never been cleaner nor more scrupulously shorn. Each morning, with decreasing conviction, they spoke about plans and projects and future excursions. The Royal Academy. The National Portrait Gallery. The designer shops of Bond Street. The Tate. But when they were almost on the brink of departing on any of these expeditions, the day seemed mysteriously to have passed. The following day, they resolved, they'd take a walk down Park Lane or to Piccadilly Circus or – well, anywhere outside the walls of the hotel.

But the sun rose and set again and there they were, arrested by apathy in their sumptuous cocoon. Lily happened to see in Eva's meticulously-maintained ledgers that two weeks had set them back more than fifty thousand pounds, but so inured had she become to boundless extravagance that the amount didn't even make her blink.

'How much money *does* the old girl have?' Tom kept asking – with decreasing frequency, for even he had begun to lose his zeal for profligate spending. He'd worked his way four times through the Room Service Menu, sampled each possible permutation and, ridiculous as it seemed, sometimes found himself wishing that Eva would hurry up and die and thus set them all free.

At night alongside Lily he found himself yearning for the carnal pleasures of Shepherd's Bush. It was unbelievable that they were here, in this perfect set-up for an extravaganza of bonking – endless booze, a mattress that made Jimmy's seem like horse-hair, a view to die for – and neither of them could be bothered. He couldn't understand it. It wasn't as if *Eva* was a disapproving presence. On the contrary, she kept hinting that if things had been otherwise she'd have been up for it herself. That Hildegarde dyke was a turn-off, but luckily Tom had little to do with her. When she wasn't attending to Eva, she sat stiff-backed in the bedroom watching daytime telly.

No, it was something else that disturbed him and flattened their libido. No one spoke about it – they all averted their gaze as though it were an unzipped fly or an inappropriate fart. But Tom knew deep down, he couldn't pretend otherwise, that the ignored but potent presence in their merry little party was death.

'Is she prepared?' he asked Lily one night.

'In what way?'

'Has she made a will? Does she talk about it?'

'She's made a will. I heard her asking the nurse to witness it. But, no. She doesn't talk about it, not really. She just keeps saying that at least she'll be a *person* till the end. Whatever that means.'

'The end,' he repeated. 'She's not arguing with that, at any rate.'

'But she still seems to think she can put it off somehow. And it's amazing how well she'd succeeding. My mother seems to have more energy than both of us put together right now.'

Tom, flopping back into the feather cushions, couldn't disagree.

But Eva was aware that her own frenetic and apparently untiring vigour was nothing but a fragile mask. Beneath it she was terrified. Behind its brittle façade she was being consumed by foreboding so potent that it couldn't be touched even by doses of morphine strong enough to knock down three unhabituated sumo wrestlers. Her pain, granted, was under control. But there was no doubt that the disease was worsening fast and she frequently coughed up blood, which triggered ever more manic efforts to dispel her gathering dread.

But nothing helped. Manipulating her international shareholdings and her po-faced nurse gave her only fleeting satisfaction. As for Lily and Tom – what a disappointment they were turning out to be. A total and non-tax-deductible write-off. For what they were costing, Eva had expected distraction and vicarious enjoyment. At least. Instead of which they merely consumed. No questions, no apparent appreciation, no interest at all it seemed in how she'd come by such immeasurable sums. The pair of them seemed to spend their days slumped in a quasi-marital tedium so dire that, in comparison, life with Max had been as racy as the Grand Prix.

This wouldn't do. She'd have to do something to perk them up, to perk herself up. Something drastic. Something that would take her mind off the terror-monster that lurked within.

A couple of days later she announced that she had an amusing idea. They would all three play a game. Lily was mystified and uneasy. 'What kind of game?' she asked suspiciously. She had never known her mother to participate in any game at all, much less suggest one. Eva had always maintained that all games but bridge bored her stupid. 'Not bridge, I hope?'

'Of course not, silly girl. We'd need four to play bridge. And anyway I'd get frustrated since I'm far, far better than anyone I've ever met. Actually, when I come to think about it, *you*, Lily, might be quite good. She has a surprisingly clear head for figures, Tom. Perhaps one day, when I have time, I'll teach you —'

Her voice faded away and she suddenly looked bewildered and reproachful. Then she seemed to catch herself.

'No, not bridge,' she said firmly. 'I was thinking we might play a version of charades. That's always quite a lot of fun, isn't it?'

'Yessirree,' Tom enthused. 'Don't listen to old spoilsport here. Playing a game's a great idea and charades is a *brilliant* game! You mean movie titles and such-like? Once we've got ourselves nicely pissed, it will be hilarious.'

Eva stopped him with a stern look. 'I said a *version* of charades.'

'What version are we talking about?' Lily asked. She wasn't sure she liked the sound of this.

'You'll have to wait and see!' Eva cocked her head mysteriously. 'I'll give you a clue, though. It's called "Lies and Secrets".'

That confirmed it. 'Lies and Secrets' sounded not only mad but also bad and potentially dangerous. Instinctively Lily wanted out. 'I'm not in the mood,' she said.

'Go on, Lily – you're the one who keeps saying we should be *doing* stuff,' cajoled Tom. 'The evenings are so long for your poor mum. A bit of amusement's not a lot to ask – and, anyway, it sounds like a laugh. "Lies and Secrets", eh? Is it an acting game or a memory game?'

'A bit of both,' Eva answered with an enigmatic smile. 'Each person taking part – well, each of *us* really – has to produce evidence of a lie they've told or a secret they've been keeping. Often they're one and the same thing. It's a bit like Show and Tell, except that it's up to the rest of the party to guess the secret and to decide how successfully it's been kept. Get it?'

'Is there a prize?' Tom asked. He seemed buoyed up by the novelty of the evening and unfazed by any sinister implications.

'Maybe,' Eva answered tantalisingly. 'Lily – I assume you're going to join us?'

She didn't answer for a moment. Maybe she was seeing too much into this. It could be that the incarceration was affecting her nerves. 'I'll think about it,' she said. And as she spoke she was beset by the same sense of inevitability that had overtaken her before taking Eva from the hospital. There seemed something fated about this dreadful game. It was their incontestable destiny.

The prospect of the evening ahead somehow impelled her to leave the hotel for the first time in eighteen days. 'I'm going for a walk,' she told Tom, who seemed bemused by her flurry of agitation. She needed air, natural light – urgently. She wanted space to think, to breathe. A reprieve from imprisonment with a bored dying woman and a facile young man.

'Shall I come along with you?' he offered, clearly out of duty.

'No. Thank you.'.

'Ok.' He looked relieved. '"Lies and Secrets" – your mum's got you going, hasn't she? I bet you're scheming to win that prize. But wait till you see what *I've* got up my sleeve. If it isn't the greatest secret in the whole fucking world, then I'm the Queen's bastard son. If there's any prize to be had – and knowing Eva it'll be *huge* – I'll bet you anything Tom Kennedy will sweep the board.'

'Good,' she said distractedly. He could sweep whatever he wanted. She'd get out and clear her head and then return to tell Eva decisively that she and Tom could play 'Lies and Secrets' to their hearts' content. Lily herself was done with all that.

'Well, then,' he was saying, 'if it's all right with you, I'll be off on a little mission of my own.' He winked at her and tapped the side of his nose, a meaningful gesture that asked for further questioning.

But she wouldn't give him the satisfaction. She merely nodded.

'To do with the game,' he goaded.

'I gathered.'

Eva overheard the exchange. Her daughter, she knew, was none too happy about the impending revelry. 'What kind of game?' she'd asked, warily, in a way that warned Eva that any deviation from this routine in which they'd become entrenched – eating, sleeping, waiting for the end, an end – could be dangerous. Lies. Secrets. What had she been thinking when she'd proposed such a dark diversion? She imagined she knew all of Lily's and she guessed that smoking dope behind the bike shed would be the beginning and end of young Tom's. Which left herself. Eva. Did she really want Lily to know about the worst of her?

Yes, she probably did. In the absence of belief in a man of the cloth who might grant her absolution, she'd quite like her daughter's forgiveness. If not that, perhaps, her understanding. When Lily had looked at her in that timorous way, Eva had seen beyond the specks of green and gold into an ocean of losses and might-have-beens. For an instant she'd wanted to reach out to her daughter and, risking tears, to communicate something beyond the distractions one devised to make existence tolerable. But she had stopped herself. Life had made her a games-player and she wasn't about to change the rules, not at this stage.

So she decided to go right ahead with the arrangements.

'Hildegarde,' she commanded. 'I want you to see that my linen suit is pressed for this evening. We've planned a little party.'

'Mrs Green,' countered the nurse, 'first of all, as I have told you many times, I am employed here to look after your health and not your wardrobe. Secondly, on account of your health, I forbid you to take part in any party.'

The rage that suffused Eva at this refusal of her order was a welcome antidote to unease. She exploited it to the full.

'You – *forbid* me?' She could hardly speak, she was so angry. The arrogance of this overpaid scivvy, this high-handed fascist. With the fee she was getting, what right did she have to deny Eva even a single whim? And what in God's name was so harmful about a party? Was there anything healthier Sister Grün could suggest? A session in the gym, maybe? Weight training? Since medical science had failed so miserably with her body, what else could she do but indulge what was left of her morale? 'Just you wait,' she told her – not as a warning, as a curse. 'Just wait until your health is like mine. You won't have the *balls* to party. You'll just lie down and die.'

Sister Grün seemed at first stunned by the barrage, but recovered smartly and levelled all six feet and two inches of her robust frame at her assailant. 'I have no intention of descending to your state of health, Mrs Green. I neither smoke nor touch alcohol and am very careful about my diet. I do intend, however, to inform the agency that I would like immediately to resign from zis job. I will also ensure the management of zis hotel is properly aware of your condition. Until now we have been maintaining a little fiction —'

'Thank you Sister Grün,' said Eva icily. 'That is quite enough. I'm sure you will do whatever you think is right and proper. In the meantime, since you're still in my employ, will you please help me to my desk. I have work to do.'

Her steady tone belied her turmoil. Surely the nurse wouldn't carry out her threat? And *surely* the Dorchester, grand as it was, wouldn't eject so profitable a guest – especially one who, although undoubtedly expiring, was managing to do it with such perfect decorum?

But however fiercely she tried to reassure herself and however hard she tried to distract herself by spending and shocking and celebrating, she couldn't hold down that sharply escalating sense of doom.

Then, to make matters worse, she did her daily arithmetic and it seemed that, due to some ill-judged futures and misplaced hedge funds, the sum of her assets had suddenly and steeply plummeted.

On a good day she'd have seen this as a challenge. The phone and email would have crackled with deals and counter-deals; in no time at all she'd have recouped her losses and made a little extra on the top. A flagging market had always been for Eva like an untested peak to a mountaineer; the prospect of a conquest had been irresistible. Now it seemed hardly to matter. Her only response was to think that maybe she ought to tell Lily she wouldn't be inheriting very much.

'Lily,' she called. And then, when there was no response, more sharply: '*Lily*!'

At least half a minute later Sister Grün appeared. 'Your daughter has gone out. She left the hotel at ten thirty-eight.'

'I see.' Eva remembered. Lily had mentioned she was going out for a walk. 'How about him – Tom?'

'Mr Kennedy is out as well. He set off shortly before noon.'

'They might have told me,' complained Eva, annoyed. 'We normally have lunch together. What am I supposed to do?'

'Eat alone,' said the nurse, the blunt practicality of her advice not masking its insolence. Eva glared at her furiously but didn't deign to react. Instead, she harnessed her anger in an effort to pull herself to her feet and, brushing aside the nurse's assistance, dragged herself arduously along on her Zimmer frame.

'I'll have a little siesta now, I think,' she managed. 'I want to be fresh for this evening.'

She didn't sleep. She'd become increasingly frightened of succumbing to sleep, which allowed her no reprieve from the terrors that haunted her. The nurse kept offering to further increase her doses of morphine but Eva, who still clung to her determination not to be a Sick Person, steadfastly refused. She would not give in. She wanted to be there right until the moment of not being there and beyond. Beyond would be – beyond would be —

'Sister Grün,' she called. 'Hildegarde. Please come here.' Whatever ill feeling there was between them, the nurse was still contracted to carry out her professional duties. She remained biddable, for now. 'Perhaps, after all,' Eva said, 'I could do with a little more sedation? The pain is suddenly much worse.'

'A moment,' said the nurse, and disappeared to prepare the drug. She returned, armed with a syringe.

By which time, Eva had changed her mind. 'On second thoughts, it's not *that* bad. Maybe I exaggerated. It's bearable. But would you mind asking my daughter to pop in and see me as soon as she gets back?'

'I will tell your daughter,' she said stiffly. 'Or maybe night nurse will tell her. Now I must leave.' She turned to the door.

'Hildegarde.' Eva summoned her back. She couldn't bear to see her go. 'Where do you come from?' she heard herself asking, she had no idea why. She had no affection for this woman, yet the urge to know this was overwhelming.

'Me?' The nurse stopped in her tracks, clearly astonished. 'I am from Wiesbaden, Mrs Green. That is near Mainz, in Germany.'

'I am from – Berlin,' Eva countered, full of wonder at making this claim. It had been many decades since she'd acknowledged her origins. 'I am German too. German-Jewish, actually.'

'I see,' said Hildegarde. 'I, personally, have nothing against Jews.' She paused for a couple of seconds before proceeding on her way.

'Hildegarde,' said Eva, barely managing a strained whisper, 'before you leave, please would you help me – to get up. And to get dressed – for the evening?'

But the German had gone.

In the continuing silence Eva dozed, then awoke, then dozed again. She became vaguely aware of a murmur of voices in the adjoining room and heard the click of a door. With difficulty she rang the emergency bell at her bedside, and Lily appeared. At last.

'Mother...' she began.

And Eva could hear her saying it as though it were yesterday. Her big lie. *I'm engaged to be married.* How brave that had been. How foolish. How sad. 'You don't have to play this game if you'd rather not,' she said. 'We both know about *your* secrets – far be it from me to embarrass you in front of your young man.'

Lily nodded.

'A charming fellow,' Eva went on, shaping each word laboriously. 'He's been good for you, Lily. But one of life's freeloaders, I know the type. It will be interesting to see what will happen to you next.' She stopped and managed a wry smile. 'It *might have been* interesting,' she amended, shutting her eyes and thinking how naturally she was using the conditional form of the verb, how complicated it had seemed when she'd first battled with the English tongue.

It was haunting her, this sense of being alien. Other. She needed to grab onto it somehow ... to make some connection. With difficulty she turned to face Lily.

'There's a small leather box inside the desk drawer,' she managed. 'Brown leather. You might have seen it when you emptied my safe. Bring it here. Please. And while you're up,' she added – for she was still Eva, albeit the last vestige of herself, 'would you draw the curtains. I'm cold.'

Lily complied without saying a word. She identified the box, wedged behind a stack of alphabetically annotated ledgers, and delivered it into Eva's frail hands.

'Help me open it,' her mother said irritably, pushing it towards her. 'Go on. It won't hurt. It's not a bomb.'

It hadn't occurred to Lily that this ancient box might harbour an explosive but, now that Eva had said it, she held it as far from her body as she could. Gingerly she untied the tape that bound it shut. 'Is this what you were bringing to the game? Is it *your* – secret?' she asked.

'It was. But I've lost interest in that game,' Eva said. 'I want only *you* to see it.'

'Tom will be disappointed.' She grappled with the knot. 'He's gone to collect whatever it is he plans to show us. He's looking forward to it.'

'Ah, well.' Eva's distracted gaze was following her fumbling hands. 'Lily, haven't you ever been curious about how I spent my first thirty-nine years?' she asked.

'I've sometimes wondered.'

'Sometimes wondered,' Eva repeated bitterly. 'Is that all?'

'Recently, I suppose, I've been thinking about it – quite a lot.'

'*Recently*? You mean when you learnt how rich I was?'

'Maybe,' Lily said cautiously. The interrogation was making her edgy. Worse than that, the smell of decay that hung in the room was making her sick.

'And how did you imagine I got so much money?' Eva persisted.

'I don't know.' This stupid box seemed to resist being opened. Lily had an urge to smash it against the wall. She was desperate to get out of here. Air. She needed air. 'I have no idea how you got your money,' she said edgily. 'I haven't wanted – I've been afraid to ask.'

'I see.' Eva paused, considering. Then she said slowly, 'You've been worried that the money may not have been honestly acquired? That I may have stolen it, embezzled it? Maybe even *murdered* for it?'

There was silence while the words reached their target, slowly, as though impeded by the glutinous air. Then Lily, appalled, sat up sharp, the box almost falling off her lap.

'Mother!' she said. 'Why would I think something like that?'

Eva didn't answer. She lay back and closed her eyes.

And Lily, watching her, was beset by the dawning conviction that her mother hadn't alluded randomly to the third possibility, absurd as it seemed. 'Murdered for it?' Might she have done that? Could she have? It was certainly within her capability. There was a ruthlessness about Eva that suddenly made sense.

'Here you are.' Her mouth was dry and her hands trembled as she handed it over to her mother. 'Your box. It's open. But I've had enough. I don't think I want to see what you have inside.'

Lily's tone was gruff and, having placed the box on Eva's lap, she stepped away and turned her back. Stubborn girl. Surely at this stage she'd indulge her dying mother's wishes, her last ever game?

'Lily,' she ordered, with as much authority as she could imbue in a voice now so quivery and thin. 'Will you please turn round. There's something I want to show you. Something you should see.'

Nothing happened. Lily's back remained motionless, her shoulders stolidly square.

'Peek-a-boo,' teased Eva, certain that curiosity – if anything – would impact on Lily's obstinacy. She knew that her insinuations had been dangerous but tantalising and, in Lily's place, she'd have been gagging to know more. 'You're not *interested* in my little relics?' she asked, unable to stop herself sounding a little forlorn.

'No, I'm not.'

'Ah well, then.' She sighed, she couldn't help it, as she glanced at the contents of the box. Maybe Lily was right. They *were* only relics, trivialities, after all. Of what account were they now? An ancient train ticket, Berlin to Port of London, February 1939. And here – a letter introducing her to the foster family that took her in. She pulled out two ancient crumbling newspaper cuttings. DEVONSHIRE FARMER DISAPPEARS ON FAMILY PICNIC, was the headline above one; MUSIC HALL LEGEND DIES PEACEFULLY, above the other. What would Lily make of them without Eva's excuses or explanations? And where, how, to begin with so little time left?

'Are you done?' Lily asked, still adamantly looking away. Like a cross parent awaiting a bowel action from an obdurate child.

'Not quite yet.' No, she wasn't. There were two more items to be accounted for. Another newspaper cutting and a small item of jewellery. These she would place on the top of the box so that afterwards (what a strange notion – even now she couldn't conceive of her imminent non-being) – afterwards Lily might understand what, in the end, was important. She shut the box. 'Here,' she said. 'You can take it away. You'll see what's inside in good time.'

Silently Lily turned round. Wordlessly, she accepted it.

'And just remember two things,' Eva added, placing a hand over Lily's. 'First of all, it was *my* financial genius, mine alone, that turned a tidy sum (however I obtained it) into a fortune. I've a feeling that you might have inherited that genius, Lily. Cultivate it. And secondly ... secondly ...'

'What?' Lily asked, interested at last. That laggardly curiosity seemed at last to have been tickled.

Too late, thought Eva. All at once, her power of speech seemed to desert her. Her tongue was thick, thoughts in a dark tangle. What was it she was going to say? Secondly ... ? Something about connections – her origins – her only descendent – her daughter ...?

'What?' Lily asked again, for there had been a change in Eva's tone. She had shed that perpetual note of mockery and, for once, sounded sincere. But the claw-hand on hers, so urgently clutching, had gone limp. Her mother's eyes were shut and she seemed to have slipped into a trance. Lily, watching her, felt empty and lonely and sad.

Great, she thought. What a brilliantly rip-roaring party. And, as predicted, what a ridiculously ill-conceived game. All she could be grateful for was that Tom wasn't here to see or hear about the mysterious (and no doubt dastardly) contents of the box she now replaced in the drawer.

Close thing, though. Just as she returned to Eva's bedside, she heard the clunk of the outer door to the suite being opened and shut. He was back. 'Howdy pardners,' she heard him calling, which immediately told her that he was more than mildly drunk.

The fun starts now, she thought – with dread rather than anticipation.

'Yoo-hoo! Where's everyone? It's time for your favourite game show, Shhhkeleton in the Cupboard.'

Laughing uproariously, he appeared at the door to Eva's room. 'What the fuck's going on here?' he slurred. 'I expected a knees-up, not a bleeding morgue.'

'Tom,' Lily cautioned. 'Take it easy. She's not —'

'I. Am. Fine.' From some ultimate reserve tank, Eva seemed to have extracted sufficient life force to thrust her eyes open and raise her head. 'Tom, bring me a Scotch. Now.'

'Sure thing. See, Lily? You fuss too much. You joining us?'

'No,' she answered.

'No? Well, then – two doubles coming up. You're welcome to change your mind later.' He reversed into the sitting room. She heard loud clunks and crashes as he fumblingly prepared the drinks.

This wasn't exactly the level of shindig he'd been getting himself oiled for, he thought, aiming the Chivas Regal roughly in the direction of the pair of tumblers he'd laid out. Oiled and psyched up, and for what? The two of them miserable as sin in that darkened room, killjoy Lily in particular. At least the old lady had been up for a drink – no stopping her, one had to admire her fortitude.

'Coming,' he called. 'Just getting my kit together for the game. We're all still on for it, I assume.'

Without waiting for an answer, he placed the tumblers onto the most commodious silver tray he could find. Then, out of the extra-large freezer bag he'd bought for transportation purposes, he lifted his most precious possession and set it down on the tray. He'd be a bantam cock's boxer shorts if this didn't win him first prize.

'Duh-duh-duh-*dum*,' he sang, as he made his appearance at the bedroom door.

'Tom?' She'd turned round to look at him. Satisfying puzzlement was written all over her face. 'What have you got there? Your dictionary? Why on earth would you want to bring *that*?'

'Aha,' he said mysteriously. 'Drinks, ladies? Lily, it's not too late to change your mind.'

'I'm fine. Thank you.' Her eyes were still glued to the book.

'Have patience,' he teased. 'All will become clear. Eva? Your Scotch. Top-of-the-range, as ever. Can't beat this place for quality.'

He held the glass out and the old lady tried, and tried again, to grasp it. Full marks for effort. Too weak, though. If there wasn't that gleam in her eyes, he'd have sworn she was on her way out.

'Lily,' she ordered, croakily but peremptorily. 'Put the glass to my lips.'

Lily complied. She was beyond resisting anything now. If her mother wanted pitch herself into an 80-proof coma, she certainly wouldn't stop her. And if it turned out that she never woke up, it might be better all round.

'Thank you,' Eva said, and her voice sounded better. Was this the same person who had, only minutes before, been comatose, on the brink of oblivion? Was she inhuman, the way she kept bouncing back? A malign immortal spirit? 'And so, Tom?' she was asking. 'What is it you've brought to show us?'

'Can't you see it's a dictionary?' Lily put in quickly. 'The Shorter Oxford English Dictionary. I've seen it in his flat. It's most impressive.' She wished he'd get this over with. Lexicography, at this point, seemed wildly out of place.

'Impressive, indeed.' Tom drained his glass and went to pour himself another. He came back with the bottle and offered to top up Eva's.

She nodded, her eyes glittering. 'So tell us what makes this dictionary of yours so impressive, Tom?

'Well,' he said. 'In the first place it was my old dad's. A family heirloom, if you like. Secondly, it was where I learnt to spell my first long word. Want to know what that is?'

'No,' said Lily.

'Yes, please,' said Eva. She seemed more perky by the moment.

'Right.' He grinned at her, ignoring Lily. 'I'm going to ask your daughter, Mrs Green, to have a go and look the word up.'

'I won't need to,' Lily said. 'My spelling's always been —'

'Lily,' Eva warned. 'Do as the gentleman says.'

She felt the weight of the hefty volume as it was deposited on her lap. 'The word in question,' Tom was saying, 'is *omnipotent*. Recognise it, Lily?'

'Yes,' she said. Was this happening? A spelling bee? Here? Now? Maybe she was featuring in her own hallucinatory dream. 'Didn't you once say it meant having power. Infinite power?'

'Good girl. An excellent student. But let's make sure you're correct. Open it, Lil. Go on. Have a look inside. You want to, you know you do. You've been sniffing around it for a long time.'

He was dizzy with anticipation, almost falling about with fear. This was the moment he'd looked forward to and dreaded ever since the day Hector had revealed the secret to him. In a moment it would be out.

She was turning the first few pages very slowly.

'The letter O,' he urged. 'Get a move on.'

And then, all at once, the dictionary lay open – and there it was. His father's precious Luger.

Black and malevolent.

Lily gasped. This was the last thing she'd expected.

'Ha ha,' she said nervously, for surely it was a toy, a childish practical joke? But he didn't laugh along. He was staring at it, as though it was as shocking to him as it was to her. 'Tom?' she said. 'It's not real, is it?'

'My dad's personal Luger P08.' He spoke with a mixture of awe and pride. And fear as well. She could see by his expression and the way he shifted from foot to foot that he was afraid.

'Let me see?' Eva was straining to raise her head. 'Lily! Show it to me.'

She couldn't move. The heavy book and its contents were weighing her down. 'I – can't.'

'Tom, will you show me what you have there,' Eva directed. 'Now.'

Her peremptory tone brooked no hesitation. Even now. Like an automaton, Tom slid his hand into the hollowed paged and – holding it as far away from himself as he could – lifted out the gun. Lily was a novice when it came to weaponry, but even she could see that he wasn't holding it like a seasoned shot.

Eva frowned and sniffed as she eyed the Luger. 'Yup. The real thing,' she declared. 'As genuine as they come.'

'Course it's genuine,' he said, his self-assurance flooding back as he saw the approving way she considered it. There was no way that a person as rich as she was didn't know something about guns. No-one could have accumulated such a fortune by *honest* means. 'My dad was Hector Kennedy,' he confided, for there was a fair chance she'd be on nodding terms or more with the leading lights of the underworld. 'Famously known as The Hedge. '

'Hmm,' she said in a noncommittal way. She sank back looking buggered again. Definitely not long for this world.

But he was pumped up. Adrenaline and alcohol were charging through his system. Nodding vigorously to himself, he examined his tool. The real thing. As genuine as they came. It felt warm now, alive. He was Tony Montana, ready for the kill. 'You wanna fuck with me? Okay,' he muttered. 'You wanna play rough? Okay. Say hello to my little friend.'

'Tom,' Lily said warningly.

But he took no notice. 'This little beauty has seen some real action,' he said. 'Take a look at her, Lily? Look at these lines?' He brandished it flamboyantly. 'Eva?' he said, though it seemed clear she was beyond further applause.

But no. There was life in the old girl yet. She was raising her head again, higher, looking directly at him with her blazing eyes. It was like in the movies when the corpse arises from the bathtub and is not dead after all.

'Shoot me,' she was saying.

'Shh-shhoot you?'

'Yes, shoot me.' She sounded like she really meant it. 'Go on, Tom. I'm ready for it. Put your finger where your big fat mouth is. You'll me doing me a favour.'

Bloody hell. In the rush of the moment, he pointed the barrel at her. Never had he felt so powerful.

'Stop, Tom. Don't do it!' Lily sprang into action. In a single movement, she shoved the book off her lap and jumped to her feet. She had to stop him. He was going to fire at her mother. 'Don't!' she cried. 'Are you crazy? Are you off your head?' She lunged towards him and tried to knock the gun out of his hand. He dodged.

Squeeze, he told himself. Squeeze the fucking trigger. A criminal chorus was egging him on.
Welcome to the party, pal. Crawl out from under that rock You're one psycho son of a bitch...
He was sweating like a trooper, shaking like a leaf.

She managed to grab hold of his arm. Again he almost slid away. But she took hold of his forearm and held his wrist with her other hand, twisting it so that the gun pointed to the ceiling.

'Get off,' he said through clenched teeth. He kicked her but she held firm. 'Let go,' he muttered, but – like a crazed creature – she clung to his arm. 'Get away, Lily,' he said. 'Ok, I won't shoot —'

As he was saying this, she made another grab for the gun and he gripped it tightly, he couldn't help himself, and pressed down on the trigger. There was an almighty explosion and the lead crystal chandelier shattered into a million costly shards.

At which point Eva's heart gave in and she quietly expired.

19

This was not the ending Lily had envisaged for her mother but suspected it might have been the sort of send-off Eva would have aspired to for herself. Inglorious, yet in its way magnificently surreal. There she lay, lifeless on the bed, with Lily aghast and still glued to Tom's arm. The Oxford English Dictionary with its broken spine was buckled on the floor, with the smoking Luger alongside it. Hanging over everything was the pungent smell of gunfire and scattered everywhere like sparkling confetti were the splinters of glass from the smashed chandelier.

Once Security had been alerted it took only minutes for the Mayfair Suite to be heaving with doctors, hotel managers, ambulancemen and police. Lily, in a state of shock, was helped to a chair. She saw the gun on the carpet near her feet, a viper still waiting to strike, and – without meaning to – reached out for it.

'Leave that alone, miss – it's evidence,' someone bellowed.

'It's the daughter,' warned someone else. 'She's probably in shock.'

They led her to the sitting room and gave her tea.

'Where's Tom?' she asked.

'They've taken him in for questioning. He claims ownership of this unlicensed and dangerous weapon. We must eliminate all the suspicious circumstances surrounding your mother's death.'

'Is she really dead?' Lily asked. 'Have you checked properly? My mother has a way of – you know —'

The sombre-faced way they were nodding convinced her. She thought about the leather box secreted among the files in the drawer. Had it been only a few hours before, not even that, when her mother had tried to unleash its contents like a latter-day Pandora? It all seemed irrelevant now.

It seemed fitting and satisfyingly punitive to summon Elsie, Sylvia and Mattie back to England for Eva's funeral. Lily thought her mother would have enjoyed her posthumous power to curtail their cruise and, anyway, who else was there to invite? The only other person who gave a damn about Eva, alive or dead, was Tom.

And he was otherwise engaged; busy – as he put it – 'pleasuring Her Majesty'. When she visited him in Pentonville Prison, the first thing he wanted to know was whether it was his Luger that had killed her mother.

'Of course not,' said Lily. 'You fired it into the ceiling. She was dying anyway. Her heart just gave out.'

'I don't mean killed, as such. I'm talking fright.'

'Do you think that's likely, my mother dying of fright? I must tell you, Tom Kennedy, self-proclaimed son of the supposedly infamous Hedge, you seemed more frightened than she did.'

He looked indignant – and younger than ever in his prison garb, with his closely-cropped hair that showed his vulnerable skull. 'And *I* must tell you,' he retorted, 'that my dad was one of the most notorious crooks ever. The tool's my inheritance – my father's legacy.'

'And until now have you had much opportunity to use it?'

'Oh, yes,' he said quickly. Then caught her eye. 'Actually, no. Not yet.' He paused and looked away. 'It's not *in* me, Lily,' he confessed. 'I've been trying all my life. It's like – like Mozart's son being tone-deaf, or Einstein's being thick, or Churchill's kid having no stomach for war.' He fell silent.

'Tell me about it?' she urged. 'Please tell me?'

So he told her – about his high-born but weak mother Beatrice and his tyrannical father and three nasty sisters. And how his mother had died and his father had been assassinated. And boarding school, and how desperately hard he had tried to be bad. And Jimmy's friendship and sudden demise. And then, of course, there'd been Lily.

'How about you?' he asked.

So, speaking softly, for visiting rules at HMP Pentonville were strict, she told him. About her dull childhood and secret dreams. And how Max had died and Eva had seemed to thrive in his absence. And how Lily in desperation had told her big lie. And about coming to London. And how hard she'd tried to find a surrogate for the fiancé she'd called Jeremy. And, finally, there'd been Tom.

'Finally?' he asked. 'You mean finally as in for keeps or finally as in it's over?'

She wasn't quite sure which alternative he preferred. 'Who knows?' she said. 'Who can tell? Let's wait until you're out of here. I'm sure they won't keep you inside very long. Your transgressions seem to me to be quite minor.'

He glared at her indignantly. 'What do you know about such things? They're serious enough in the eyes of the law. Apart from illegal possession of a firearm, they've booked me for tax evasion, social security fraud and resisting arrest. Even though I didn't.'

'You went like a lamb,' she said. 'You can't be *liking* it here, surely? It's supposed to be punitive.'

'It is. It's *fucking* hard,' he insisted, with enormous relish. 'One of the few virtues of prison life is that, after the excesses of the Dorchester, it's good for the flab.'

They were silent for a moment. 'I thought you adored the Dorchester,' she said, slightly offended that he was belittling her mother's hospitality. Not to mention that, given a shortfall in funds he wasn't even aware of (for she was embarrassed to tell him), she'd be paying off the bill until she was about a hundred and two.

He shrugged. 'Maybe it was too much of a good thing? You liked it too, at the start.'

'At first I did,' she agreed. 'But then I started thinking that even paradise could pall after a while. Heaven must be full of frustrated saints who are sorry they didn't get to hell.'

He laughed, and it cheered her that he found her amusing. It gave her hope. 'Now that's a possibility,' he said. 'We're going to have to ask Eva to keep us posted on that one.'

'My mother in heaven?' she asked sardonically. 'You don't know the half of it.'

'Well, maybe you should tell me about it then —?'

'No. I'll leave it there. One thing I will say, though, is that if they let *her* in, then standards are slipping. Badly.'

She was smiling when she left him, which was abnormal for a departing prison visitor, and engendered a few suspicious stares and an extra-thorough frisking. Next thing they'd refuse her entry to Pentonville, never mind Eva into the Elysian Fields.

Much more pressing, though, was how she would be received when she went back to the Dorchester. A stern letter from the General Manager had 'invited' her to call in at her earliest convenience in order to discuss the substantial outstanding balance and to collect the personal possessions left behind by Lily and her fellow occupants of the Mayfair Suite.

She hesitated for a long while outside the hotel, Park Lane traffic roaring behind her and taxis shunting to and forth with affluent-looking guests. She'd arrived here in style once. This time there was a good chance that they would grab and detain her, maybe set her to work in the kitchens for her mother's temerity to die on the premises. Plus a few other minor inconveniences, such as the presence of an illicit weapon and the destruction of an antique Murano glass chandelier. The last, alone, would swallow any profit that remained after she'd sold the Hatch End house.

Which would leave Lily in possession of a legacy that was a nicely-rounded zilch. She didn't care, though. Any money she might have inherited from her mother was tainted, as far as she was concerned. All of it smacked of ill-gain.

Bracing herself, she stepped into the lobby and walked to the desk with proud, determined strides. There was little they could do to her. Fortunately, she had nothing left to lose.

'I am Lily Green,' she announced to the concierge, remembering how she'd once felt it necessary to elaborate her name with the addition of an extra e. Now it seemed concise and self-sufficient. Like Lily herself. 'I have a letter here from the General Manager. I believe he's expecting me.'

'Could you take a seat for a moment, Miss Green? I'll tell Mr Conway-Smith you're here.'

Sitting as elegantly as she remembered how ('Knees together, ankles crossed,' Carla Devine had counselled. 'Dignity, decorum, deportment.'), she tried not to think of the reception awaiting her. Scorn and derision. Accusation. As the only available vessel of retribution, she deserved all of it. But she could take it, she decided, straightening her back with enough resolve to make it ache.

After such trepidation it was almost a let-down when, after being ushered into his considerable office, she was greeted by George Conway-Smith with a crushing handshake and his deepest, most heartfelt condolences on her bereavement.

Was that all?

'The – um – money —?' she began to ask.

He stopped her. This was clearly a subject one put into writing rather than discussed. 'All in good time,' he said soothingly. 'We understand how easy it might be to be taken in by a young scoundrel like that Mr Kennedy —'

She was about to put him right. 'No, Mr Conway-Smith,' she was on the brink of saying. 'It wasn't like that.'

But she stopped herself. The Tom she'd just visited in jail would, she thought, like nothing better than to be officially endorsed as villain of the peace. What difference would it make if she were perceived by hotel management as a dutiful daughter who'd been diddled by him? Her mother, the real offender, was dead.

'What I mean is,' she said, 'that I intend to pay the bill, every last penny of it, as soon as my mother's estate has been wound up.'

'I'm sure you do, Miss Green,' he said. 'And I appreciate your concern for us at such an – er – awkward time. But let it rest with us for the meanwhile. As it happens, we have comprehensive insurance against such – eventualities. Our assessors are doing all they can and we'll keep you fully informed of what transpires. Fingers crossed, eh? In the meantime, though, I'll have my staff arrange for the delivery of your belongings. I believe the family property is in —'

She was about to say Chelsea. Instead, drawing herself to her feet, she said, 'Hatch End.'

'Good,' he said. 'A lovely part of the world. By the way' He held out a smaller carrier bag with the Dorchester insignia. 'I thought perhaps I should give this to you personally. It was found among the – er – debris and may contain items of value.'

Her reprieve was miraculous. She had fully expected to find herself despatched to the kitchen on long-term washing-up duty. Instead of which, she deported herself to the Bar for one last celebratory (and valedictory) martini cocktail. The room was quite crowded. Most of the tables were occupied. Lily seated herself on one of the chairs that lined the long bar and thought how self-conscious she might once have felt at being there alone. The days of haunting laundrettes and supermarkets in tremulous search for an available man seemed distant indeed. Ah, yes – she was done with all that.

While awaiting her drink, she glanced inside the carrier bag she'd been given – guessing, even before she saw it, what it would contain. Yes, suspicion confirmed: it was *that box*, the one bearing her mother's iniquitous secrets, the revelations she'd so strong-mindedly spurned.

'Huh!' She could almost hear Eva chortling. 'You thought you'd got away?'

'I have,' she retorted. Inwardly, of course. Having been reprieved ('Fingers crossed') from debt and disgrace, she wasn't going to risk impropriety. 'I am, mother dear, fancy free.'

Her defiant thoughts, however, were unmatched by her gesture. Full-blown curiosity, more potent than she'd ever experienced before (was this, in the absence of cash, Eva's legacy?) drove her to open the box and to peer inside. The first thing she saw was a discoloured locket on a faded gold chain. She lifted it carefully. It was old, very old. It occurred to Lily that everything she'd owned until now had been new, or newish. There was something deeply and unaccountably affecting about holding this item that her mother had kept, that her mother had chosen to pass onto her. She had to blink to hold back tears. Inside the locket were two tiny sepia photographs – Eva's parents? Her grandparents? Did it matter? She felt no particular kinship with the stern-faced man or his coiffed wife (was that a Star of David round her neck?) but would wear this, always, as a token of connection, of belonging. Whatever that meant.

She was about to shut the box – the necklace had evoked sufficient emotion for one day – when she was drawn to a newspaper cutting that had been conspicuously placed. A birth notice that had appeared in *The Times*, no less: *To Eva and Max Green, a healthy daughter, Lily*. Terse. Official. And again she almost cried, not about the notice but the fact that Eva had cared enough to keep it all those years.

Enough, she told herself. She was getting soft. What had happened to tough conniving Lily Green with her mendacious audacity – daughter and heiress of the impenetrable Eva with her ill-gotten but now-dissipated gains. Firmly she put the box away. 'Cheers,' she said, as she raised the martini to her lips – and this time she couldn't help saying it aloud.

'Cheers,' came another voice from a little way along the bar.

Lily started. How embarrassing. She glanced at the speaker, a man, who seemed to be eyeing her with amusement. How dare he. She would not submit to being an object of mirth. She sat up primly and took a ladylike sip, but couldn't hold back another discreet sideways peep.

He noticed. She looked away and then, irresistibly, back to him and saw that he had raised an enquiring eyebrow. Cheeky. What sort of woman he think she was? On the other hand, it was a rather attractive eyebrow. Most refined. Lily had to admit he was not a bad looking man.

She smiled. Oh, God – what was she getting herself into now? And look: he was smiling back. Who was it who'd said, 'Look, smile, say something'? Jennifer Flowers, she remembered, and smiled even more broadly at the recollection. How funny and irrelevant that all seemed now. Yet how utterly relevant. She'd looked, she'd smiled, and now if she wanted to detain this attractive man, she had to speak. Quickly. No time to be lost.

'I – er —' she began.

'Would you like another drink?' he broke in.

'Another drink?' she hedged, not wanting to seem loose or louche. God forbid. On the other hand ... 'Why not?'

He moved a couple of seats towards her until they were side by side, facing the bar. He smelled as he looked and as he spoke. Elegant. Distinguished. She hoped that her air of refinement matched his, and her lips twitched again at the thought. If only he knew.

'So?' he said.

'So,' she answered, withholding information until he showed his hand. Never mind Flowers et al, it's what Eva would have done.

'Isn't this the most wonderfully civilised place in London?' he remarked, to which there was only the possibility of assent. They continued in this vein, exchanging pleasantries, until at last Lily turned to him and said, 'This is ridiculous. You don't even know my name.'

'Oh.' He seemed embarrassed. 'I didn't want to be – what is it? What *is* your name?'

Nothing for it. 'Lily,' she said. 'Lily Green.'

'Lily,' he repeated. 'It's lovely. It suits you.'

'And yours?' she asked – and, even as the words left her mouth, she knew what the answer would be. It was as if someone – Eva? – were whispering it into her ear.

'I'm Jeremy,' he said.

Jeremy. Could this be her mother's revenge or reward? Would her first great lie continue to haunt her forever?

'I'm very pleased to meet you, Jeremy,' she said, extending her hand. 'At last.'